Beautiful Star

YUKIO MISHIMA

Beautiful Star

Translated by Stephen Dodd

PENGUIN BOOKS

PENGUIN CLASSICS

UK | USA | Canada | Ireland | Australia
India | New Zealand | South Africa

Penguin Books is part of the Penguin Random House group of companies
whose addresses can be found at global.penguinrandomhouse.com

First published in Japanese 1962
First published in Great Britain in Penguin Classics 2022
001

Set in 10.5/13 pt Dante MT Pro
Typeset by Jouve (UK), Milton Keynes
Printed and bound in Great Britain by Clays Ltd, Elcograf S.p.A.

The authorized representative in the EEA is Penguin Random House Ireland,
Morrison Chambers, 32 Nassau Street, Dublin D02 YH68

A CIP catalogue record for this book is available from the British Library

ISBN: 978-0-241-54556-0

www.greenpenguin.co.uk

MIX
Paper from
responsible sources
FSC FSC® C018179

Penguin Random House is committed to a
sustainable future for our business, our readers
and our planet. This book is made from Forest
Stewardship Council® certified paper.

I

Under a cloudless mid-November sky in the dead of night, a 1951 Volkswagen emerged sputtering into life from the garage of a large, well-to-do residence in the city of Hannō, Saitama Prefecture. The stone-cold engine required a few minutes to turn over before the car was ready to depart. All the while its passengers glanced around uneasily.

This old-fashioned household had only recently built the ramshackle garage for their newly acquired second-hand car. Blue-painted garage doors fronted some bamboo lattice fencing that had seen better days. The garage was a sign that the family had broken free from a long rut and was stirring into action.

But no one could guarantee the course of the action they had embarked upon. As scions of Hannō's premier lumber family business, they had inherited a sizeable fortune, but none of the interest in the light-hearted, run-of-the-mill pastimes that had enthused their predecessors. Akiko, the beautiful daughter, was a quiet type with no close friends. Just a couple of doors from their home was one of those old-fashioned post offices built with thick earthen walls, but she would walk right past it and take her stack of mail all the way to the main depot by the train station. Some looked askance at this, and tongues wagged. Her letters included airmail bound for every corner of the world.

The car sped along the wide, flat Hannō roads in the deep of night. The son, Kazuo, was Akiko's elder brother, and he sat in the driving seat alongside Akiko. Their parents, Mr and Mrs Ōsugi, were in the back.

'I'm so glad we left early,' said the father, Jūichirō. 'Things often take longer than you expect, so it always pays to be a bit early.'

'Exactly. If we're late, our *friends* will take offence,' replied Iyoko, the mother. All four looked steadily ahead through the car's windscreen at the night sky as it slowly unfolded between low, unlit rows of houses. The whole family had inherited the same beautiful, crystal-clear eyes.

There was not another soul on the road. The car passed the city's Chamber of Commerce and turned right, made a left at the police station, its presence marked by the faint glow of the night watch, and soon reached the front of the new City Hall which also served as the city bus terminal. The pure-white City Hall building, rectangular and modern, loomed out from the darkness of the night that gathered thickly around Mt Rakan, immediately behind. The family was going to climb that mountain.

Mt Rakan stands 195 metres above sea level. In the Kōji Period (1555–1558) during the reign of Emperor Go-Nara, the Venerable Onoya, first abbot of Nōninji Temple, founded a temple on a mountainside which he named Mt Atago. Later, in the fifth year of the Genroku Period (1688–1704), Keishōin, mother of Tsuneyoshi, the fifth Shogun of the Tokugawa Dynasty, donated sixteen *rakan* (important saints') statues to the temple, and the site's name was changed to Mt Rakan.

Kazuo parked beneath the huge windowpanes of the deserted City Hall. On the other side of the dark glass, traces of light from the streetlamps reached out to the absurdly high ceiling and the hundreds of chairs. Semi-circular rows of empty seats faced an empty onstage rostrum. Emptiness reflected emptiness in a way that seemed to maintain a tense equilibrium far more effectively than during the daytime when the hall was packed with people.

After taking a peep, Kazuo went to open the boot of the parked car. He dragged out a rucksack packed with things to eat and a blanket to ward off the cold, and slung it over his back. The others would be carrying cameras, binoculars and flasks to the top.

Akiko sprang nimbly from the passenger side, well wrapped up against the cold in grey slacks and a gaudy ski sweater, with the ends of a woollen muffler dangling from her neck. The ethereal beauty of her face shone in the darkness, while her shawl set off her slender frame nicely. Energized by the night cold, Akiko used a silver torch to draw bold circles of light around herself in order to test its strength. It looked like a deadly weapon in her hand.

Next out was Jūichirō, with an extra sweater on to keep warm, and Iyoko, dressed Japanese style, with a muffler peeping from the neck of her thick full-length overcoat. After graduating from university in the liberal arts, Jūichirō had dabbled for a while as a schoolteacher, but he never gravitated towards any other particularly intellectual occupation. And yet his splendidly long, bespectacled face endowed him with an elite academic weightiness. His distinguished, rather bony nose immediately conveyed an air of loneliness and desolation to those around him. Iyoko, in contrast, had a warm, homely face, the same dull-witted, gullible features she had passed on to her son.

The party set off up the mountain in silence, the lights from their four torches criss-crossing the ground before them. By the time the white lettering of a sign emerged from the gloom to inform them they were on the path to the top of Mt Rakan, sharp-tipped cedars were already pressing in around them. From this point, street lighting was non-existent.

It had been virtually windless at ground level, but the higher they climbed the more powerful grew the rustling of trees in the night. Through gaps among the cedars, deep wells suddenly opened up that led to the night sky, revealing ever-brighter clusters of stars. Kazuo was in the lead, and his sharp, probing torchlight happened upon a group of gravestones at a roadside cemetery. Since the path was wide and the incline gentle, they took a wide detour around the stones, and emerged into an open space halfway up the mountain. Their lights fell on empty benches and a scattering of white scraps of wastepaper.

Not a single bird was in song. After they crossed the open space the path narrowed, becoming steeper and tougher to negotiate. Logs were set horizontally into the ground to serve as footholds, but rocks and tree roots had invaded the path from all directions, and the path's unevenness was exaggerated even further by their torchlight, as rock shadows flickered wildly along the way. The wind stirring through the trees above their heads grew steadily louder.

But none of them appeared at all distracted from their noble objective. Even the womenfolk remained fearless.

If the moon had been out over the mountains the landscape would certainly have seemed brighter. In fact, the moon had made an appearance the previous day at dusk, but quickly disappeared. Moreover, it was such a thin sliver of moon that it would not have helped much even if it had remained in the sky. The four urged each other up the arduous path. Had they made the climb during the daytime, it would have been child's play.

They eventually came to a small grassy spot where their torch lights struck a set of four or five dilapidated stone steps. The stones cascaded down through the dark cedars like a small waterfall.

'At last, we've made it! The observation deck is just up there,' said Jūichirō, short of breath.

'It took twenty-seven minutes from base to here,' said Kazuo, holding the luminous dial of his watch close to his face.

The observation deck was a level patch of rock-strewn ground about 300 metres square. To the north stood a stone monument that marked an imperial visit, surrounded by a forest behind it. The ground lay entirely open to the south. Apart from two or three straggly pine branches and the tops of some dense low-lying woods, a completely uninterrupted view of the southern sky spread from directly above them all the way to the horizon. Down to the east was a scattering of lights from Hannō, but they were outdone by the cluster of green, red and yellow illuminations emanating from Johnson Military Base, visible on the horizon due east.

'What time is it?'

'Seven minutes to four.'

'I'm so glad we got here before the hour. I really wanted to arrive at least thirty minutes before things are due to kick off.'

They had worked up a sweat during the ascent, but this dissipated immediately, and they became aware that the cold of a November dawn on a mountain top was not to be taken lightly. Kazuo removed the scruffy blanket from the rucksack and spread it on the ground, while the women, their backs set against the wind as it howled through the northern forest towards them, strove to make their surroundings a little more comfortable. Iyoko poured hot tea from a flask into plastic cups and offered them around, and she unwrapped the sandwiches. At last, they all had a few moments to contemplate their individual patches of the starry sky.

'How clear it is. And no moon, either. We're so lucky.' Iyoko's eyes brimmed with emotion as she spoke.

It was one of those magnificent starry skies never visible in the big city. The stars were embedded in the firmament like spots on a leopard's fur. The atmosphere was crystal clear, and the arrangement of stars – some distant, some closer – revealed the true depths of the night sky. Light flowed into haze-like clusters, in such a way that those looking on thought they saw nets being cast into a misty expanse of starlight. Far too many stars to count, thought Akiko. Still no sign of dawn in any corner of the heavens. The horizon was cut at right angles by the Milky Way, and the Great Square of Pegasus was about to sink out of sight. The ceaseless twinkling of myriad stars flooded the night sky with those hyper-charged vibrations that linger even when the note on a stringed instrument has already been played.

'What a pity, though.' Jūichirō's tone was sonorous yet direct. 'This morning, neither your mother nor I managed to see our home planets. Just a glimpse of those tiny points of light would have brought so many forgotten memories flooding back. When I was still living on Mars all that time ago, I can tell you I looked at Earth in exactly the same way.'

'It's not possible to see Mars in November.' Kazuo's response was rather curt. 'Because it rises and sets about the same time as the sun. But Jupiter, where Mum comes from, is visible in the early evening.'

'I was too busy to look yesterday,' sighed his mother. 'I can't tell you how happy it would have made me here this morning for us to see our native planets all together.'

'Mine will come into view soon,' said Akiko, turning back affectionately to her brother.

'Mine too. Poor *humans*, you've got to feel sorry for them.'

'Now, now!' His mother admonished him with a smile. 'Remember, that kind of language won't do. It might be OK around here because no one can overhear us, but if you make a practice of saying things like that in front of strangers, you could get into terrible trouble.'

Behind them to the north, the wind crashed like ocean waves, flailing through the upper branches of cedar and pine trees, then rising up at a distance before dropping down to pummel them like a sudden avalanche. Their hands were frozen through, but they had equipment to carry – cameras and binoculars – so none of them wore gloves. A constant flurry of leaves pelted their backs. The strange sound they could just about catch turned out to be the rattling of a zinc door in a deserted teahouse nearby.

The constellations turned quietly, invisible to the eye. Orion's Belt hung in the sky to the south-west, its three stars lining up with a fourth, below, Rigel, to form the shape of an old-fashioned kite. The whole family was watching out for movements of light, but they kept getting distracted by extraneous things. There were meteors. There was an aeronautical beacon nestled among the mountains far to the south which they had never noticed until then. And head-lamps from cars travelling along the main highway flickered in the dimly lit outskirts of Hannō.

'They promised they'd appear in the sky to the south between four-thirty and five.' Even as he spoke, Jūichirō's bespectacled eyes remained firmly trained in that direction.

'Just another ten minutes to go. I wonder what tidings our *brothers and sisters* will bring. What sacred mystery will they convey?

'The Soviet Union has finally managed to test a fifty-megaton nuclear bomb. They're on the point of committing a heinous crime that will break the harmony of the Universe. And if America goes on to follow blindly in their footsteps . . . The end of human beings on Earth is already in sight. Our family's mission is nothing less than to ensure it doesn't happen. And yet we remain powerless, while the world seems utterly oblivious!'

'Don't despair, Dad.' Kazuo offered soothing words while his bin-oculars continued to scour the heavens. 'Compared to the timescale that frames the Universe, the period of our suffering pales into insig-nificance. I don't believe earthlings can all be that stupid. At some point they'll wake up to the error of their ways, and a time will come when they submit to our way of thinking about complete harmony and eternal peace. In any case, we should write that letter to Khrushchev as soon as possible.'

'Akiko's been working on a draft. You're almost finished, aren't you, dear?' said Iyoko.

Her beautiful daughter replied with a monosyllabic grunt as she searched the starry sky.

Finally, it reached four-thirty. Total silence reigned as the family attended to the sky with a mixture of tension and expectation. Jūichirō had received notice early the previous morning that several flying saucers would be making an appearance at this time.

It was summer the year before when the family suddenly awoke to the fact that they were all extraterrestrials who had descended to earth from their respective celestial bodies. This supernatural insight began with Jūichirō, but within a few days it had possessed both parents and children. Even Akiko, who had just thought it funny at first, was no longer laughing.

The easiest explanation was to assume that the souls of extraterrestrials had suddenly taken up residence in all the family members, and they now had total control over each person's body and spirit. At the same time, while the family still retained clear images of past events and things like the births of the children, such earthly memories had been transformed instantaneously into false histories. It was highly regrettable that their personal memories of other worlds (that is, their true histories) had been irretrievably lost.

Jūichirō was no man of action, but he was thoughtful and had a clear understanding of the world. It was his belief that, in order to protect his family, it was absolutely vital to prevent society at large from getting wind of their secret alien identities. But how to do that?

Jūichirō had enough common sense to understand that human purity and honesty could only be protected from harm if they were kept carefully under wraps. This thought never entered his wife's head, and his children were still young, but he did make every effort to alert them all to this reality. Let them feel proud about being

7

extraterrestrials all they liked, but even the tiniest display of arrogance might leave them highly vulnerable and in real danger of being exposed to the world. It was essential that they conceal any feelings of superiority. After all, the world was obsessed with sniffing out why some people stood out even a little from others.

There was no way Jūichirō could have anticipated that he, of all people, would suddenly develop such a clear sense of his higher calling at the age of fifty-two. As a young man, he had been tormented with an inferiority complex. Held in contempt by his father, a complete philistine, he had sought salvation in the gentle and forgiving world of the arts. As long as his father was alive, Jūichirō at least made a minimal effort to help out in the company business. But once his father was dead, he felt no further obligation and turned to a life of idleness. He would accompany his wife to Tokyo from time to time to see a play or an exhibition, and he had put his son and daughter into Tokyo schools. He created an untroubled, isolated and cerebral family in this provincial city just an hour's train journey from the big city.

Then one day in his early fifties, and with no thanks to personal effort or accomplishment on his part, he was touched by the grace of a superior understanding which awakened him to his life's mission for the first time. The lack of purpose that had characterized the first half of his life now struck him less as a mistake, and more as a half-finished, though flawlessly preserved condition that allowed the universal truth to seek him out when the time was right to make him its vessel.

During the earlier, inactive phase of his life, he was the sort of person who could not stop wondering why, for example, the top branches of garden trees were slenderer than their trunks, and why these branches shorn of leaves became so delicately embedded into the blue sky. The structure of giant elms in wintertime reminded him of fine river tributaries on a map. It was as if the wellspring of the trees was hidden away somewhere in the heavens, and numerous treetop branches, cascading down from the watershed in the blue above, forged together into black trunks and suddenly melded into the shape of a tree. Perhaps it was precisely because trees were delicate streams pouring down from the heavens in crystallized form that their abundant branches and leaves also stretched upwards, struggling to find their way back to the celestial realm.

But these fantasies were no proof that he possessed a poetic nature. Constantly troubled by the way his worldly illusions got smashed into tiny pieces, he could never quite trust the structure and effectiveness of individual objects in the world. For instance, he had thought long and hard about the shape of scissors. When you spread them wide, the extended tips centred on the fulcrum spread out in the shape of an open fan, creating two areas diametrically opposed to each other. Scissors are simply something you hold in your hand, but they readily bisect the world, forming spaces that incorporate mountains, lakes, cities and oceans. But a simple snapping shut of the sharp metal tool obliterates the wide earth, and you are left with nothing but a cut sheet of white paper and a strange, beak-like implement.

In this way, the world expands and contracts around us – suddenly brought to life, and then extinguished – in an endlessly fretful series of transformations. Jūichirō had doubts about the effectiveness of all the everyday objects, and the wretched limits they constantly force upon us. When he opened the mysterious structure of a black umbrella above his head on a rainy day, how jarring the curved handle he felt in his hand, and how merciless the steel frame as the black silken material tautened above him, almost to breaking point. And that endless, persistent pattering of rain, forming rivulets that scattered in all directions!

There was a shop that made wooden tubs in the corner of an alleyway near the Ōsugi home. On sunny days, straw mats would be spread out all the way into the deserted alley, and two or three workmen would hammer nails into new bathtubs. As Jūichirō strolled by, he was nauseated by the thought of families who would soon be taking dips in those very same tubs. He could just see the husband, the wife and the children as they straddled the bath before getting in, with their flabby naked bodies and body hair, flecks of white soap foam still clinging to their waists, and looking horribly smug about life.

Every time Jūichirō and his wife went on an outing to Tokyo, he was distraught about the growing number of huge new buildings, their fluorescent lamps left on even in daytime. In every window, people constantly talked as they beavered away. But to what end?

Jūichirō sensed a total lack of coherence in the world. Everything was horribly broken. There was no connection between the steering wheel and tyres in a car, no link between brain and stomach in a human being.

On top of that, he was a kind and delicate soul who found it difficult to gaze upon such a fractured world with indifference. Cold war and global insecurity, the veneer of pacifism, people hurtling downhill towards imbecility between moments of respite, the illusion of economic prosperity, crazy hedonism, the effeminate vanity of the world's political leaders. All these things pricked his fingers like thorns in a bouquet of roses that he could not resist picking up.

Later, such things came to strike Jūichirō as harbingers of grace, and he prepared himself to take on the heavy responsibility for a world that had fallen into such adverse circumstances. Someone had to suffer for it, he thought. There had to be at least one person willing to walk the earth with bloodied naked feet on broken shards of glass.

Whenever he got news of a child knocked down and left covered in blood on the roadside in a hit-and-run accident, or a train crash resulting in dozens of injuries, or some major flooding where hundreds of homes were swallowed up, he would recoil, trembling with feelings of self-reproach. After all, he inhabited the self-same earth, the same incoherent world, so how could he claim himself innocent of all offence and all scandal? But perhaps his heartfelt suffering was the very key to restoring a sense of wholeness to the world. One morning, as he was plucking a single flower from a tea bush in the garden, it occurred to him that somewhere on this planet, thanks to some mysterious act of fate (connected to the plucking of this very flower, perhaps), someone was probably getting dragged under a 10-ton truck.

Yet how could it possibly be that his own body felt no pain? If the suffering of an individual writhing in their death throes produced not the slightest ripple on the rest of mankind, how could anyone make sense of that? Confronted by the bald fact that physical suffering never extended beyond the experience of a single person,

Jūichirō was plunged once more into deep despair. Why should even the fearful agony of the atomic bomb be reduced to individual suffering? Could it really be categorized simply as a physical experience? He thought he knew exactly why the person who dropped the bomb went mad. That man had lacked the ability to feel the tiniest bit of pain, not even an itch, and this must have driven him crazy.

Just as Jūichirō was coming to acknowledge the pettiness and limitations of his own suffering, and to feel ashamed of his own conceit, he read a book published in London, entitled *The Home of Flying Saucers*.

Until then, Jūichirō had hardly shown any interest in such things, but once he read it, particularly the section on the famous Mantell UFO incident, he became firmly convinced of the existence of flying saucers.

The incident took place at the United States Godman Army Airfield in Fort Knox, Kentucky, on 7 January 1948, when Captain Thomas F. Mantell lost his life while in pursuit of a flying saucer.

At approximately two-thirty that afternoon, a Fort Knox military policeman was notified by the federal police that an unusually large object was flying towards Godman. Police had sighted the object over Madison, Indiana, 150 kilometres from Godman. Several hundred citizens in Madison also spotted it.

Having received this communication just before three p.m. from the military policeman the officers at Godman Airfield kept their eyes on the sky over the base, which was cloudy, with occasional clear patches. Suddenly, through a cloud break to the south, what looked like a gigantic metallic object momentarily caught the sun's glare as it came into view, but just as quickly disappeared. Instructions were issued immediately for three pursuit planes to take off from the base under Captain Mantell's command.

All the officers in the control tower sighted *it*, shaped like a huge disc, with a top that resembled an inverted cone, and a tiny red light flickering on and off at its vertex.

At eight minutes past three, the two wingmen in the accompanying aeroplanes made radio contact with the control tower to say they had been in tight pursuit of the object, but it had outflanked them. They had watched the captain's aeroplane disappear after it.

About five minutes later, Mantell's voice was heard over the control tower tannoy.

'Object ascending. Speed increasing. Now proceeding same speed as aeroplane. Three hundred and sixty miles per hour. Now ascending to seven thousand metres. If capture is impossible, I will abort.'

This was the last living communication from Captain Mantell. A few minutes later, his F-51 fighter appears to have broken up in mid-air, and its wreckage was discovered over a range of several square kilometres.

The witnesses who verified the incident included multiple experts. There was also an abundance of supporting materials, so that the possibility that people might have been carried away by their imagination was completely ruled out. As he read on, Jūichirō became convinced that the flying saucer had carried inhabitants from another planet. From that moment, he was possessed by the study of flying saucers, and he devoured every book on the subject he could lay his hands on. His open and intellectually curious family shared the books passed on by their father, with the result that flying saucers and extra-terrestrials became the sole topic of their conversation.

And then something unforgettable happened during the summer the previous year. It started with Jūichirō.

He was asleep upstairs in the middle of the night when he awoke to the sound of something calling. Iyoko was conscious of her husband getting out of bed, but it was not unusual for him to pop down to the toilet during the night, so she went straight back to sleep.

Jūichirō was still in his pyjamas when he stepped out of the house. The moon was almost full, and the road brightly lit. He later remembered the clear outline of the moon reflected in the dusty front mirror of a three-wheeled motor bike parked outside the nearby sawmill.

After walking for a while, he came to an unmanned crossing on the Seibu railway line. Red gravel on both sides of the tracks was sprinkled with silver dust, rubbed away from the rails, which sparkled beautifully under the moon. As Jūichirō crossed the tracks, he was conscious that he had no idea where he was going. It just felt like he was on the right path, as if he were being pulled by a thread.

On the other side of the tracks was a large vacant plot, a factory site under construction, apparently, with just a single grubby tarpaulin sheet rising out of a dense blanket of summer grasses. It was covering up some building materials, but there was no sign that construction work was underway. As Jūichirō stepped through a gap in the barbed-wire fence into the deep grass, he sensed the tops of his feet getting soaked in dew, while his ears were inundated by the din of countless insects.

The insects suddenly fell silent. He looked up into the sky. Above the roofs of the surrounding low-lying houses there hung a flying saucer, tilted at an angle.

It was light-green, elliptically shaped and apparently utterly stationary. But as he watched, a wave of orange swept across it. The colour change took no more than four or five seconds. The vessel suddenly shook and shuddered, and no sooner had it turned orange all over than it flew off in a straight line at extraordinary speed into the south-eastern sky at an angle of about 45 degrees. At first it appeared as large as a full moon, but it shrank in an instant to the size of a rice grain and finally melted into the night sky.

Jūichirō sat, overcome, among the summer grasses, tears streaming down his cheeks. He felt that this fleeting apparition had touched the deepest core of his memories and triggered something within himself.

During those few seconds when the flying saucer was in sight, he had savoured an overwhelming emotion of supreme bliss. The bliss was the product of an indisputable realization that the fragmented world had attained a clear sense of harmony and unity, and the world was instantaneously healed. In the twinkling of an eye, heaven's glue had reconnected the broken shards, and the world reposed once more like a crystal globe in a state of unblemished peace. There was a merging of people's hearts, strife was no more, and his gasping sensation that he was on the verge of death had given way to calm, orderly breathing.

To think that Jūichirō was capable of glimpsing such a world for a second time! For this was a world he had certainly witnessed with his own eyes in the distant past, before he lost it. Where did he see it first? Sat among the summer grasses, his pyjamas drenched in dew, he racked his brains and dug deep into his memories. Various images of childhood emerged. All those flags in the marketplace, soldiers marching, rhinoceroses at the zoo, his hand thrust into a jar of strawberry jam, weird faces looming out from the woodgrain on the ceiling . . . like old exhibits crammed along both sides of memory's corridor as it rose into mid-air. And at its end, doors flew open to reveal nothing but a sky full of stars. The corridor was set at exactly the same angle as the path taken by the flying saucer.

'I get it. I know where my memories come from!' thought Jūichirō. It was just that he had been blind to the reality until then.

Now he knew. He was not from Earth, of that he was sure. That flying saucer had carried him on a mission from Mars to save this planet from its critical situation. The supreme bliss that accompanied his sighting of the ship just now obviously involved some sort of exchange taking place between Jūichirō, as he once was, and the occupants of the flying saucer.

All this thinking had left him so exhausted he could barely keep his eyes open. He rose to his feet and somehow staggered back along the way he came.

Next morning, he awoke to find himself in the same bed he had got into the night before. His wife was completely oblivious to his excursion in the small hours of night.

Jūichirō's heart was bursting with happiness the whole day long, but he wondered whether he should tell his family about what he had experienced that night. In the end, though, he could no longer contain his joy, and he came clean to the whole family as they sat around the dinner table. Akiko laughed the loudest.

But that evening Kazuo had a similar experience, and the next morning Iyoko had already sighted a silvery-grey flying saucer in the bright sky before anyone else was up.

Akiko laughed even more.

The next day, Akiko got off the train at Hannō Station on the way home from school. She was in no mood to go straight home to her deranged family, so she stopped by the Hachiman Shrine and ascended the steps to the grove inside the shrine. It was still light and the air was fresh, so she thought it might serve as a good place to prepare for the next day's classes. No one was about, and the shaded cedar thickets, brimming with the cries of evening cicadas, felt pleasantly cool.

Akiko went northwards up the stone steps, and, just as she reached the Torii gate at the rear of the shrine, her attention was drawn to what looked like a white dot flickering in the sky above the main hall of worship. Upon closer attention, it seemed to be hovering somewhere over the Komatōge Pass, which was nestled among the mountains, although Akiko first mistook it for a star that had appeared in the fading sky light.

But this 'star' was moving in a strange manner, and it suddenly came to rest over her head. There she was, standing in the precinct of a deserted shrine, surrounded by cedar groves with a round silver-gleaming body above her. It circled slowly in the sky over the trees. Akiko trembled.

It spiralled around and around in increasingly smaller circles, its underbelly silver-grey with a faint green tinge, like a sparkling jewel. Akiko almost cried out. All the mistrust and derision she had ever harboured seemed to have been turned inside out.

And then, in a flash, *it* disappeared from view like a phantom.

. . . from that day on, Akiko stopped laughing. She had become convinced that she was from Venus, and that the family she was a member of actually comprised of an interplanetary federation of extraterrestrials.

For the next six months, Jūichirō did everything he could to protect his family by concealing their true origins from the world at large. He taught his children to apply themselves even more strictly to their academic studies, and never to neglect activities that would make them appear as earthlings. He was particularly insistent that Akiko should throw herself into her study of handicrafts and cookery, and act in a way that followed conventional custom. After all, he was aware how easily honesty and purity could be damaged.

It was Akiko who took on the most obvious visible signs of change. Once she became aware of her Venusian roots, she grew more stunning by the day. She had always been a good-looking girl, but this did not affect her behaviour as long as she remained oblivious to the fact. However, now that she knew where she got her looks from, her beauty immediately took on an extra sheen of refinement and coolness. The neighbours gossiped that she must have met someone, even though Akiko had begun to demonstrate an increasingly disdainful attitude towards the opposite sex.

The family greeted their neighbours with a smile even though their hearts were not in it. But they were naturally standoffish, and their smiles were so contrived that they put their neighbours off. People kept their distance even more than before.

'Dad, people still push up against me when the train is full, but I don't get upset like I used to. Because now it feels like I'm looking down on them from a higher plane. Only *my* eyes seem to see clearly. Only *my* ears hear music from the heavens. Those sweaty oiks have no idea that their fates actually lie entirely in my hands.'

When Kazuo spoke in this breezy manner, Jūichirō scented danger. If the mob could read Kazuo's mind, it would never forgive him. In fact, it would kill him.

'Act like you're an ordinary guy,' his father remonstrated gently. 'Ordinary, no matter how distasteful you may find it. People superior to others have a duty to act like that. And it's the only way to protect yourself.'

. . . When spring arrived six months later, Jūichirō had an abrupt change of mind. He began to say that, if they wanted to carry out their mission effectively, they ought to make every effort to find kindred souls rather than waste time worrying about secrecy. The world was in imminent danger, Jūichirō mused, yet here he was, a slave to old-fashioned family sentiment, with his thoughts too hemmed in by timidity.

He racked his brains before coming up with the idea of placing an advertisement in the 'Common Interests' column of a tabloid magazine: 'If you are interested in ◉, we would like to hear from you. Let's work together as members of the Universal Friendship Association in the pursuit of world peace.'

◉ was the symbol that Jūichirō had devised to stand for a flying saucer, and responses were eerily spot on. Eighty per cent of letters arriving from every corner of the country surmised that the sign referred to a flying saucer.

Jūichirō produced pamphlets, copies of which the whole family helped to print, and he began to correspond frequently with members nationwide. Early that summer, Jūichirō had liquidated all the stocks bequeathed by his father and transferred the cash into a bank deposit to help with future activities. To everyone's surprise the stocks had appreciated enormously, increasing five-fold. And then, later that summer, there was a major financial slump. The family was now firmly convinced it was in the hands of someone watching over them from above.

However, until that moment, the flying saucers had always chosen to reveal themselves to one family member at a time. Of course, they all trusted each other when they asserted that they had seen one, but they had never had the opportunity to witness one as a group. As head of the family, Jūichirō had been gradually honing his extraterrestrial communication skills since the summer, and he yearned for the chance for them to make contact en masse.

It was early on the previous morning that Jūichirō had finally received advance notice.

'There's no time to waste. Khrushchev and Kennedy should meet and sit down together for a simple breakfast. Nothing special. Fancy food dulls the mind.' Jūichirō was talking to himself. Maybe he was tired and losing patience as he searched the sky. He vigorously rubbed his hands together, numb from the cold. 'All they have to do is pick up the phone on the desk and say one word: Washington. They should throw away their pathetic pride and all the trouble they've got themselves into, and get down to some serious talk about the future of humans. And as for all their half-baked plans! They're so far from everyday concrete reality that they've brought disaster down on the world. My father used to be like that. And that's precisely why I can see right through them. Father's life was so distanced from everyday objects like scissors, umbrellas, garden trees and vegetable salad that these things simply passed him by. Just like the stars have fled from humans.

'Halting nuclear weapons testing, disarmament and the Berlin question should be up for discussion just as much as soft-boiled eggs, baked apples and raisin bread. If you look at things from the commanding heights of the Universe, they all have equal worth. We've got to get earthlings to understand that. People commit murder precisely because they think it's such a big deal and they can't resist the temptation.

'Khrushchev and Kennedy need to sweep up their breakfast breadcrumbs with their napkins, set the napkins back on the table and emerge from the room arm in arm. They could make an announcement to the waiting reporters basking in the morning sun: "We are of the same opinion. Humankind should live and prosper."

'No need to release pigeons, or for a military band. The moment they utter those words, a bright fresh day will burst into life. The whole Universe will recognize that, from that moment on, Earth has become a *beautiful star*. So, what do you think? How about we find the strength to make them embrace each other as quickly as possible?' But he had barely finished speaking before adding, more darkly, '. . . that is, if we have the strength. How sad that I've been assigned this temporary human body. But there again, it's obviously all part of the Universe's foresight and underlying plan.'

There was no reply from his wife and children. All had their eyes glued to the southern sky.

Astronomy is still an unreliable science, but Jupiter's surface temperature is said to be about 100 degrees below zero. A native of that planet, Iyoko was huddled shivering inside her blanket, lamenting her own pitiful lack of resolve in the face of even this trifling cold. She was barely interested in politics. If the world was reformed and peace established in the way advocated by her husband, she would probably be assigned the domestic task of keeping the world neat and tidy. Iyoko loved the abundant cereals that were to be found on Earth. The sweet-smelling fragrance of wheatfields in the summer, and the golden heads of rice bowing in autumn. These were worth preserving for ever for the sake of earthlings. But whatever planet she found herself on, she would probably end up in charge of the kitchen. Despite that, she had no confidence she would be able to properly manage just the two different types of kitchen found on Jupiter and Earth.

Every time Kazuo's binoculars shifted from one area to another, the lingering trace of starlight would fool him into thinking he had spotted a flying saucer.

He tried to remain focused, but his father's chatter was putting him off. His heart overflowed with a decisive will to power, that gained traction from a mixture of unadulterated good intent and sentimental affection towards the world. He dreamed of an utterly pure form of power capable of maintaining eternal peace on Earth. This was something that the Earth had never experienced before, so it needed instruction from the other planets. Moreover, this power was not religious or spiritual in nature, but blemish-free, pure as a new towel, and able to exert control over every aspect of life.

Akiko ignored the others, devoting all her attention to the sky to the east. If the flying saucers were going to arrive slightly off schedule, might they not also come in from a different direction?

The cold sent occasional little shivers across Akiko's shoulders. She was concerned her lips might chap, so she fumbled to apply a thick coat of lip balm. The cold had numbed her fingertips, and she was worried about making a mess. But it was better than deliberately shining a torch onto her compact mirror and getting ticked off by her parents.

Now that she knew she was from Venus, Akiko increasingly grew to accept the comfortably lazy indifference that formed part of her very nature. Close scrutiny would probably have revealed that her coldness was no different from the comfortably lazy indifference of a clever, self-satisfied little minx. And it was to the young woman's advantage that, having no desires of her own, she appeared to have conquered all desires . . . Akiko was all for bestowing peace upon the Earth, but in the same way that someone might offer a sweet bun to a scruffy urchin.

It was almost five o'clock, but there was still no sign of flying saucers in the southern sky. Not one family member voiced their frustration.

How they longed for the red-tinted elliptical crafts to fly towards them, turn pale green and shoot off at a different angle. Witnessing this as a family for the first time would consolidate the sense of solidarity that underpinned their drive to save the world. Even if the ships turned up but failed to impart anything new, their mere presence would provide a huge boon to the family. All four of them harboured the same thoughts in their hearts.

The roar of the north wind behind them grew even fiercer. Kazuo glanced down at the luminous dial of his watch. The aqua minute hand pointed to five o'clock.

'It's not over yet. I said before that sometimes their timing is a bit out.' Jūichirō spoke in a deep and phlegmatic tone. And yet all of them, in their hearts, experienced the dousing of their passions, like a cold wind scouring some inert planetary body. They found themselves abruptly scurrying back to their respective corners. A mood of harmony and unity had kept them finely tuned like a harp, but suddenly the strings seemed broken and all sound had died.

'I see it,' Akiko suddenly spoke out in a clear voice.

'You do?' The other three looked eastward, ecstatic.

But it was not a flying saucer. She had seen the red glow of Venus rising above the eastern horizon.

'What I mean is, I see my home planet,' said Akiko. Her parents were kind enough to indulge their charming daughter with their heartfelt blessings towards Venus. And then, they cast once more their long-suffering gaze towards the southern sky. Kazuo recognized the modest glow of his own planet, Mercury, as it rose simultaneously to the left of Venus. He set aside his binoculars and cried with delight, 'I see mine too.'

The sight of that tiniest glimpse gave him strength.

The siblings could not bear to tear their eyes away from the eastern sky. Venus and Mercury arose at a dignified, ceremonial pace. The red hue of Venus slowly paled into the same clear white light of Mercury as they rose in unison.

The twin planets stood out above a dark purple bank of clouds while the shadows of surrounding trees gradually broke free from the darkness. Trees framed against the eastern sky etched particularly delicate silhouettes, while the shadows of individual leaves fluttered gently in the wind quite enchantingly. The stars were beginning to fade, but dawn remained a reluctant reddish brown, while assorted coils of cloud – from ink black to purple, and of various depths – lurked on the eastern horizon.

'It wouldn't surprise me if they turned up after dawn. After all, that's what they did with you,' Jūichirō addressed Iyoko.

'That's right, mine appeared after the newspaper was delivered.' Jūichirō was already able to make out the general features of her face as she spoke, and the check pattern of the blanket wrapped around her stood out sharply. But he never imagined that the first stirrings of daylight could envelop his heart in such bleakness.

Autumnal leaves, scattered by the morning storm, came clearly into view along the uneven stony surface of the ground. Jūichirō was distressed to notice that the more things became visible, the more insistent the existence of all those things he had failed to notice on their way up.

'It's still early. Too soon to throw in the towel,' he said to himself. For her part, Iyoko showed no sign of giving up.

At five-thirty, Kazuo could read his watch without needing to depend on its luminous markings. The clouds in the east had turned burgundy, the sky pale white. Mountain ridges to the south-west emerged clearly, while the three stars of Orion's Belt lingered ever so faintly.

'My home is disappearing. Look how the light . . .'

Akiko rocked her brother's shoulders as she spoke.

'Mine, too.'

Dawn was breaking hesitantly, emerging like a withered, pressed flower the colour of bitter orange. But just as it took on a dark vermilion colour, it swallowed the light from Venus and Mercury.

Tears flowed down Akiko's frozen cheeks.

'My star . . .' Pale white roofs of village houses appeared out of the dark foothills, and the old familiar green of the mountains began to emerge. The first Seibu Line train, the five-thirty, wove like a bright thread through the trees among the foothills. From the distant mountains to the south-west, gloomy like a copperplate engraving, Mt Fuji's white peak came into view.

'What time now?' Jūichirō asked his son, and continued, 'Ah, I can see easily now with my own watch. It's six. That's an hour since they said they'd come. I think we're going to have to call it a day. You know, we've been waiting all this time and they haven't turned up, but maybe that was exactly the message they meant to convey. Perhaps it was a kind of test, checking to see how brave and resilient we were as extraterrestrials.'

His son tried to encourage him with a cheerful tone. 'But, Dad, we made such an effort to come here. Let's stay at least until sunrise. They could still arrive any time now.'

'You're right. Maybe it's a bit early to throw in the towel.'

Chimes announcing six o'clock reached them from Hannō, where a line of street lights still shone. The green fields and white-walled storehouses emerged vibrant, while several crows cut diagonally across their vision, cawing. To the south-west, the mountains south of the Sannōtōge Pass had come into view, their snowy peaks already tinged scarlet.

To the east, layers of cloud piled up further. Sharp red shafts of light broke through a section of the clouds, as though through a pair of smiling lips.

'Whatever happens, we mustn't stop believing.' Iyoko was usually slow to offer her thoughts, but this time she demonstrated an old-fashioned steeliness. 'When human beings set out to do something, they get all excited and then they're disappointed. It's quite normal for them to give up. But *we are not humans*, we must never forget that. Not for a moment.'

The sun finally rent the clouds and exposed its dazzling face. Like a powerful javelin, the first bolt of light pierced the south-west flank of the snowy peak of Mt Fuji, immediately turning it the colour of roses.

2

Akiko finished the English version of the letter to Khrushchev a few days after the family had climbed the mountain. Once she had worked on the original Japanese and Jūichirō had added some rhetorical flourishes, she was assigned the role of translating it, since she was an English Literature major. They were concerned that a letter in English might not go down well on the Russian side, but no one in the family knew any Russian and they could hardly get outside help.

Dear First Secretary Khrushchev of the Soviet Union,

It appears that you recently carried out a 50-megaton nuclear missile test, and we are so concerned that we felt forced to write you this letter. When we heard newspaper reports that, immediately following the test, radioactive material damaging to the human body was contaminating our rainfall here in Japan, our home in the Far East, we became even more despondent. But it should be stated from the beginning that we humbly compose this missive not merely from the perspective of individual Japanese nationals. Rather, it reflects the demands and warnings from all humanity, or to be more precise, from the entire Milky Way. As representatives of various planets now resident on Earth, we find it particularly hard to allow your behaviour to pass unanswered.

Of course, we in no way hold you alone personally responsible. This is a major problem not only for human civilization, but also for peaceful order within the Universe. Mankind is now at loggerheads with the advanced civilization that it has created by its very own hands, and it is left with only two choices: to become wise rulers of that civilization, or to perish as slaves under the yoke of that same civilization. Actually, your adversary is not America, but yourself. The greatest enemy of mankind is mankind. If only you could over-come your demons in order to save the Earth and humankind from destruction, and summon up a dauntless spirit in order to eradicate for ever the threat of war by the accidental push of a button, then you would truly earn the honour of becoming the greatest benefac-tor in the history of mankind. America soiled its hands when it dropped the atomic bomb on Hiroshima. That stain will never be expunged from their history. But why, sir, do you compete with America to sully your own hands? America is cursed with an indel-ible sin against humanity, so why do you not distance yourself from them, take wise counsel and keep your hands clean? . . . It is still not too late. The stars above keep watch, day and night, over the Earth's fate. We are distraught that half the planet is already contaminated, but we never lose hope that it will revert at some point to the ancient beautiful star it once was . . .

Having reached this halfway point in the letter, Jūichirō blithely sang his own praises, as was his wont.

'Brilliant! I love the way the letter avoids the hectoring tone a religious fanatic might use. It's written in a way that addresses Khrushchev with respect, but also urges him to be ambitious. It would be wrong to adopt the tone we use towards our fellow believ-ers. With humans, you have to go out of your way to follow human logic and psychology to make your argument. It's the same patience you need when you're humouring a dim-witted dog, or when you're developing skill in the arts.'

'What if there's no reply?' asked Kazuo.

'If there's no reply, there's no reply. The reply itself doesn't mat-ter. Because the only thing you can be sure of is that the letter will have dyed Khrushchev's heart for ever with indelible ink.'

The letter was typed out, and at the end all four family members inscribed the symbols of their respective native planets, next to which they affixed their signatures. They passed it around for a final read, and they had some fun trying to predict what the outcome would be. They felt that the letter truly expressed the wisdom of the stars.

The next day Akiko's English History class was cancelled, so she took the day off. She was entrusted with delivering the letter to the post office.

'After dinner tonight, let's have some warm sweet-bean-and-sticky-ricecake soup. Could you drop by at Murata's on your way back from the post office and buy about a litre of adzuki beans?'

Mother always decided amounts intuitively, and a litre of beans to make soup for four was way too much, but Akiko did not challenge her about it.

The clerk at the post office counter gave not a second glance to the name of the addressee, and accepted it like any other airmail letter. Whenever Akiko went to send mail overseas, the clerk would exchange a few pleasantries with her. Aware of his growing familiarity, she worried he might begin to take greater interest in the letters she handed over and grill her about them. But there was no sign of that yet, and the young man's interest was confined solely to Akiko's face.

Akiko took the bus and got off close to home, then walked towards Murata's, the general store. There were no hills in Hannō, but it did have many wide, unpaved roads. Red and blue shop awnings, struck by the warm morning sun of early winter, stretched down over the white roads to even lower than people's height.

When the shop boy spied Akiko slowly walking towards them from the bus stop with a shopping basket on her arm, he rushed inside excitedly to inform the shopkeeper.

'Mr Ōsugi's daughter's coming. She's got a white coat on with a red beret.'

'Nothing to get worked up about,' said the shopkeeper, busy with her children. 'Just palm off whatever rubbish you can on her at the highest possible price. That family doesn't have a clue.'

Having lost 50,000 yen during the financial slump, it was only natural that she got wind of rumours that the Ōsugis had disposed of all their shares before the summer. She was convinced the family had been tipped off by an inside source, and she resented it bitterly.

She was determined to pass off shoddy goods onto such a conceited family. At the same time, she ordered the shop boy, Tarō, to redouble his efforts in winkling out the family's secrets. Such was the peculiar nature of the shopkeeper's interest in Iyoko and Akiko.

If I had my way, I'd serve them poison, she thought. The whole family's making money on the sly, all the while living their stuck-up lives and looking for all the world as if they're better than the rest of us. They're so full of themselves. The husband puts on the airs of a scholar, while his wife plays the wise wife. The son is a moronic philanderer, and when it comes to their daughter, well, she may look as if butter wouldn't melt in her mouth, but they say she's hanging out with boys in Tokyo. And another thing, a girl who walks like that is a slut who will never have children. An honest, hard-working family like us loses big money, while that lot pose as intellectuals but rake it in. There are some odd things afoot in the world. Just a few days ago, the whole family went for an outing somewhere in the car in the middle of the night. I bet they're involved in drugs, or something. I've had enough. I'm going to catch them out, rope the whole family together and take them down to the police station. They can deal with them there.

In the store, there were rows of apple and orange crates covered with boards, with all sorts of things heaped on top. Seasonal fruits, onions, potatoes, pickles, giant radishes, red pickled ginger, boiled beans, sweets, chewing gum, instant curry and the like. In summertime, they sold ice cream too. The lowered blinds made the interior gloomy, and it gave off a ponderous smell like an estuary backwater afloat with multicoloured objects.

Akiko's pale face peeped through a gap in the blind, and she spoke in a beautifully clear voice.

'Do you have any adzuki beans?'

'Ah, so nice to see you again. We happen to have some really good beans in,' said the shopkeeper from the back. 'How much would you like?'

'A litre, please.'

As ever, Tarō threw himself into giving the beautiful Akiko a raw deal as to the quality and weight of the goods. The young man felt that, by pulling the wool over her eyes, he was actually sharing a secret with her. His stingy malice was a way of compensating for the despair he felt about his own acne. As he kept his eyes on Akiko's face and measured the beans, he hummed an indistinct tune at the back of his throat:

> '. . . Drifting like ducks asleep on the water,
> Such love unfulfilled . . .'

In this manner, he sold Akiko some adzuki beans soiled with grain husks at 130 yen for the litre, and he even pressed her to take a damaged can of mushrooms at 200 yen, twice the normal price.

What lovely people they are, thought Akiko. She had left the shop and was taking the shortcut home. The whole family always looks happy, and they bring such energy to their work. It's true the children are grubby, but they get along with their mother like peas in a pod. And they always greet me with such a nice smile! I'm no expert on the matter, but that's the goodness and happiness of human life in a nutshell. We need to do our utmost to protect them from the hydrogen bomb.

It was a really clear, beautiful afternoon in early winter. The path that Akiko followed was lined on both sides by tea hedges with small white flowers, dead and shrivelled, shaded by dusty leaves. The sky was burnished with countless persimmon trees, their withered branches tangled together. Through the hedge she spotted a farm courtyard where shirts had been hung out to dry, along with some large taro leaves and a cluster of faded chrysanthemums. A dark rundown barn leant against the fence, reeking of goats.

Akiko was content. The flying saucers may have failed to show up over Mt Rakan, she reflected, but at least today she was fulfilling her duty as an extraterrestrial.

However, as she continued along the meandering path, she noticed a couple walking ahead, chatting as they went. Recognizing one of them, her face darkened and she stopped in her tracks. The young man walking with an unknown girl was Kazuo. He should have been at school right now.

He's up to his old tricks. And, of all things, to think he's hanging out with a human girl!

Beside herself with anger, Akiko's cheeks flushed. It was not the girl's purity that her brother was dishonouring, she felt, but her own.

He was obviously making a mockery of Jūichirō's admonition: 'Act like you're an ordinary guy . . . no matter how distasteful you may find it.' Is this what Father's words ultimately boiled down to?

That morning as Akiko had watched Venus rise solemnly in the eastern sky, it felt like she had reached a deeper understanding of the roots of her own purity.

To speak of Venusian purity was a paradox. As the planet arose, bathed in the cold air of dawn like the goddess emerging into life from the green froth of the Phoenician shore, she seemed oblivious to any unwarranted injunction against passion. What had possessed Akiko to end up in a place governed by laws other than those of planetary motion? Those planetary laws were scrupulously kept. They drove the elliptical orbits around the Sun. They ensured that the lines tying the Sun to the planets moved at a determined time, and that the surface area of the fan-shaped plane they sketched remained constant. They maintained exact correlation between the square of orbital periods and the cube of the average distance from the Sun.

These laws alone informed Akiko's ethics. Unlike the purity of Earth women, trapped in their petty morality, her purity more closely resembled a hard, glittering star that superseded all ethics! Purity! Purity! The word rang constantly within Akiko like a musical refrain and its echo never ceased, whether she was packed in a train on the way to school or sat in a lecture on American Literary History in Classroom Sixteen.

Once, for example, sunshine pouring through the windows threw half the blackboard into light, so that it was difficult to read what was written in chalk from where she sat. The name 'Nathaniel Hawthorne' had been scrawled across the board in large romanized script, but when the area around 'Hawthorne' appeared to fuse into the glare, Akiko felt that the light from the windows had folded its wings tightly over those chalk letters, and replaced them with one joyfully scribbled word that only she could read. Purity.

Another time she accompanied some fellow students into an unfamiliar coffee shop. Numerous rubber plants were dotted around strategically, Latin music was blaring out of the record player and young couples canoodled in dark booths where they had been holed up all day. The sight of this did not lead Akiko to immediately stand up and leave. Instead, she leant back into her chair for a while with her eyes firmly closed.

'What's up?' asked a friend.

'My eyes, they're tired. Just let me be for a while.'

At that point, the insistent, suggestive refrain of a vulgar samba record suddenly cut right through: 'Pure! Virginal! Oh, oh, virginal!' it seemed to say. All at once, the small dark coffee shop was transformed behind Akiko's closed eyelids into an ice-cold inner sanctum, filled with the chill of daybreak, with every wall catching the first flush of dawn. People dressed in glowing, white, long-sleeved robes sat around in contemplation. This is a coffee shop on Venus, thought Akiko. They'll be bringing in Venusian coffee pretty soon, I'm sure of it.

There were so many examples.

In late spring at the time of its greatest eastern elongation, Venus had shone so brightly as an evening star that she noticed it during rush hour beyond the fields through the window of her Seibu Line train. She was squashed by the bodies of foul-smelling men, and tilted her head away from the rawness of their breath. Unable to move even the bag she was clutching in her hand, she twisted her body, but staggered with every lurch of the train. Just when it felt as if her body might break under this clamour of unyielding, insensitive, rude human flesh, Akiko's serene pale face floated above the dingy shoulders like a lily flower, and she gazed towards Venus beyond the fields through the window. As the carriage swayed, so did Venus. The star seemed to pursue them on their speeding train. A twinkle of indestructible purity suspended in that late spring sky in the evening . . .

Eventually they came to a branch in the path. Straight ahead led to the Ōsugi home, but her brother and his girl turned right. Akiko was worried they might turn around and spot her, so she kept her body pressed against the hedge as she followed. The litre of red beans and the can weighed heavily in her shopping basket.

The right-hand path came out next to an Inari shrine, dedicated to foxes. Swinging his bag, her brother laughed happily and pecked the girl on the cheek. As she twisted her body to brush lightly against his, his hands passed carelessly over her. The exaggerated cut of his navy-blue trench coat set off her brother's broad shoulders surprisingly well.

The girl was petite. It was the fashion at the time for girls to wear chunky, deliberately oversized men's sweaters with the sleeves rolled right up. But the face that looked up at Kazuo appeared child-like and soft, with fragile, delicate lines running from her mouth to her chin. She was the same age as Akiko, or possibly a couple of years younger. Her rouged lips, ripe and glossy, appeared to cling effortlessly to the surrounding air. A purple skirt stretched tightly over her backside, which caught the sunlight and rolled smoothly from side to side as they ambled along.

The pair entered the park that bordered the approach to the shrine. Benches were nestled among old towering cedars and cherry trees, and beyond that were a swing and a horizontal bar where children could be heard shouting. There were also mothers with babies strapped to their backs gathering fallen cedar leaves to build bonfires. The couple seemed in two minds about which bench to settle on. In the end, they avoided the cold shade under the trees and sat on a sunny bench next to a stone handbasin, inscribed with the words 'The cockerel's first cry'.

Akiko tucked her conspicuous red beret into her shopping bag and trod stealthily between the cedars. She crept up slowly behind the pair. With just a single cedar trunk between them, she could make out their conversation clearly.

'So, you're skipping school and your family don't know anything about it?'

'Relax. I never stay away longer than the class I'm avoiding, and today we really did have time off. There's a cold going around, and all those batty old teachers have gone down with it. And I never take any schoolmates home. We all do the same. So, there's no chance of getting grilled by our mothers and spilling the beans.'

'You've got your head screwed on,' she chipped in cheerfully. Even from where she was standing, Akiko sensed a really big smile on Kazuo's face in response to the girl's remark. He was easily flattered.

'Kazu, you're really good at mind games. I'd better watch out.'

'I'm nothing special.' His tone betrayed someone pleased as punch. 'It's fine having fun in Tokyo, but you get a real thrill hanging out close to each other's homes like this.'

'I'm not into thrills. A big, thick, solid cushion on the floor. That's the kind of happiness I prefer. Like one of those flashy cushions monks sit on.'

'That's all well and good, but I prefer a small plump one. Like you.'

'Oh, you're awful.'

Akiko steamed with anger as she listened. But just as she was about to pounce, they started kissing and it threw her. This was the first time she had ever seen her brother kiss. His squashed lips were pushed out of shape and he wore the most ridiculous expression.

Akiko closed her eyes tightly. In the darkness, several hundred Venuses burst open in all directions. She thrust her hand deep into her shopping bag and approached the bench. The girl was lost in the kiss, her head inclined upwards with eyes closed. Akiko took a big handful of adzuki beans and dropped them over the girl's face.

The girl sprang up with a shriek and, staggering a few paces away, turned back around. Akiko was smiling. The girl suddenly sobbed:

'Monster! I should have guessed it would be some girl,' she shouted repeatedly.

'You're wrong. I'm his sister.'

'I just don't get this!'

The girl turned tail and took a few slow steps, before sprinting back up the path they had just walked down with extraordinary energy.

Kazuo was surprisingly calm. Still sitting on the bench, he spoke to his sister with adzuki beans in his hand.

'What's all this with adzuki beans?' He raised his drowsy, long-lashed eyes. 'What possessed you to do that, Akiko?'

Akiko did not reply. She walked right around the bench to stand in front of her brother and quietly sat down by his side. Taking out the red beret from her shopping bag, she pulled it tightly down over her ears.

'So, what's it all about, Akiko?'

'I don't think I ever realized how much you've been leading lots of girls astray. And now I've seen it with my own eyes.'

'And that's why you flew into a rage?'

'Well . . . she was human . . .'

Kazuo said nothing. The wind stirred slightly, scattering some worm-eaten leaves from a cherry tree onto their knees. It was an inexpressibly sweet moment.

'OK, let me tell you how I feel.' Kazuo glanced briefly around before beginning. 'First of all, I've never revealed my secret to any of those girls. You're probably afraid I'm going to let something slip, but as Dad says, it would do more harm than good if someone were to find out we're aliens. We should never forget it's the Universe that entrusted us with maintaining peace on Earth. The Earth never asked anything of us. We don't owe the Earth anything, and in the end we're not responsible for it. Unlike humans, we have absolutely no liability towards earthlings or their affairs. Ethically, of course, there's nothing to stop us killing humans, but we just don't go there because it would get messy with their legal system. Dad even pays all his taxes to avoid any such difficulties.

'But when it comes to human girls, I just can't keep my hands off them. They strike me as so exotic, so curious and elegant, and absolutely bursting with originality. And it's all a matter of what angle you view them from. Human males love to look up to them from below, whereas celestial beings like us tend to gaze down from on high. That's why we generally get a full view of the smooth valley between their plump white breasts, without even really trying.

'To tell the truth, they're not really such a serious temptation. I realize I have no responsibility towards them, and I'm confident they'll stay none the wiser about that. And even if one of them gets pregnant . . .'

'What, you've got some girl pregnant?' Akiko cried out in despair.

'Relax. I mean *if*.'

'Even the possibility is terrifying. It would result in a half-breed born from an extraterrestrial and an earthling. Has it never occurred to you what a harsh life such a child would have? It would be catastrophic. The child would have human responsibilities and be tied by the laws of this world. At the same time, its heart would beat with traces of its father's sense of universal freedom, which would make it feel it could do whatever it pleased beyond the limits of earthly good and evil. A child like that would lead a terrible life of suffering and hardship!'

'You're worrying too much,' her brother continued, calmly. 'Even if a girl got pregnant, as a human mother she'd rely on her maternal love to overcome any hardships that ensued. As I said before, I wouldn't bear the slightest responsibility . . . And if mother and child found it too hard to cope, we'd just have to work out some clever ruse to quietly kill them off. That would clarify how totally useless it was for them to suffer for my sake, or on my behalf.'

'I'm with you there.' Akiko expressed agreement with an unexpected level of compliance. 'My own feeling is that, somewhere, there must be a wonderful girl from your own planet for you to love. I'm sure you still retain memories of pure and elevated celestial love in your heart, unlike the coarse, animalistic love they have here on Earth. If you don't, I can only conclude that you've been tainted and poisoned by wicked earthlings. I really lost control just now. There'll be less sweet bean soup to go around tonight. But you're to blame for that.'

Their argument seemed to have cooled a little by this point and, relieved, Kazuo looked mischievously towards his beautiful sister.

'Come on, out with it. You're trying to drag me into the way you do things yourself, aren't you? Venusians are so self-righteous.'

'What do you mean?'

'You know what I mean. You're exchanging letters with a

Venusian boy who lives in Kanazawa, aren't you? Is that what "pure and elevated celestial love" is all about?'

The words caused Akiko to blush. But deep sincerity prevented her from hitting back with a quip. Humiliated by the thought that her true feelings were being ridiculed, she flew off the handle and glared angrily into her brother's face. Her clear, bright eyes were extraordinarily blue. Her cheeks had momentarily blazed, but now they were drained of colour, and her composed features were etched under the bright morning light with the coldness of a night sky suddenly studded with stars.

Kazuo recognized his sister's expression when she was really angry. He now regretted having gone too far, but it was too late. Akiko addressed him with a display of withering contempt on her beautiful lips:

'You're a big talker, aren't you? But you know, you might actually be a big phoney.'

'What are you talking about?'

Guessing at what she was implying, Kazuo immediately became animated too. This was the first time anyone had ever doubted him, and in this all-out fight between brother and sister she was prepared to hit him where it really hurt. All he could do was adopt the same tactic.

'Yes, a big phoney. Maybe you're nothing more than human. You say you come from Mercury, but I've never heard of a Mercurian who spends all his time chasing skirt. You claim to have seen a flying saucer, but you're lying. Mum and Dad both saw one, so you decided to climb on board by pretending you had too. You just didn't want to miss the bus.'

'I've seen one, I really have. You're the one we can't trust.'

'I saw one with my own eyes. As you'll recall, I was the one full of doubts at first, and I laughed it off. But ever since it appeared in that wood at the Hachiman Shrine, I've been a believer.'

'You have witnesses?'

'No.' Akiko faltered. 'What are you implying?'

'You have no witnesses, yet you claim to have definitely seen it.

Look, those stuffy alien airs you put on are all very suspect. If you really were extraterrestrial, you'd act more naturally.'

'Don't use those grubby human words on me. They have a nasty human stench about them.'

'Do you really doubt me?'

'Absolutely.' Akiko spat out the word. But no sooner had she uttered it than she was assailed by an indescribable sadness, and tears gathered in her eyes.

She looked down. Beneath her feet was the cracked dry earth, across which spread the rectangular shadow of the stone basin. The basin contained no water. It was buried under a heap of crinkly leaves. Children had drawn vein-like red crayon marks on the stone surface. They were not exactly drawings, more like morose and sinister patterns left behind by the children as they passed by. The squeaking of the horizontal bar in the distance reached them through the cedars, like a sick man grinding his teeth.

Both lapsed into silence as they caught a glimpse of an unpleasant, disordered world. Surely it was the same world that frequently vexed their father Jūichirō so much. A world in which nothing had meaning, a higgledy-piggledy mess without harmony or unity.

'Absolutely.' Akiko's word was immediately followed by the collapse of the beautiful crystalline world they had both inhabited, to be replaced by an alternative, horrific world that welled up from the earth. Its ghastly back speckled with bluish-black marks.

They said nothing more until the evening. They could hardly maintain their silence during mealtime. The sweet red-bean soup their mother had worked on so hard was somewhat lacking in flavour, but their tempers were gradually cooling and they ate it with relish. That night, Akiko visited her brother's room, which reeked of gas-heater fumes. Kazuo had just opened the window to clear the air.

The south-facing window opened onto a magnificent starry sky. Orion was yet to appear, while Scorpio had already sunk in the west, with Sagittarius in pursuit. Only the head and tail of neighbouring Capricorn were visible. In the centre of the sky, the constellation of

Aquarius was formed from the giant star Sadalmelik, representing the beautiful head of the youthful water-carrier, and the four stars that gave shape to his water jar. A torrent of stars spilled southwards out of the jar's mouth, where Pisces swallowed every drop.

As they gazed in silence at the starry sky, their hearts were completely healed. The order of the stars had restored their trust, and the need for words of apology or justification had passed.

'Of course, we came from up there. It's just that the memory fades sometimes . . .'

'You're right. That's why we need to look at the heavens sometimes, to allow those memories to return with the old intensity.' Kazuo spoke gravely, then sneezed.

There had not been a high-school class reunion in ages, and this one was to be held on the first floor of a little restaurant in the Nihonbashi district. Jūichirō was going into Tokyo anyway to request some books on flying saucers at the Maruzen bookshop, so he decided to attend.

Passing some garishly dressed young hikers who had alighted at Hannō Station, Jūichirō went through the ticket barrier to wait for his train. The city of Hannō was the main gateway to the Oku-Musashi Natural Park, and every season of the year there was no end of hikers. They revealed a tawdry understanding of 'nature's mysteries' in their rainbow-coloured mufflers, walking boots and overly water-resistant watches. On the one-hour journey to Ikebukuro, Jūichirō's thoughts were fixed entirely on ways to battle the madness that was rampant in the world.

He left Maruzen and killed time at the department store opposite, shopping for a few items his wife had requested. He was so taken by the rich variety of products on display from around the world that he ended up staying until closing time. The range of goods was fascinating. Dazzling gold boxes of raisins, plumped-up sweaters, flowery embroidered panties, train sets equipped with stations, tunnels and railway bridges, beautiful nappy covers. They were all masterpieces of human civilization in their ability to replenish the human heart with life's charms. Each object, perfectly suited to its usage, and restricted specifically to nothing more than that purpose, provided the confused and half-crazed customers with fine-tuned ways to improve the minutiae of their lives. The essential nature of things never faltered – brooms were brooms, and shoes were shoes – and they formed a gigantic structure of cords that bound human beings tightly into human life.

So long as I'm here, I'm safe, thought Jūichirō. Just for a moment, human insanity is healed. That's the purpose of department stores. They are like hospitals.

He was well aware of a pathological tendency among earthlings. The masses in every country were really healthy, passionate for novelties and old-fashioned ways in equal measure, mean-spirited yet tender-hearted, wary of both danger and violent emotion, and fervent fans of an anodyne atmosphere . . . But despite all these characteristics, they were quite capable of going insane.

By the time Jūichirō reached the restaurant on the first floor, most guests had already gathered and were noisily catching up with old schoolmates.

He presented an air of mystery. No one knew what he had been up to since the war ended. Someone had mentioned his name and sent an invitation to his old Hannō address on the off chance, and was surprised to receive a positive response. Until Jūichirō turned up, the whole group had been engaged in speculation about him.

Jūichirō had been a completely nondescript student at school, so his classmates recalled him only dimly. He had joined the literary society, where he wrote odd, indecipherable poetry, and the art club, where he painted nice, agreeable landscape pictures. He also attended the music club religiously. The government crackdown on Socialism that began specifically on 15 March 1928, along with the winding up of Marxist literary movements, had an effect on quite a lot of people, even at school level. However, as the son of an affluent Hannō lumber businessman, Jūichirō had avoided all the fads, as if he were walking along with his eyes closed.

At a push, the only thing that had made him stand out a little was his dislike of shabby clothes and his comparatively neat personal appearance. He had stubbornly rejected any interest in the outside world, and he repaid sentimental friendship with a wan smile. On warm winter days, he would stand apart from others in the play-ground and crouch down in a sunny spot under the big acacia tree, with his black overcoat still on. That was how he earned his nick-name, 'Black Fly'. But he had shown no signs of anxiety or dejection. Whenever he wanted to borrow a notebook from a friend, he would ask nervously, as if he were dealing with a stranger, and if a friend borrowed money from him, he would quickly hand over the cash without even looking his friend in the face. He never had any roman-tic interests.

In short, Jūichirō had left no lasting impression on any of his assembled classmates. Indeed, the only thing they had retained was a sort of small empty space that their memories could not pos-sibly fill. In the class commemorative photograph, his face alone amounted to a featureless face under a school cap. Their fractious efforts to summon memories of him concealed something close to envy for the utter blankness of his adolescence, in which not a single seed of the usual putrid self-loathing, common among other young-sters, could be found.

'The guy barely left a shadow. I guess that means he's lived a long life.

> Though hated,
> he lives long:
> the winter fly.

Or maybe not,' said Satomi, chief of the General Affairs Depart-ment at Tozai Denki Company and an accomplished haiku poet, quoting the famous verse by Takarai Kikaku.

'I wonder. Docile men can be surprisingly tyrannical at home, loathed by their wives and kids,' said Maeda, company director at Dainippon Rayon.

'You must be talking about yourself there,' teased Sakaki, a law-yer with a sharp tongue.

While all this was going on, Jūichirō slid open the door and entered. In the past, no one had wanted to know him, but now they all clamoured to greet him.

'Oh, you've got white hair. That's a pity. I made a bet you'd be bald.' It was Ōtsu who spoke, the completely bald owner of a famous draper's shop in Ginza.

Jūichirō was beckoned to the empty seat of honour, where he sat cross-legged in his homespun trousers, with a shy look on his face. All eyes were focused on him, observing every move of his body as if he were a woman. By the look of things, they did not have to worry he was going to ask them for cash. Perhaps he was attending his first class reunion in twenty years in order to makes some contacts and help his son find work. Everyone seemed to think that was the situation. If that was all, they could relax.

Since most people had arrived by now, the organizer made a few opening remarks, and the self-introductions followed.

Tamagawa stood up to speak. 'Right now, I'm the deputy minister at the Ministry of Finance. At the ministry, we're working as hard as we can to reduce next year's taxes. I'm sure that's what you're all desperately hoping for, so please rest assured.'

'Hey, you can't fool us!'

Tamagawa continued. 'I have two sons and three daughters at home, and we all look like those Billiken dolls from America, with their monkey-like faces and tufts of hair on their pointy heads. They're definitely all chips off the old block.'

He really did look like a Billiken doll. It might be possible to patch together an affectionate, young, smiling face if you gave him a few retouches: sticking some tufts of black hair onto his receding hairline, removing the bags from under his eyes, smoothing out his cheeks and tautening his lips. And there was something about him that made you think of the June breeze passing through the acacia treetops, or the smell of an unmade bed in a third-class dormitory. It was quite impossible to tell whether he was an old person caricaturing youth, or whether he was a caricature of youth itself.

Finally, it was Jūichirō's turn to speak. He stood up and addressed them in a pensive tone. 'You probably don't recognize me, but I am Jūichirō Ōsugi. I have no job. I have one son and one daughter. My wife is in good health. There's nothing else to say, so I'll just leave it at that . . .'

For someone who should never forget to act like an ordinary guy, his words fell rather short of the mark. Far from laughing, people remained silent and even forgot to clap.

As the self-introductions continued, it felt as if people at the prime of their careers from every sphere of life in Japan were openly jostling over who had the biggest desk. The drinking began, and their conversations grew louder and louder, as if they were giving speeches.

'This summer at my store, sales have gone through the roof, thanks to those tropical shirts. Textiles are a fine example of how you don't have to lose out to new ideas and the technological revolution.'

'The lawyers working on the Nagai case aren't going to make any money. In fact, while they're getting bogged down in the trial, all the profits are coming my way.'

'Buy my shares! We shifted five hundred and fifty thousand electric fans this summer, and now we're gradually moving into electric stoves. I guarantee that winter is not going to be especially warm this year.'

'As things stand, Ikeda's in trouble. But look, no cabinet ever falls because they failed in economic policy.'

'You say his diabetes is getting worse and worse, but there are exceptions.'

'I love the liver supplements your company makes. I want my customers to enjoy them too, so would you consider passing them on at wholesale price?'

'You don't have a phone connection? Why don't you come to our place? We can install one tomorrow. That's right, tomorrow.'

'Essentially, the haiku is a poetic composition on flowers and birds.'

'A downturn? Nothing wrong with that. That's what keeps the Japanese economy healthy. The same thing happens in the West. We have a hot bath, followed by a cold shower, then another hot bath, and another cold shower. Come on now, it's what makes the Japanese economy fundamentally strong.'

'Now, when that geisha made her debut in Yanagibashi three years ago . . .'

Jūichirō stood alone among them, unable to avoid overhearing their raucous conversations. His ears were particularly drawn to the shrill voice of Deputy Minister Tamagawa nearby, who was gossiping with a small group of people standing around him. They were not cabinet members, but they were discussing a well-known politician whose eye was on the prime minister's position.

'I never realized Kuroki had such a compassionate side. During the wake for my wife, he took time out from his busy schedule and offered incense with tears in his eyes. Such natural tears . . .' said one of them, obviously showing off that he and Kuroki were on good terms.

'Nah, it's all just a monstrous show. He seems honest and upright and brings in the younger crowd. And actually, it's not often you get such a clean-cut figure in the Conservative Party. So, as long as he appears that way, who cares about his integrity? That's one way of getting things done, and he attracts easy popularity.'

Kuroki was a few years younger than Jūichirō, and he appeared to have eclipsed the prime minister in popularity among the young. Meanwhile, he had opened a small private academy for young men and was pouring all his efforts into what he called 'New Education'. This was a major project that aimed to protect the future youth of Japan from the 'poisonous fangs of the Japan Teachers Union'. He remained a loyal devotee of the old Conservative politicians who had now passed away.

He was slim and sharp-looking, with a youthful body honed through physical exercise. His speech-making skills were dazzling, and it was rumoured that women drooled over his stern countenance and eloquence whenever he appeared on television.

'If things are as bad as that, why not come to our place? You're just not getting phone calls. But if you come to Nozu's office . . .'

Jūichirō was gradually going crazy, and he regretted having decided to come. What possessed me? Maybe it was my mission that unconsciously drove me here, to open the eyes of this gaggle of well-connected men. Otherwise, why else would I have put myself in a place so removed from world unity and harmony?

He suddenly recalled the orderly piles of beautiful merchandise in the department store he had just visited. When you thought about it, all those products depended on this lot!

In an instant, Jūichirō envisaged these people stripped naked by the wind, lying face down on the earth, groaning in agony. The skin of their bodies half hanging off, torn clumps of hair in their hands. Eyes inflamed, lacking the strength even to stand. Raising their slumped heads from time to time to utter barely audible cries for help. Air-conditioning units and telephones, twisted out of shape, lying scattered about. Bodies slumped against a collapsed wall, with only their red ties standing out, dangling like flickering tongues. Sheet after sheet of paper that escaped the flames, filling the sky like flocks of birds.

Jūichirō could not resist the urge to stand.

'Excuse me,' he called, throwing out his frail chest. 'Please, listen to what I have to say.'

Everyone quietened down in surprise and locked eyes on Jūichirō's long, bespectacled, rather pale face with its pronounced, bony nose.

'Gentlemen, our world confronts danger right now. The world could even end tomorrow. This is not the time to invest in telephones, to buy drugs wholesale, to worry about the next government cabinet, or to write the next haiku on the theme of the electric stove. We must join hands and struggle hard to warn humankind about its own stupidity. We should tear away the blinkers from deluded fools, strip religion from those who are blinded by their beliefs, and open their eyes so they can return once more to what they once were. If we don't, we're in deep trouble. If we fail to establish eternal peace on earth here and now, a huge dark grave will yawn wide open before humankind. Forget your immediate everyday matters, I implore you, and join me on the first step towards the great mission of saving the world.'

When he had begun his speech, they took it as a joke and for the most part it went down well. But as he continued, the whispering increased. Some turned away in displeasure, while others creased up in an attempt to contain their laughter. Before long, the forceful, barely repressed hoarse guffaws of middle-aged men began to spread, until the restaurant's sliding doors were shaking with laughter. The organizer eventually came and took Jūichirō by the arm.

Brushing aside the hand, Jūichirō spoke with a serene gaze.

'I'm not mad, you know.' His voice was hushed but perfectly audible to the whole group, which had ceased chattering so as to catch his reaction. Finally, amid the ensuing laughter, someone spoke out in a way reminiscent of the rebukes that police used to issue at those politically 'dangerous' gatherings they had all attended as young men before the war.

'Enough talk!'

The organizer was a considerate, reasonable man, and he forced Jūichirō back along the corridor to address him even as the laughter continued to reverberate.

'I'm so sorry. They're all such plebs. They're not capable of hearing what you have to say. Your words really struck home. I'd love to have a long chat with you about it somewhere else, but not here.'

'How much would that be?'

'Eh?' The organizer was taken by surprise, and he looked as if the bags under his eyes had grown larger.

'I mean, for today's party. I must be off now.'

Jūichirō did not take the bus from Hannō Station, choosing instead to walk home slowly. As he stopped from time to time to gaze at the starry night, a new courage welled up. Fragments of laughter came back to him, seeming to reverberate down through gaps in the stars above. Jūichirō had caught a cold. He was feverish for several days. At night in his febrile sleep, dreams frequently breached a dam and overflowed like a flood, as a diversion from the irredeemable weakness of the human body and sensitivity he had inherited.

3

On the first of December, the *White Swan* semi-express turned around at Naoetsu Station and set off in the opposite direction. The view from Akiko's window shifted from mountains cloaked in dead, yellow grasses and endless small, blighted, spindly poplars, to sun-soaked desolate plains that stretched before her like pools of water spilling through breaks in the cloud.

This was Akiko's first ever solo trip. Her mother and father had both voiced their opposition, appalled by their young daughter's reckless behaviour. They were anxious for her well-being and desperate to stop her. Akiko was incensed by her parents' concerns and misgivings, which were so *human*.

'*We are not humans*, we must never forget that. Not for a moment.' Weren't those the exact words her mother, Iyoko, had used that dawn on top of Mt Rakan?

'That young man from Kanazawa claims to come from Venus, but what if he turns out to be a total fraud, a "human" trying to hood-wink you? A hidden flower like you will be ripe for the plucking.'

'He's not "human". No way. No mere human could possibly inspire me like that.'

'Can you really trust in inspiration just from a letter?'

'All we need to do is meet. I'll know the minute I see him. If I think there's anything fishy, I'll turn around on the spot.'

Akiko's journey was motivated in part by something which she could not speak out loud. A lack of trust in her father. During the month of November, her father had received advance notice three times that flying saucers were on their way, and three times they had been let down. On top of that, the family had announced these arrivals with great fanfare in mimeographs which they had printed out and distributed nationwide to members of the Universal Friendship Association.

Jūichirō communicated by telepathy, secretly, in the dead of night, so there was no way the family could tell if his methods were off, or whether he was just incompetent. Lacking her father's long experience with all sorts of difficult situations in the world, Akiko had never yearned for ways to put things right. All she required was indubitable empathy and unshakeable proof.

Akiko could not suppress her envy of the way earthlings visualized empathy. For instance, imagine a single rose in a bud vase on the table. Every person who has studied the rose, both as a name and as a concept, in the course of a standard human education will know for a fact that they are looking at a rose. No one could doubt its rose-like existence. Next thing you know, poems centred around the word "rose" emerge, so that no matter how much a poet may feign loneliness, even an obscure poem will still evoke empathy in accordance with the common associations of that word.

However, Akiko found it hard to convey her feelings through poetry. Even to her family! If she had been an artist like Van Gogh, for instance, she would have been able to produce the true likeness of a strange sun which she had seen with her own eyes, and evoke the empathy of all. But there was no way she could turn her home planet, Venus, and the flying saucers that carried its emissaries into art.

Akiko was becoming less and less inclined to wear make-up for the sake of earthlings. If she was not going to appear beautiful in the eyes of Venusians, what was the point of lining up her lipsticks and fancy foreign face powder next to her triple mirror? The year's 'in' colour and changing skirt lengths held no meaning for her. Humans told her she was beautiful, but she was assailed by doubts that she might be uncommonly plain according to the Venusian aesthetic. She felt willing to pay any price to gain evidence to the contrary. In this way, Akiko luxuriated in a beauty which could not be satisfied, even though the whole world told her she looked gorgeous. At the same time, it was a solitary beauty, lacking the slightest hint of coquetry.

The young Venusian man living in Kanazawa was called Takemiya. He insisted that his letters to Akiko, whom of course he had not even met yet, were not written to flatter. It was just that he had the ability to predict the appearance of flying saucers, predictions rather limited geographically and never extending beyond Kanazawa. He wrote to Akiko frequently that, were she to visit Kanazawa on one of those special days, he could guarantee that they would both witness the arrival of a flying saucer together. He specified the next date as December the second, at three-thirty in the afternoon. Akiko brushed away her parents' objections and wrote back to accept his offer. When her brother, Kazuo, got to hear about it, he grinned without saying a word.

Akiko had been neglecting her make-up recently, but now she had some fashionable black velvet clothes made to order for the trip, and she put her all into making herself as beautiful as possible in human eyes. That way, I'll test his judgement and get a good sense of how I rank. If he tells me my looks are truly hideous from a Venusian perspective, then it will overturn not only my own eye for beauty, but the whole of humanity's. If he tells me I'm beautiful, well, I'll realize that human taste is not all bad.

Akiko had never had a manicure, but now she painted even the nails on her feet a cherry-blossom pink. The middle-aged woman sat next to her on the train was blissfully asleep, and when Akiko went alone to the dining carriage, men could not keep their eyes off her. She was like a star under observation by a pack of amateur astronomers through grotty telescopes.

It had been cloudy all day since morning, and the landscape through the window was repeatedly drenched in rain. But when the train approached the Japan Sea shore, sunshine appeared increasingly through gaps in the clouds. As she glanced over the slate-grey surface of Toyama Bay to her right, a westering sun that blazed like a furnace appeared to sink through heavy, red clouds on the left. But the horizon remained cloaked in dense cloud, obscuring the boundary between sky and mountains, with only white beards of snow floating up from the mountainsides like vivid phantoms.

Akiko laid the half-read English book face down on her knees.

She compared the glossy finish on the nails of both hands as they caught the distant sinking rays of the sun. Her nails formed beautiful rows. She recalled her brother's passionate taste for the exotic when it came to the beauty of human girls. These thoughts gave Akiko a mixed sense of oddly warped pride and faintly pleasurable humiliation. The thoughts were not entirely negative.

The *White Swan* pulled into Kanazawa Station at five o'clock, just as the lights were coming on. Akiko had sent ahead the details of her carriage number and what she would be wearing. She had barely descended from the train before an expectant voice reached her: 'You must be Miss Ōsugi.' The front carriage occupied by Akiko had stopped in an uncovered section of the platform, and the lighting was poor.

'Yes, that's me.' Stepping onto the platform, Akiko spoke quietly. The young man had already taken possession of her luggage.

'Welcome to Kanazawa. I am Takemiya.'

Kanazawa was exceptionally warm for the time of year, so at her first intake of the local air Akiko experienced no adverse reaction when she alighted from the heated train.

This is how two extraterrestrials, from the same distant home planet of Venus, came to greet each other. In the eyes of the world, it must have seemed like a commonplace tryst in some dark corner of a train platform, but from a universal perspective it was the moment of a truly ceremonial encounter between Cygnus and the Great Square of Pegasus, on a platform in full view of the heavens above. The train had already departed, the platform bustle had faded, and the keen silence that occasionally visits even a noisy station now reigned. This allowed the wind, cradling the multicoloured signal lights as it passed through the night sky, to rustle discreetly like the pages of a sacred document being turned in the hands of twinkling witnesses who watched over the couple's encounter from their celestial vantage point.

It took a while for them both to recover from their surprise at the other's good looks. Akiko had never imagined Takemiya would be so beautiful, and the feelings were mutual. In fact, there was not one odd thing about Takemiya's youthfulness and, compared to other young men, not a single abnormality or blemish in his outward appearance. If Akiko could appreciate the beauty of a being from Venus in this way, her own looks could hardly be viewed as ugly from a Venusian perspective. The realization made Akiko extremely happy.

An abundance of sleek, dark hair set off his white skin. He looked doleful, with firm, nicely shaped lips. His demeanour was relaxed, although the crimson tie around his neck under a navy-blue trench coat had been pulled nervously into a small knot. The one thing that betrayed his non-human origins was the slightest hint of an in-organic echo, like pieces of rusty metal rubbing together, that had crept into his clear, resonant voice.

'I've booked a nice room for you in an inn that overlooks the Sai River. Let me take you there first. I'd love to have had you to stay at my place, but there are lots of us in the family and it's cramped.'

'By family, you mean . . .'

Picking up what she was getting at, Takemiya blushed.

'No, I'm single, of course. But, unlike your family, my parents, my brothers and sisters, my uncles and aunts, they're all human. It's a pain.'

Akiko looked into Takemiya's eyes as he spoke. The whole Ōsugi family had clear eyes, so she was not surprised to see that he shared the same feature. However, in his case the beauty of his eyes was truly unworldly. His pupils were the night sky in crystallized form. All earthly things reflected within them seemed purified, and they clearly bore a celestial imprint. Akiko had no doubt that his eyes revealed their common origin.

Their taxi avoided the congested Korinbō district, followed the direction of the Sai River south alongside a long earthen wall until they came to the great Sai River Bridge and arrived at a well-known inn on the south bank of the river. The tea-ceremony-style room overlooking the river had already been heated, and incense was burning.

Takemiya sat Akiko in the seat of honour and bowed deeply as he stretched out his hands across the tatami floor. His lustrous hair hanging from his forehead almost brushed the brand-new matting. Akiko had never seen a young man in Tokyo perform such an elaborate bow. Her brother was from Mercury, and his manners were awful!

The landlady came to greet them. She addressed Takemiya as if they were good friends. The few words they exchanged revealed that she and Takemiya were fellow students of Noh drama.

'Do you practise chanting the texts of Noh plays?' asked Akiko in surprise. She tried to envision him chanting old Noh texts as a kind of performative song.

'Yes, Takemiya also does Noh dances on stage. He's so good at it that he debuted in *Dōjōji* this spring on the Hōshō Noh stage. He puts me in the shade,' said the plump, slightly grey-haired woman.

This first evening, Akiko and Takemiya dined together at the inn. The maid brought them a dish of appetizers, including dried seacucumber ovaries, stuffed *shiso* rolls from Aomi and sweet shrimp, garnished with a single autumn leaf, together with a heated bottle of the local sake. Akiko struggled, but with little success, to imagine the face of this modern-looking young man before her on stage wearing a *fukai* Noh mask and a long wig, and dressed in a *Tsuboori* kimono with an elaborate red Chinese design.

After sending the maid away, Takemiya clearly had something on his mind, but he hesitated for some time before eventually speaking up with a resolute smile.

'I really understand how it must have confused you when you heard I practise Noh chanting. But it relates to a big secret that I can't tell other people. It was only when I made my debut in *Dōjōji* this spring that I first got an inkling that I come from Venus. I realize it's weird, but ever since then all my contacts with extraterrestrials have been connected to the Noh mask.'

This strange turn really aroused Akiko's curiosity, and she remained tantalized by the young man's polite, composed tone as he told his story.

Takemiya hailed from one of Kanazawa's renowned families, and they still lived in an old samurai residence. Notwithstanding his reluctance, he was obliged to take up the study of Noh chanting in accordance with the common custom of his neighbourhood.

These chants had begun to infiltrate the masses at the time when Kanazawa was still a feudal domain. The Daimyo had noticed a wonderful conflation between the breathing of his craftsmen and breathing in the performing arts, and he allowed his workmen to practise chanting. These workmen were engaged in a range of trades – swordsmith, painter, sculptor, scroll mounter, silversmith and the like – in artisan training schools established within the castle walls. Whenever the Daimyo was absent from Edo and resident back in Kanazawa, he would invite top-class Noh actors from Kyoto to perform for him over several days. Even commoners were allowed to come and watch, and sometimes the Daimyo himself would take to the stage.

After the Meiji Restoration the custom went out of fashion for a while, but it soon underwent a revival. Even gardeners and fishmongers would gather to practise chanting under the guidance of minor teachers who had been accredited by their respective neighbourhoods. When people finished their work shifts at a restaurant, they would gather at the reception, still wearing their aprons, to discuss whether to perform *Feather Mantle*. At the ridgepole-raising ceremony, carpenters would chant *Hall of Longevity*, and *Stumbling Beggar Priest* would be performed during wakes and at Buddhist memorial ceremonies. Ever since the Tokugawa Period, the Kaga-Hōshō School of Noh had emphasized lots of strong chanting and magnificent singing voices, but in the last twenty years the Tokyo chanting style had undermined it.

Takemiya was not the type to recklessly oppose established norms and old customs. From his youth, he had felt a deep penchant for the quietude of beauty, and he felt no disappointment in a beauty that never changed and offered no salvation. Unlike other young men, he was an ardent admirer of anything that precluded the possibility of self-redemption.

He preferred solitude and walks, and he loved the colour of the northern sea. He had a premonition he would end his days secluded in this old northern town. His youthful thoughts were comforted by the prospect of losing himself in the town's dusty beauty, completely unbeknown to the world.

The clear, bright atmosphere of the northern provinces, the cool, pure, porcelain-like decline of this town famed for its ceramics, and the quiet reflection of glazed roof tiles all suited the image of an old castle town sunk in the depths of time. He found it impossible to get close to human beings. Their turbulent lives were distant from him. In the end, a comforting core of solitude took root within him and the concept of death became ever more magnificent. He turned into something approaching an accumulated sediment of beauty, like a *Kutani* teacup embossed in gold dust and vermilion. He was perfectly aware how the show of gold, his interest in death and the sweet loneliness of youth marked him out as a solitary beauty. He kept his distance from any girl who came close.

He saw nothing but vulgarity in the ardour of young people and the obstinately 'progressive' ideas typical of people from the northern regions. His interest was directed towards the pursuit of individual refinement, exceptional dreams and anything that seemed to go against the grain of the times. The things he considered essential for the world did not exist. But if these things were not there, they ought to exist. Surely this was the ethical basis of beauty and art. His only option was to be an artist. All he had to do was to superimpose the world of dreams onto what already existed with the aim of creating a new, double-layered reality, in which everything could be appreciated in its dual form.

He began as a child with an aversion to Noh chanting, but ultimately developed the affection, shared by other northerners, for its icy, sumptuous passages. Its literary style was a brocade of decorative excess that withstood the indoor gloom of the northern winter. Like the overly gaudy *Kutani* ware and embossed gilt lacquer work, the chanting maintained an equilibrium with the dark, murky sensitivity of the locality.

Kanazawa was also a town of stars. The sky was clear throughout the seasons and, apart from Korinbō, the one district blighted by neon, stars twinkled like gentle raindrops over every roof in town. But even as a child, Takemiya had felt no special affinity to stars or astronomy. Some of his friends used to bring star charts to school and make a show of explaining the constellations, but he was never particularly influenced by his schoolmates. When he thought about it later, his interest in stars must have lain dormant within him so far back that he had no conscious memory of it, like the reflection of stars buried deep among weeds at the bottom of a pond. It was only when he made his debut with *Dōjōji* in springtime that these stars first revealed themselves in his heart and in his eyes.

That happened in April, when spring was at its peak in the Hokuriku region. Cherry and plum were both in blossom, and there was a riot of iris, azalea, peach and apricot flowers. The funny rabbit-shaped ridge tiles and hemp-leaf tiles on the roofs of the old samurai residences glittered in the sunlight.

Takemiya stood between cold mirrors as he put on his costume, and awaited his entrance. His heart overflowed with pure tension! Perhaps at that blissful moment when he was about to plunge to the depths of his own existence, he was aware of rippling wavelets of musical rapture from the other side of the brocade stage curtain as they reached out to embrace him. He would escape the dual existence that had animated him for so long, and move towards oneness with nature.

Now that he was about to change into the stuff of human dreams, his purified heart no longer needed to dream of other things. The tips of his toes enveloped in pure white *tabi*, as if carved from wood, glided onto the polished bridgeway that led to the stage.

'With great pleasure. I will dance for you as best I can.' With these words, the dancer rested momentarily at the stage assistant position in order to don a tall court cap. Then, standing by the first pine on the bridgeway, he initiated the *ranbyōshi* section, a dance of mixed rhythms, exclaiming, 'I am so happy! I will dance for you!'

A small hand drum beat out a steady rhythm like sighs arising from a deep chasm. Takemiya raised the big toe of his right foot, and let it hover. Then, with his fan held open by his side, he began the difficult motions that would last about twenty minutes. A large, purple damask bell hung in the air on the Noh stage, silently, as if heavy with suffering.

The drum's fierce rhythm sounded once more, like a storm blasting through a wilderness. Narrow slits for the eyes in Takemiya's *fukai* mask. Through which the uncertain world is glimpsed. That outer world barely had meaning for him. The dance, rooted in medieval entertainments for priests, in thanks for their performance of ritual festivals, depended entirely on the shouts of encouragement from the audience to keep the feet moving in harmony with the beat of the drum. The performer constantly paced himself through the regulation of his breathing . . .

Weathered bark on the inside of the mask touched his sweaty cheekbones, constricting his breath within to produce a feeling of hellish intoxication. His eyes took in the obscure theatre light, but inside the mask he sensed a vast deep darkness. The rhythm of drumbeats reverberated clearly through the gloom like blasts of cold wintry wind.

No sooner had he experienced this darkness dividing the inside of the mask and his own face than he felt something strange. It was as if the outer surface of the beautiful *fukai* mask, invisible to him, had become his true face, while his original face, separated from the mask's inside layer by a huge darkness, had turned into something else. This original face had assumed the form of his unconscious existence that, arising from a deep well of unfamiliar memories, directly confronted the enormous field of darkness.

Flesh steeped in music. Feet bound by clean *tabi*. A pristine emptiness of the heart born from the constant effort to maintain the body's equilibrium. He seemed to be standing at the very centre of beauty, and suddenly the world seen through the tiny slits of the mask was transforming into something else.

The damask bell swaying in mid-air and the hesitant light that pervaded both stage and theatre seats disappeared. At that moment, he was glimpsing another world through the slits of the Noh mask. He seemed to advance quietly, one step at a time, through the vast dark plain on the inside of the mask, his ears packed with a screeching gale. The distance was considerable, and his legs grew tired. But he foresaw that the core of his existence, the extraordinarily intimate home of his essential being, lay on the opposite side of that darkness. He walked. The air filled with terrifying, cracked music. The occasional snatch of a flute, its song passing like a steam iron over his soul. He walked. The closer he came to his destination, the larger grew the slits in the mask. Light spilling from those holes cut through the darkness before him.

It must have been when Takemiya heard the flute's song that the star came to mind. The thin flute music was like a beam of starlight reaching him through the darkness of space. Its intermittent, blurry sound took the shape in Takemiya's ear of bright starlight fading away in the bright dawn. What else could the flute's sound be but the light of the morning star?

Little by little, his home, unmistakably, came into view. He had suddenly arrived. The world glimpsed through the slits of the mask was radiant. That world was Venus.

'So, what happened? What was Venus like?' asked Akiko, breathless.

'I don't know how to describe it,' said Takemiya, a troubled look crossing his brow. 'A truly wonderful place. I just can't put it into words. I guess you might call it beauty in its perfect form.'

'But how? Just tell me what you saw.'

'You come from Venus, yourself. You should know.' With these stern words Takemiya lapsed into silence, and Akiko felt inhibited from pressing him further. Takemiya continued with his story.

From that day, Takemiya developed an obscure belief that he was Venusian. But he lacked certainty. On a visit to his barber's one week after his stage performance, he was leafing through a new tabloid magazine when his eyes happened to catch an entry in the Common Interests column: 'If you are interested in ◉, we would like to hear from you. Let's work together as members of the Universal Friendship Association in the pursuit of world peace.'

Takemiya was not especially knowledgeable about such matters, but a strange intuition told him that the symbol, ◉, must have something to do with spaceships. This was how his extended correspondence with Akiko began. Spurred on by her unwavering belief that she came from Venus, Takemiya nervously disclosed that he, too, had Venusian roots. But he did not let on about his experience with the Noh mask and the many other strange subsequent incidents, fearful they might be less than convincing via a letter.

As time went by, he began to hear the distant call of the Universe whenever he placed the *fukai* mask, a family treasure, over his face.

This renowned mask owned by the Takemiyas was reputedly an *Echi* masterpiece. Its name was derived from the sixteenth-century Chief Abbot of Echiyama in Echizen province, Yoshifune Echi, famed for his Noh women's masks at the beginning of the Muromachi Period.

Takemiya often shut himself in his room and wore the mask over his face. Ultimately, he came to hear a voice announcing the time and place when flying saucers would be visiting. Three were due to fly in from Venus at eight in the evening on the sixteenth of June near the Uchinada sand dunes. He went there and, sure enough, they appeared at the allotted time. This was his first ever spotting of a flying saucer.

For a long time, Takemiya had been contemptuous of the human capacity to understand anything, so he did everything to keep his secret from the family. Without letting on to anyone else, he travelled alone about once a month to greet the flying saucers that would appear at exactly the designated time and place.

His trip with Akiko the following day would be his first encounter with flying saucers in the company of another person.

. . . Takemiya's long story finally came to an end. Akiko drew a deep breath. Ordinary people of the world would have met his story with a smile, but it inspired nothing less than unshakeable belief and empathy in Akiko. He saw flying saucers. He really did. As he had told her, 'If these things were not there, they ought to exist.' The flying saucers and all of their related miracles had appeared to him in accordance with this aesthetic demand.

Takemiya's thoughts and experiences were entirely different from those of her father. The younger man really identified as a

Venusian, whereas her father seemed merely to have thoughts about being a Martian. Were Martian thoughts (the only reason that qualified him as a family member!) strong enough to hold sway even over Venusian thoughts?

Jūichirō earnestly yearned for peace to all mankind, but Takemiya showed not the slightest interest in caring for others. The latter considered this world to be false, and the only things he believed in were the existence of flying saucers and the dazzling beauty that pervaded the entire planet of Venus. Takemiya and Akiko's extraordinary good looks spoke of the exceptional natural blessings found on Venus. On that world, their beauty was probably nothing out of the ordinary.

Now that his story was told, Takemiya felt worried that Akiko might be tired from her journey, so he courteously took his leave from the inn, saying he would come to fetch her the following morning at ten o'clock. Once he had gone home, Akiko took a bath and gazed intently at her own beautiful white flesh, feeling nothing but gratitude for this body that Venus had put together from a selection of the very finest materials available on Earth. That night, Akiko fell into a pleasant, deep sleep.

The next morning, they had plenty of time to get to Uchinada. Since the weather was good, Takemiya decided to give her a tour of the city. They took a leisurely stroll together around Korinbō before the Saturday crowds had gathered, and then went to see the famous main gate of Oyama Shrine, which was set back a little from the main street where the trams ran.

They walked shoulder to shoulder, appearing to all the world like a couple of lovers. Passers-by seemed startled by the beauty of their faces, and looked back a few times. Why on Earth would they not be thought of as lovers? They were rare visitors from another place, and they were not ashamed to show it.

Akiko was delighted that the cool, clean impression left by Takemiya the previous evening was not betrayed by the morning light. It was a gloriously cloudless day. Even in this downtown district the air was limpid, and it permeated her skin. The clamminess of human sensuality was entirely absent. A bolt of pristine blue stretched across the clear winter sky.

'Yesterday, when I met you for the first time, it felt like I'd finally met someone I'd given up thinking I'd ever meet. It must be the Venus connection.'

Takemiya raised this matter of great importance with such simplicity, and the expression he wore was so unruffled, that Akiko easily concurred. 'Me too.' As she spoke, Akiko sensed that they were raising up their serene conversation to the sky, proudly and together, as if it were a beautiful garland. Having despaired of the ugliness on Earth, this conversation gave Akiko the means to fully vent her contempt for human beings. To put it another way, right now they were engaging in a hypocritical conversation, frequently based on impure motives, in order to transform it into one that followed celestial laws, even though the words they used were identical.

How amazing it was to converse in a way that exactly replicated human speech! Their beautiful language was shot through with scorn, and their hackneyed words of love bore a silver lining of disdain. Akiko would not have been surprised in the slightest if Takemiya had suddenly expressed his love for her. Such a declaration would have provided a humorous rhetorical means to construct a double structure of heavenly fellowship and harsh contempt for humanity.

They reached the main gate of the shrine. This gate was highly eccentric in design, built in 1875 under the guidance of the Dutchman Holtman, and one of the few remaining examples of an exotic foreign style. Not a single section of the huge three-storeyed gate conveyed a sense of nobility. The twinned Chinese lions flanking both sides of the gate stood guard over the immature structure that evoked parallels with a gaudy undersea Dragon King's palace. Moreover, its three layers of tiled *karahafu* gables were divided by fretwork transoms based on a pine-tree-and-crane pattern, studded all over with Chinese plum insignias, while the Dutch-style windows on the third tier were inlaid with green, blue and red glass. Once, copperplate lamps fitted into the hipped roof had emitted such powerful beams of light from behind the multicoloured glass that they even served as markers for the shipping routes far out in the Japan Sea.

'You know, this place makes me think sometimes,' said Takemiya, tapping the gate's brown-and-white horizontally striped pillars with his slender fingertips. 'The Dutchman who built this was probably aiming to erect a glittering multicoloured lighthouse. He must have been mortified to receive such a vulgar commission from the Japanese of that time, with China and the West all jumbled up inside their heads, even though I'm sure he had his own heart fixed on the gloomy northern sea and its everlasting nights. I wouldn't be surprised if he saw flying saucers. Perhaps he locked himself away in that room on the third tier and manipulated the multicoloured lights to communicate with the craft as they flew in over the sea at night.'

'I guess you were still on Venus then.'

'You too.' A cool tension was at work in their hearts as they continuously sought to establish the source of what each was feeling at the moment. Each and every thing that they shared, no matter how small, no matter how detailed, could be traced back to Venus. The way they ordered the same drink at a tea shop when they got thirsty on their walk along the road. The *Kutani* vase that caught both their attentions when they glanced into a shop. Their spontaneous exchange of smiles at the sight of a supermarket billboard claiming to 'Sell Happiness'. The fact that they just happened to walk in unison up the stone steps of the shrine gate. The longer they spent in each other's company, the deeper grew the conviction that they were being tugged by invisible strings with direct links to distant Venus.

Takemiya hailed a taxi and ordered the driver to take them straight to Kenroku-En. This famous park was a must-see for anyone visiting Kanazawa.

The park's entrance was directly opposite the imposing white turret of Kanazawa Castle's Ishikawa Gate, and yellow leaves had blown in from afar to scatter on the surrounding gravel path. The couple ascended the broad path's gentle incline towards the wooded heights in the park.

The more they climbed, the more Akiko felt overwhelmed by a profound sense that every step was leading not so much to somewhere new, but to a place she had fallen in love with many moons ago. Even the individual trees lining both sides of their route bore the barely discernible traces of once-buried memories, like faint pencil lines that had escaped the eraser. The pine branches, thrusting into the blue sky like trailing smoke, evoked familiar visions from ages past.

Coming to the edge of the Kasumiga-ike Pond at the top of the hill, they watched several swans at play on the water. Akiko finally put into words the firm conviction that had been building in her heart.

'I've been here once before. I'm sure of it.'

'But this is your first time in Kanazawa.' Takemiya spoke coolly. 'Ah, I've got it. You're picking up exactly what's happening inside my head.'

If Takemiya's words were correct, loneliness could not exist on Venus. Her father, who had agonized so much over human loneliness, would have been better off as a Venusian. What a pity for him that he came from Mars. Akiko and Takemiya even held memories in common.

But what she was remembering through Takemiya did not extend as far as the world of Venus. Akiko found that very galling. And even memories related to Earth failed to cover intimate details of his daily life. Her recollections were strictly limited to landscapes that had struck him several times in the past as beautiful, poetic memories. Certainly, Takemiya was spot on to have registered the beauty of this park on a previous occasion. The scenery around the pond offered Akiko a beauty of unparalleled tranquillity that blended intimate memories with fresh impressions.

As she watched, three swans glided across the water, their red beaks taking them in different directions. The Uchihashi-tei Teahouse jutted out from the opposite side of the pond, and her eyes were assailed by the white glare of its firmly shuttered *shoji* paper screens. Next to the Kotoji stone lantern a rivulet fed into the pond, carrying its inexhaustible supply of pure water. How green the pine trees on enchanted Penglai Island in the centre of the pond! And the vibrant colour of new straw wrapped around their trunks to protect them from snow . . .

All human traces in this garden had been tucked out of sight, but artificial nature was not entirely bad. Various human characteristics were hidden away – hatred, jealousy, selfishness – but a splendid facsimile of heavenly peace hung in the pristine atmosphere.

Takemiya may have been a little overfamiliar in his language, but Akiko liked his manners. He never slipped his arm around her waist or took her hand. This cannot have been due to excessive modesty on his part, and it was certainly not a matter of decorum. Did a melding of hearts such as theirs necessarily lead to a melding of flesh? Was the body obliged to imitate the actions of the heart? What if fleshly entanglements were originally patterned on the erotic union of minds, and merely served as inevitable compensation born from despair?

Their hearts possessed the landscape in tandem. A flow of images across the eyes, swans adrift on water, sky reflected in pond, red- and white-petalled camellias. All these beautiful fragments they shared as one. Words were no longer necessary. When they sat down to rest on a bench by the water's edge, for instance, they acted together. When Akiko gave her tired legs a rest and then found new life, inspired by the traveller's endless drive towards the next new thing, the two stood up independently but at the same time.

They left the pond behind them and crossed Gankobashi Bridge, made from layers of tortoiseshell-patterned Tomuro stones to form the shape of geese flying in formation, and came out on the eastern side of the rivulet where the yellowed leaves of the famous cherry trees swayed apprehensively in the breeze. The couple ascended the hill to the viewing platform that looked out to the north-east, and Akiko took in the expansive view under Takemiya's guidance as he pointed out first one place, then another.

It was the pleasure of the journey in its purest form. Akiko savoured the thrill of being away, not only from everyday matters but also from the troublesome members of her own family in Hannō, each from a different planet, with their own personalities and ways of thinking. It was also an escape from school life in the city where she faced threats to her 'purity' every minute of the day.

'It feels lovely. The weather's so clear, with just a slight chill to the air.'

Akiko put away her scarf in her handbag and let her fragrantly oiled hair flutter in the faint breeze. The cool air playing around her hair brought a flush to her small, well-formed ears. People always said there was something cold about her refined face, but now it was melting in the soft, pleasant sunshine.

'In the springtime when I was a kid, I'd often go and gather bracken there,' said Takemiya, pointing north-east to the gentle slopes of Mt Utatsu that rose up on the other side of the Asano River. The locals had given the mountain another name, Mt Mukō, written with Chinese characters that meant 'Mt Yonder'. Poets also called it Mt Mukō, but they used different characters meaning 'Fragrant Dream Mountain'. A health centre building stood out, white, close to its peak.

Below them, the glazed tiles of countless old roofs in Kanazawa's network of streets glittered in the sun. Next to a temple, its tiled rooftop rising into the sky, stood a new middle school building. The mesh of telegraph poles and electric cables seemed not quite suited to the city. A white-bricked bank from the Meiji Period was covered in a tangle of cables like fine cracks in a mirror, while city trams, painted red and yellow, sped single-mindedly along their tracks through intermittent patches of clear winter sunshine.

'What a lovely city. It's almost as if we've lived here together in the past.'

'Are you saying you'd like to live with me here in the future too?'

Akiko looked up at Takemiya, slightly surprised, but his beautiful face maintained its unruffled composure. Akiko tried to interpret their conversation in accordance with cosmic grammar. He was only asking if she was willing to spend all her days with him here on 'Earth'.

'The future? Well, maybe for the short time before the world is blown to smithereens.' Akiko's retort was playful and refreshingly direct.

'Look, that's the Kahokugata Lagoon over there.' Takemiya pointed to a hazy strip of sea far away to the north.

Wisps of factory smoke, scattered over the sunlit yellow plain, were visible, extending as far as the lagoon. Notwithstanding the glorious sunshine, the hazy boundary of the horizon looked remarkably like a bright withered field that would go on for ever.

★

They returned to Korinbō and had a light steak lunch at a place called the Tanuki Teahouse. It was finally time to go to Uchinada. Akiko spread out her travel guide on the table and asked Takemiya: 'Are we taking the Awagasaki train there, or the Hokutetsu bus?'

At that moment, the empathy that had operated so subtly between them since morning seemed suddenly to break. Takemiya's expression still betrayed no sign of ambiguity, but his beautiful eyes fell upon the bitter dregs left in his coffee cup.

'Why not go by taxi? We could keep it waiting there for an hour.'

This exchange forced Akiko to reinstate their mutual empathy. As a matter of fact, she was the one at fault. A Venusian should never, even for an instant, entertain such lowly human concerns. No wonder there had been a breakdown in their empathy. Akiko had received a considerable amount of spending money from her father for the journey. All she needed to do was to take a taxi and keep the meter running for a few hours, no questions asked. Although, come to think of it, Takemiya had not paid for a single thing since morning. It had all happened quite naturally, with Akiko picking up the tab. For the coffee, for the taxi, probably even for this lunch-time beer . . .

It took no more than thirty minutes to reach Uchinada by taxi from the city centre. The Asano River divides into two tributaries, one of which leads to the Japan Sea, while the other flows into the Kahoku-gata Lagoon. The taxi followed the regular Hokutetsu bus route along the former tributary.

It was two o'clock when they hailed the taxi. The sky had been perfectly clear until then, but the weather is changeable in the Hokuriku region. No sooner had they entered the vehicle than dense black clouds suddenly rolled in from one corner of the town. The clouds immediately covered half the sky, and by the time the taxi had reached the river basin in the lower reaches of the Asano, surrounded by the stubbly yellow of harvested rice fields, even the stones along the dry riverbed had darkened. But there was no sign of imminent rain.

As the couple gazed at the gently sloping Mt Hōdatsu under layers of cloud to their right, their thoughts turned to the nearby sea and the sacred moment that was to come, and they fell into silence.

Akiko recalled those sad times when her father had failed. That dawn cold on the summit of Mt Rakan in November. The solemn ascent of Venus in the sky as it grew light, like a lost hope.

The Ōsugi family may have avoided the loneliness of the human world, but in its place they experienced *interplanetary loneliness*. For not one person in the family had witnessed a flying saucer in the presence of another. Wrapped in silence, Akiko was caught between two emotions. Delight at having been born on Venus. Unease that her happiness might disintegrate in an instant. Akiko could tell from Takemiya's reluctance to speak that he shared the same unease and tension.

'Look! The dunes!' There was a nakedly cold, metallic tone to Takemiya's words as he pointed through the windscreen to the smooth hills ahead.

They arrived in no time. The driver was afraid the sand might get the better of his tyres, so he parked a considerable distance from the dunes to let them off. The couple set out along a wide road that passed between impoverished, sandy onion fields and patches of chrysanthemums with their faint blush of rouge, heading for the dunes ahead and the sea beyond. The road felt quite solid underfoot, like any other road.

It was a considerable walk before the freely undulating sand dunes would come into sight. Monotonous groves of young pines lined both sides of the road, still blocking their view of the water beyond. It was only when the road rose a little that they caught their first sighting of a stretch of black sea. Across the hill to the left lay acacia trees, their delicate desiccated branches pricking the overcast, light-filled sky. The sky seen through the tangle of treetops and trunks felt somehow different. It seemed to brim with a more pensive light. Awesome clouds, emitting powerful beams at their edges, crowded into the patch of blue that had opened up between sullen clouds and the horizon.

Akiko was fascinated by the strange energy of the hill and woods. The acacia branches, ash-coloured and covered in sharp dry thorns, were entirely shorn of leaves, yet the hill itself was cloaked in a warm green undergrowth that stood out even from a distance.

'How about climbing that hill?' said Akiko.

Takemiya hesitated. He checked his watch before replying.

'Well, we do have some time . . . But sometimes their timing is a bit out, so it might be better to get there early.'

These happened to be the exact words her father had used late that night, and Akiko could bear the anxiety no longer. Thoughts of potential sadness and disappointment sprang to life. She scrambled up the steep bank adjacent to the road with no assistance from the young man. Takemiya had no choice but to follow.

But the hill they climbed did not have much to offer. There were traces of logging here and there, with trees left where they had been cut, stretching over the greenery like skeletons of gigantic animals. Takemiya stood with his hands stuck in his coat pockets, looking bored.

Akiko immediately sensed that the poetic sentiment she had ascribed to the beautiful wood was a mistake. At this moment, she had discarded universal poetry in the search for Romantic verse. Come to think of it, the chirping of sparrows gathered in the treetops suddenly grated, and the deserted grove of withered trees began to feel like a place with no meaning. But Akiko was definitely waiting for something. Was it flying saucers? Or something else, maybe? Akiko had failed to notice that the desolate air of this wood reflected her unfulfilled heart. Inside her head, however, Akiko exclaimed loudly and unreservedly: How happy I am! Free to swim in purity, such utter purity. Those stupid human customs are a world away from here!

They descended the hill and finally stepped onto the sand dunes overlooking the sea at just past three o'clock. No workmen were in sight, but they did find a roadside sign:

UCHINADA VILLAGE, KAHOKU DISTRICT
UCHINADA TEST FIRING SITE, REPARATION WORK,
WINDBREAK WORK
WORK BEGINS: AUGUST 1961
ESTIMATED COMPLETION: MARCH 1962

When Akiko read this, her eyes lit up. No wonder there were so many deep lorry ruts in the road leading to the sea.

'Now I get it. There's a link here with the appearance of the flying saucers. The US military used this place as an artillery range to train soldiers during the Korean War, and now they've started planting a windbreak forest to make amends for that infamous, bloody, human conflict. All the flying saucers have to do is show up to clarify its symbolic meaning. That in itself would amount to a message of peace.'

'I'm not so sure about that.' Takemiya shook his head coolly. 'I can't believe that's true. There's no connection between meaningless human history and *my* flying saucers. It's just that *my* flying saucers love the northern sea.'

Akiko remained silent. Everything hung on the flying saucer's appearance.

These celebrated giant sand dunes had now been parcelled up into small seedling beds for forestation, and waves of dwarf bamboo hedges spread as far as the eye could see. Tiles and pebbles were mixed into the sand, and the lorry ruts extended further towards the sea. Waves on the verge of breaking could be seen from this vantage point, but the actual water's edge remained hidden by the dunes, and the crashing waves felt rather distant.

They sat themselves down with their backs against a bamboo hedge. Lowering clouds. An ash-green sea that might have been frozen. Light breaking through just one section of the western sky, and below it a patch of sea the colour of dark purple. Far to the right arose the headland of the Noto Peninsula. Clouds constantly churning. The distant cawing of crows.

The wind was not strong enough to whip up the sand, but it did insinuate itself into their ears, attacking them with its nagging whisper.

They sat leaning against each other, arms around knees. Through their clothes, they faintly sensed for the first time the other's body warmth and beating heart. Venusian or human, they were alive and had the smell of living creatures. Their flesh was exquisite, but it was still flesh that stood between them. But what did that matter? Their hearts beat as one, and the empathy that they had nurtured since morning resonated like a spinning top. There was nothing more to wait for, and they relished that moment.

Yukio Mishima

What else was there to aspire towards?

The world in tranquillity. Far from humankind. The northern sea, rolling and roaring, immovable as death. A brocade vestment stretching across the sky. The gorgeous couple . . .

At that moment, Akiko noticed a point of light twinkling deep inside the layers of dark cloud. She shook Takemiya's shoulder to alert him.

One point became two, and then there were three. They rapidly increased in size and dropped down to hover above the sea. They were in formation. It was only when all three vessels tilted and came closer that they clearly took the form of flying saucers. One half of their surfaces glinted in the light from the western sky, and the gentle rotation of the green top sections of each ship stood out in great detail. They cruised above the sea for no more than four or five seconds before coming to a dead halt in the sky, like three uncanny pupils embedded in dark clouds . . . Then, as the couple watched, a deep shudder passed through each craft and their fuselages turned an apricot colour, as if incandescent. All of a sudden, they soared directly upwards at terrifying speed from the sea's surface, and disappeared from view.

4

Akiko made it back safely to Tokyo, to the relief of her parents. But she said nothing about the flying saucers that she and Takemiya had witnessed together. Partly because she was concerned for her father's self-esteem. And partly because she felt it was a secret that only Venusians should share. As far as her parents were concerned, they asked nothing. Partly because Akiko's silence was clear evidence that Takemiya had failed to come up to expectations. And partly because they feared that any teasing about this failure would have the adverse effect of deepening her affections towards the young man. Their actions resembled the turning of the constellations, cleverly gliding past each other without making physical contact.

The New Year arrived. Jūichirō mentioned a remarkable phenomenon that would be taking place very soon in the celestial sphere. It was a scientifically precise prediction, but it also posed a huge question for the world's astrologers. For five days, from the third of February, eight astronomical objects – the sun, the moon, Mars, Venus, Jupiter, Saturn, Mercury and the invisible planet Ketu – would converge in Capricorn, the tenth sign of the zodiac. This was the first time they had been in such an alignment, excluding Mercury, for 4,974 years. 'I hear they're all worried in India that this day marks the end of the world,' said Jūichirō in a calm, straightforward tone. 'We're a really busy family, but at least we'll have the opportunity to gather together in the living room. It's been so long. I'm really looking forward to a family catch-up.'

Kazuo mentioned a strange coincidence that had occurred that day. On the way back from school, he bumped into an old elementary school friend he had not seen for seven years. And then, after they parted and he was on the train, someone else tapped him on the shoulder. It was another schoolmate he hadn't met for seven years.

'Do you really believe that was a coincidence?' said his father, sagely. ' "Coincidence" is a word devised to gloss over human ignorance and make that ignorance appear plausible.

'Ultimate inevitability, which surpasses human understanding, normally covers itself in a thick cloak, but coincidence points to that moment when it suddenly flashes a piece of its naked flesh. Perhaps the highest form of inevitability that the human intellect has grappled with is the movement of the celestial bodies. But inevitability of an even higher, more exquisite order remains hidden from human eyes, and can only be surmised through some roundabout, religious method. The very fact that religious leaders call it a mystery while scientists describe it as a coincidence confirms the hidden nature of true inevitability. The heavens simply dangle inevitability before human beings with impish, frivolous methods in order to pretend it's actually something inconsequential. Humans are really simple, superficial, inherently vain creatures, so they're happy to clutch at earnest philosophy, urgent issues of the day and other things that seem worthy of attention. But when it comes to apparently ridiculous matters and nonsense, humans just give them the short shrift they deserve. And so, humans are for ever fated to find themselves blindsided by celestial inevitability. For that reason, the beautiful naked footprints left by celestial inevitability are interpreted as pure accident.

'Lovers often end up meeting by coincidence. That's probably not so strange, but people who hate each other so much that they can't stand to be together also frequently meet by chance. In the realm of human ethics, these two examples are linked, in the sense that, whether through love or hate, people with a mutual connection inevitably meet by coincidence. Human ethics has never advanced beyond that. But we extraterrestrials have a bird's-eye view, and our field of vision is broader. From our perspective, humans encounter so many unrelated strangers by coincidence, day in day out, on the train or in town, that the number of people they

meet with whom they actually have a connection pales into insignifi-
cance. The miracle is that it's not unusual for them to chance upon
people they've met maybe only once before in their lives. The best
way to describe the coincidences that have unfolded until the present age is as a huge, invisible net of inevitability. Only Buddhists
have gained insight into this phenomenon, expressing it through
beautiful metaphors like "the shade of a single tree is determined by
past events", and "even the brushing of sleeves is preordained in a
previous existence". This insight indicates the way that the stars
have left faint traces of their own character within humans. It
acknowledges the distant reflection of the subtle movement of the
heavenly bodies. But actually, it also implies that we're caught in an
even greater mesh of ultimate inevitability . . .

'Since there's no essential difference between earthly disorder
and celestial harmony, we never fall into despondency. A beautiful
girl with old-fashioned tastes strums the *koto* in the annex of her
house. At that moment, just down the road, a young repairman suddenly slips from a telegraph pole and falls to his death. At the same
time, some children digging in the sandpit in their back garden
recover some beautiful, rainbow-coloured marbles they lost the
previous year. Meanwhile, a butterfly suddenly flies into the newly
washed hair of a woman as she dries it by the window, and she is
alarmed to discover that the hair she tended so carefully is now
tainted with yellow, powdery scales . . . These miraculous connections occur quietly, unnoticed, all over the place and in the space of
a few minutes of, let us say, a glorious spring afternoon. The rapture
of music, death, the discovery of a lost treasure, the fickleness of
untrammelled desire . . . And those major historical events of
bygone days, too, that humans believe are woven together through
inevitability, are the product of the same basic materials. And each
of those materials bears the names of distant stars.

'You know, it's only recently that I finally became convinced that
all my past worries about people and events on Earth were a blessing
from above. I mean, as the moment for universal harmony and
unity draws near, the inevitability of the heavens accelerates like a
white-hot machine. The unexpected result is that conditions on

Earth have come to resemble an overturned toybox, so that according to the human logic of inevitable connections nothing really makes sense any more. We just have to remain on constant watch about what's happening around us, and take note whenever any apparently trivial coincidence arises. My prediction is that cryptic signs of small, insignificant coincidences will become increasingly common on Earth from now on. Take, for example, what happened recently in America. In some major city, a middle-aged man called Mr James caused a minor car accident. But the man driving the other vehicle was also called Mr James. Less than two hours later, the first Mr James ploughed into another vehicle, and it turned out that the man he hit in the second accident was also called Mr James.'

The end-of-term exams had arrived. Kazuo and Akiko were asked to stay home for at least the three-day period between February the third and the fifth, and they spent the weekend cooped up in the house. The fifth was a Monday, and brother and sister felt like going to the cinema, so they agreed to meet in the Ikebukuro district of Tokyo on the way back from school. They watched an old film at the Jinsei-za Theatre and returned home in time for dinner. The train for Hannō departed every thirty minutes. While they waited in a queue on the platform, a smouldering sun was sinking into the lightly clouded western sky. The sun was in the corner of Kazuo's eye as he spoke:

'Maybe the world's going to end today. The train's taking a damn long time to come.'

'Dad doesn't believe in superstitions like that . . . But wouldn't it be great if the world did come to an end on an ordinary, quiet day like today. If it did, we'd never see the sun again.'

The faces of the growing crowd on the platform betrayed their impatience to get home quickly. You could almost hear the quiet clinking of plates being set in preparation for all those evening meals under the lights scattered across the darkening suburban plains. As ever, Akiko found such rituals of daily life unfathomable, whereas Kazuo, predictably, fantasized about being given the authority to standardize all those plates into a single design.

Local trains came and went ceaselessly on the other platforms. The train to Toshima-en. The Kiyose train, stopping at all stations. The Tokorozawa express . . . Only the Hannō train failed to turn up, and the red signal light glowing dimly through the evening mist at the far end of the platform increasingly drew their attention.

Kazuo stamped the heels of his shoes, hummed a popular tune, and said disparagingly: 'You know, Akiko, human girls are all liars.'

Akiko at first said nothing, but laughed. She found her brother's philosophical deliberation amusing. His idea was clearly based on nothing more than a kind of agnosticism, a line of thought extremely typical of humans.

But she ended up becoming angry. 'You idiot! There's nothing mysterious about humans.'

'I'm not saying they're *mysterious*. They're *liars*.' Kazuo swung his schoolbag back and forth, disgruntled.

'People lie because they're surrounded by gullible people.'

Just then, the train pulled in and people got off first through the opposite set of doors. Passengers queuing to board crowded expectantly around the doors on this side.

The two managed to find seats. When the train started off, they remained silent for a while, gazing at the darkness gathering over the fields. Once they had passed Ōizumi-gakuen, more and more clusters of *zelkova* trees stood out against the evening sky, and lights began to twinkle brightly at the far edges of the desolate plain. By the time they went through Tokorozawa Station, a twilight mantle covered the whole landscape and only paddy fields tucked among woods stood out, like handkerchiefs dropped onto a path at night.

'Don't you find the boy from Kanazawa mysterious?' Kazuo would not let go.

'Yes, I do, but he's not human.'

Kazuo kept probing his sister from all sorts of angles in the hope of discovering some sort of change within her. He was also trying to avoid getting drawn into the kind of argument they had experienced before. But ever since her trip to Kanazawa, Akiko seemed determined to keep very much to herself. She skilfully fended off all his jokes, banter and blandishments until he threw in the towel.

'Mr Kuroki asked me to visit him at home.' He had suddenly changed tack.

'Who's that?'

'That famous politician. He went down a storm when he gave a talk at our school, although some lefty students went crazy. I'm a member of the debating committee, so I went to the podium and did a good job of calming them down. Afterwards, in the reception room, Mr Kuroki took a shine to me. He gave me his business card and asked me to make sure I pay him a visit.' Kazuo pulled out a large card from his season ticket wallet and showed it to Akiko:

KATSUMI KUROKI, LOWER HOUSE MEMBER

'So, do you plan on going to see him?'

'Sure, I do,' Kazuo replied lightly. 'It's not smart to go straight for the big fry like Khrushchev.'

'Do you intend to tell him about our project?'

'Oh, right. No, when it comes to the crunch, I don't suppose I'll say anything. I'm the sort that thinks it's always best to hide your *political ambition.*'

On the outskirts of a station, a dazzlingly bright building came into view, cutting through the rural gloom of the station square. It was an electrical appliance shop, with lines of multicoloured flags hanging from the eaves. Inside were televisions, heaters and lighting appliances that sparkled in a flood of brilliant, piercing light. Even when the train had left the shop far behind, its glitter lingered in their eyes against the darkness of the trees. Akiko fancied she saw the brightness of the Venusian world that Takemiya had ultimately never managed to put into words. A bright, radiant globe, suspended in the dark expanse of space like a rural electrical appliance shop . . .

Hannō is a town without much going for it, planned down to the last detail. They got off at the station. They took a bus. When they alighted at the bus stop closest to home, a wide, empty, dark road stretched before them. On the roadside was a beauty salon operating from a private home, with a lantern outside advertising perms. A lumber merchant's had pieces of timber propped up against its outside wall, illuminated with orange light. The steam from irons curled faintly around the lattice window of a laundry.

The pair happened to pass in front of Murata's. Most of the storm shutters were closed, and only a single beam of light fell across the road.

After they had gone by, the shopkeeper addressed those inside: 'That's the son and daughter. They must be up to something to come home so early.'

She had two visitors: the local policeman, with whom she was on good terms, and the officer responsible for public order from police headquarters. She had sent for them both.

Her guests arose sluggishly to their feet and watched the brother and sister disappear down the dark road. The delicate light of a new moon fell onto the backs of the young couple, as if branding them unequivocally with the charge of thought crime. In a quiet little country town like this, the public order officer was starved of thought crimes. They were his poetry, precious gems that he rarely glimpsed. After a strict crackdown in Ikebukuro, young hooligans had begun to spread out along the Seibu Line, but the officer's work was of a different nature. He was tasked with more sophisticated matters out of the public eye.

'According to what I've managed to glean from a post office employee, Ōsugi sent a letter to Khrushchev last November. Possibly he's carrying out secret party activities. I've no idea what he's using the profits from his shares on, but he's forever taking money out. In any case, they're a very dodgy family,' he said.

The shopkeeper spoke with conviction. 'It's either drugs or the Communist Party. It can't be anything else. And to make matters worse, I can't stomach the supercilious way the whole family look down on other people. They say all the right things when they greet you, but their smiles are nothing but a front and it doesn't fool me. All the wives round here say the same thing. Doesn't it strike you as odd that a big house like that has no maid?'

'It's not a crime not to have a maid.'

'Look, if the husband really had his wits about him, you'd expect him to have thought through something as simple as that. Those people totally lack ordinary feelings, and they're hiding some big secret. Maybe you'll find skeletons under their floorboards. Then what?'

'Don't be daft.'

'I'm telling you, intellectuals with a little bit of money are the worst kind. Ordinary people like us, good, kind-hearted folk, always lose out. We spend our lives defending what's right in the world, and we have nothing but honest feelings whether we're asleep or awake. We're deeply compassionate and easily moved to tears, and our whole lives we never flinch from standing up against things we don't agree with. I don't actually hate the family. I'm just desperate to drag them out of the swamp, and put them back on the straight and narrow.'

Even at the dinner table, Jūichirō drifted off several times into a world of his own. Once he had collected his thoughts, he said:

'After dinner tonight, how about doing some exam study here in the living room? We could think of the room as the constellation Capricorn, and enjoy the final night of our first get-together in 5,000 years. After all, Mars, Jupiter, Mercury and Venus won't align with the sun and moon like this again in the same place for another 5,000 years. Once your mother has finished the washing-up, she can bring her knitting in here. Maybe I could map out a lecture tour with Kazuo as my driver, seeing as the spring holiday will be here soon. As long as we keep things quiet and don't talk, it's possible to study in here. That way, we can fulfil the sacred role bestowed upon our family tonight.'

They never had the television on at home because Jūichirō said it interfered with cosmic communications. When all four really got down to work, the total silence under the bright living-room light was broken only by the sound of pages of books and notepads being turned.

Father, with his Martian roots, was astounded by the complexity of road maps on Earth. Not a single route took the shortest distance from one city to the next. The roads would narrow and widen, and meander whimsically all over the place.

Mother was energetically knitting a light woollen sweater for her son that was primarily designed for springtime on Earth, but would also do for spring on all the other planets. Her fingers worked briskly, gradually reducing the size of the ball of wool on her knees. In her small fleshy hands, she knitted together not only an earthly springtime – in the colours of budding trees and sprouting grasses, the opaque skies of early spring, the easily sullied breast down of little birds, the hard sprays of rain – but also springtime on all the other planets, with their flames, and gaseous bodies, and ice and strange vegetation. It was as if she were unravelling each of those vast lands and reducing them to the tiny scale that pleased her most, the sweater she was knitting for her son.

The son flipped through his notes on international law, and was repulsed by the childish, abstract legislation, the timid, circuitous rules, and the antiquated principle of international cooperation. Even cosmic laws had been reduced to boorish traffic regulations designed exclusively for the thin sliver of air covering the Earth's surface. He was all for the imposition of a rigid, merciless cosmic constitution throughout the world. His legislation would ensure the destruction of the impoverished realism that had served as an easy escape for humans. A future world government would order human beings throughout the planet to be dragged into their local town squares every morning, where they would have to swear to maintain peace the whole day long. His plan was that a twenty-four-hour period of peace would continue for ever. And those who broke their oath would have their tongues cut out on the spot.

The daughter was studying the poetry of Edgar Allan Poe.

Her teacher's interpretation was uninspiring. He claimed that the narrative poem 'Eldorado' symbolized the fate of humans who sought the Ideal to the point of exhaustion. And yet, even as they despaired of any ideal that might continue for ever, they felt obliged to continue the search. But that was obvious even to a child. More likely, Poe's poem was describing the home planet of an extraterrestrial. He was, after all, the author of *Eureka*.

'Over the Mountains
Of the Moon

Down the Valley of the Shadow,
Ride, boldly ride,'
The Shade replied, –
'If you seek for Eldorado!'

Eldorado here must be a reference to Venus. Takemiya had seen it with his own eyes, she had no doubt. Of course! The 'Mountains of the Moon' in the poem indicated the desolate landscape on the other side of the moon, and hinted indirectly at Venus, whose form could be seen in the sky after crossing those mountains.

In this way, the four passed their cosmic time in the living room, each quietly engrossed in their own thoughts. The low tea table gave off a russet gleam. The four sat upon fresh tatami mats woven into the shape of neat little waves. The mandarin oranges heaped in the bowl were resplendent. Jūichirō sensed in his bones a world brimming with total harmony. Here was an ideal family beyond his wildest imagination, without worries or anxieties. Protected, this winter night, by the warm flames of the gas stove. Aware of mutual love and trust, even as each retained their respective solitude wrapped in the darkness of space. This was a model for the human family, but also the blueprint for peace on Earth. The electric lamplight fell gently onto Akiko's beautifully lustrous hair hanging over her notebook, and onto Iyoko's supple, experienced fingers while her knitting needles clacked away. It was as if life itself had been transformed into a sacred ceremony.

Jūichirō suddenly closed his eyes and recalled the grim days of his youth. He had feared the concept of happiness like the plague then. Troubled by his own indolence and beset by a serious inferiority complex, he had fantasized that this indolence would gnaw away at him until he was no more. But indolence did not kill him. That was why suicide, and the effort to commit suicide, had become such a pressing issue. The world seen through his eyes at that time appeared as a gigantic, slippery, unscalable globe that he had no choice but to confront. And yet, it was not exactly what might be described as unattractive!

After he got married and had children, he was a nice enough

husband, but how much was he capable of loving his wife and children? It was only recently, since he became aware that they were all from separate planets, that he had learned to love them. From that moment, everything became forgivable, and a blessing.

The doorbell rang.

'Who could that be at this time?' Iyoko set down her knitting and stood up. 'We're not expecting anyone. Maybe it's a member from the Universal Friendship Association who's just decided to drop by. And to think we made it so clear in our association rules that we don't do meetings like that.'

Iyoko came back, ashen-faced, name card in hand. The card read:

ROKURŌ TAKAHASHI, PUBLIC ORDER DEPARTMENT, HANNŌ
POLICE STATION

Jūichirō met Officer Takahashi in the unheated reception room. He was an unremarkable man dressed in plain clothes, and his words were polite enough. In fact, he looked more servile than polite. Only the eyes that scoured Jūichirō's face and the room as they spoke revealed his true lack of respect.

'Let me be very direct with you, sir,' he said. It was hard to sift out the good or ill intent of his words. 'The fact is, we've had quite a few strange reports coming in recently about your family driving off somewhere together in the middle of the night . . .'

The officer was afraid Jūichirō might shelter behind confidentiality with regard to his private correspondence, so he did not bring up the letter to Khrushchev.

'Oh that. We went to see the stars,' came the prompt answer.

'Stars?'

'We're all studying stars. Is that against the law?'

'No, that's not what I'm trying to say.'

'We do it because I'm terribly worried about world peace.'

'Oh, I see. So, it's something to do with pacifism.'

'If we carry on like this, the Earth will be in real trouble. It's just that you don't notice it. What is your fundamental mission as a policeman in a democracy?'

Yukio Mishima

'To protect the lives of the citizens.' Officer Takahashi's chest filled out as he spoke.

'Is that so? Well, then, you and I share the same mission. We should shake on it.'

The officer returned his gaze with suspicion in his eyes. He slurped down his tea, now almost cold, and said:

'What do you mean by protecting the lives of citizens, sir?'

'We are trying to save humanity from destruction.'

'Are humanity and the public the same thing?'

'Speaking from a broader perspective, humanity simply refers to the citizens of small towns.'

'I'm not sure I agree with you. Our work relates to citizens, but does not reach as far as humanity.'

'You just have to expand your mind a little, and you'll see what I mean. For example, try to imagine some people trapped behind bars in a zoo. How would you feel about that?'

'I'd hate it, I guess.'

'You see. That's a humane response. It's completely different to the anger of citizens. Any situation in which humans are trapped in a cage would offend your sense of common humanity and self-respect. And right now, all mankind is trapped in a dangerous cage. The cage has been locked from the outside and there's no escape.'

'Well, at least the citizens of Hannō are not in a cage.'

'You're wrong. It's just that the bars of the cage are so far away you can't see them. What I'm trying to do is break the lock and set everyone free.'

'To go where?'

Jūichirō was at a loss how to answer this simple question. At that moment he was dreaming of the vast emptiness of space, but the actual direction in which the night sky, ablaze with stars, was moving remained an utter mystery to him. That place was beyond the jurisdiction of the police.

For his part, the officer sensed that Jūichirō was raising his eyes because his sights were set on something loftier than the police. Whatever his game was, they were dangerous thoughts.

78

'So, what you're saying is that your ideas boil down to two words, "peace" and "liberation". As I'm sure you know, these are both Communist words. Freedom of expression is important, of course, but when those thoughts lean towards destructive actions . . .'

Jūichirō felt emotion getting the better of him, and he said:

'This isn't a joke. Isn't destruction the way you lot do it?'

By 'you lot', what he actually meant was 'mankind'. But obviously, this gave rise to misunderstanding and the officer immediately countered:

'Sir, are you trying to say that the police are involved in destructive activities? That shows clear contempt for the police. Only a Communist would think like that.'

The next instant, a cold smile reappeared on the officer's face, as if a layer of skin had peeled away. He was not a believer in grilling people too harshly, and he felt that his purpose for the night's interview had been achieved.

The officer announced his departure and Jūichirō saw him to the unlit entrance. As the officer put on his shoes, Jūichirō addressed him from behind:

'Don't you ever do your rounds in a uniform and cap?'

'No, civilian clothes are the rule in the Public Order Department.'

'If I'm not mistaken, you wear stars on your uniform.'

'That's right.' Officer Takahashi stood up and turned back as he reached out to the lattice door with his hand. He noted an intensely sad shadow hanging over the thin, distinguished bridge of Jūichirō's nose.

'You wear a star badge, but you've forgotten what it means. You lot have forgotten the spirit of the stars.'

After seeing him off, Jūichirō slumped down on the spot, overcome with exhaustion. A vague ache grated deep in his gut. The peaceful get-together in the constellation Capricorn had ended for the night.

The exams were over and spring holiday had arrived. A warm wind laden with yellow pollen was already sweeping across the late February skies.

Jūichirō was busy preparing the lecture he would deliver within Tokyo's inner-city area, but Kazuo had turned down the role of driver and seemed reluctant to lend a hand. He was afraid that Katsumi Kuroki might become aware of their activities, and the special treatment he had managed to receive would slip away. His father had already predicted a proliferation of coincidences, and he could not discount the possibility that he might bump into Kuroki in some assembly hall in totally unforeseen circumstances.

And so, the roles of driver and administrator fell to Akiko. Rather than give one big lecture in a large hall, her father was inclined to tour Tokyo and its surroundings in local venues such as town halls and community centres. He hoped to speak as many times as possible, developing a closer relationship with smaller audiences thereby. Akiko had sole responsibility for venue bookings and publicity, while Iyoko busied herself making copies of the bulletin which gave out details of the latest schedule to the membership. Akiko argued for an entry fee charge, but her father insisted he would bear all expenses and there was no need to take money. The lecture's details were as follows:

FLYING SAUCERS COMMAND IT: THE ATTAINMENT OF
WORLD PEACE
LECTURER: JŪICHIRŌ ŌSUGI
SPONSOR: UNIVERSAL FRIENDSHIP ASSOCIATION

One morning, with just three more halls to book in Tokyo itself, Akiko set off by car for the city. She put down deposits on two locations, and by the time she reached the third, a community centre in M Ward, it was four o'clock.

She could see the centre from a distance. It was a newly constructed Modernist building, not quite the small-scale, intimate hall her father had in mind. But M Ward was an essential location that would attract Tokyo's intellectual crowd.

It was a rather cloudy day with a strong south wind and frequent rolls of spring thunder during the afternoon. When Akiko drove into the community centre's front yard, she was surprised to find numerous wreaths adorning the entrance. Black-and-white striped cloth was wrapped around a line of narrow posts, from which black ribbons fluttered. It was a funeral curtain that stretched, flapping, all the way to the main door.

Akiko went to the community centre office, but the counter was closed and the seats inside were all unoccupied. Only one official, around forty and with a mourning band around his arm, was getting ready to go home. Akiko tapped on the counter window.

'We're finished for the day.'

He waved his hand from a distance. But then he seemed to notice Akiko's beautiful, pale face emerge at the counter window. He approached and unlocked just the window. The dust that had blown indoors made the window grate as he opened it.

'Are you interested in booking the hall? Sorry, but we can't do that today. Please come again tomorrow. You see, we only just finished the funeral for the head of our ward.'

'Can I ask just one favour?'

'Come tomorrow. We don't have that many bookings, so you'll be fine.'

'Of course, but could you possibly just let me see the hall now?'

The official pondered for a moment. The slack lips of his protruding middle-aged mouth gave off a foul breath.

'Fine. You can go in through the door at the end of the corridor. I have to go home now, so I can't show you around.'

Akiko thanked him, walked down the corridor and pushed open the door. They were in the middle of clearing up the hall. It was so gloomy that she looked up to check through the high window. The sky had become cloaked in black clouds in a matter of moments.

Inside, the funeral curtain was already taken down, but half the wreaths remained. The chairs had been pushed to the sides, so it was difficult to tell how many people it could accommodate. Akiko's shoes squeaked as she walked around alone and, with time on her hands, she read the name of one of the wreath senders. She noticed the words, 'Kanazawa City Chamber of Commerce and Industry'. It would seem that the deceased ward head was a native of distant Kanazawa. The very thought made her mind race. Surely there was some kind of link between this funeral and Takemiya.

What she first took to be a peal of thunder was actually the sound of a grand piano being dragged out from behind the stage where it had been stored away. They handled the piano roughly. The large black object, its gleaming lid propped open, was trundled to the spot where the coffin must have sat only moments before. A young man opened the keyboard cover and tapped out some playful nonsense in the treble clef.

While she listened, Akiko felt Takemiya must surely have hidden himself somewhere close by. The piano notes echoed tranquilly across the high ceiling and trickled down into the very depths of Akiko's heart.

In the three months since their meeting, they had exchanged frequent letters. Their common Venusian ancestry, along with their shared secret encounter with flying saucers, had bound their hearts together as one for ever. Takemiya's ideas about beauty had wormed their way into Akiko, and she wanted to keep a distance from her father's social activities, but the young man admonished her to cooperate with her father without any fuss for the time being. These past three months, whenever Akiko felt an urge to meet Takemiya, they would instead discuss the small photograph he gave her in Kanazawa. She kept it tucked away inside her season ticket wallet so that he could accompany her to school.

Takemiya told Akiko something which, to her own amazement, she had already discovered by herself. Living in separate physical locations empowered them to maintain a constant connection between their spirits. He wrote that, if it was true that this world amounted to no more than an illusory existence, then the innumerable illusions that filled the distance between them were both invisible and non-existent too. Likewise, he said, the only thing they could see in each other's eyes was the reality of their Venusian roots, like that multi-coloured lighthouse at the shrine gate viewed from far across the sea. This Venusian man and woman might be physically far apart in Kanazawa and Tokyo, but they stood like a pair of lighthouses towering above the sluggish night clouds of the human world.

There were artificial flowers everywhere, with silver foil and pale white blooms, and cold petals stuck into candles. The invigorating scent of death lingered after the funeral, like a spent bonfire. The piano's high notes flowed whimsically into her ears. And all the while, she felt sure that Takemiya, that strange beautiful young man, might make an appearance. Sensing that his radiant face was about to suddenly peer through that high window, filled with dark clouds, Akiko looked up.

She could not escape an inauspicious doubt that arose within her. In Kanazawa, they had shared their memories, enjoyed the same beautiful scenery, and shuddered with identical emotions. They both ended up witnessing flying saucers in the sky, an experience which left them equally in a state of extraordinary rapture. But there was one thing that Akiko was simply incapable of sharing. The exquisite world that Takemiya had glimpsed through the slits of his *fukai* mask. The Venusian landscape that, ultimately, he had been unable to express in words. Akiko's doubts lingered even now. Perhaps what Takemiya had seen was the world of death.

There was a sudden clap of thunder, causing the whole community centre to rattle with rain.

'Damn, it's pouring. And we still haven't cleared away the wreaths,' shouted a young man dressed in blue jeans.

'It's just passing. It'll soon stop. Meanwhile, how about going for a ciggie?' said a middle-aged labourer wearing rubber-soled work shoes.

The rain beat ferociously against the huge modern windowpane. No one had switched on the lights, so it grew even darker inside the community centre. The silver, yellow, green and white colours of the artificial flowers stacked against the wall emerged vividly, as if they were blooming into life. Every broad flash of lightning momentarily exposed the silver petals in all their artificiality, alive with malicious intent.

Akiko walked over to the entrance where the rain bounced fiercely on the ground, and wondered how she could reach her car, parked in front. She took out her season ticket wallet from her handbag and gazed at Takemiya's beautiful, pale, smiling face. The photo reminded her of something he had said in Kenroku-En: 'Ah, I've got it. You're picking up exactly what's happening inside my head.'

Akiko felt too far away from the bliss they had experienced in

December among the Uchinada sand dunes, and now she hungered for it. She was alone, and it was not fair. They might be living in a way that allowed them to conquer space, but perhaps it was beyond them to conquer time.

I need something in this moment, please. If I can't have you here with me, at least give me a sign right now that you exist, prayed Akiko, facing the rain.

Someone approached Akiko from behind. She turned around in surprise. Standing there was that rough-looking young man with a tousle of hair on his head, dressed in a grubby red-check shirt and a pair of worn-out jeans. In his hand, he carried the stem of a silver artificial flower that he must have plucked from a wreath. He rather pretentiously went down on a knee, straightened his torso and presented her with the flower, with the words: 'Miss, here is a token of my true feelings.'

Akiko accepted the flower without a thought. A ripple of laughter broke out in the gloom behind the young man where his friends were watching how things would develop.

Akiko seized the flower and rushed headlong into the rain.

It was late at night, two days before Jūichirō's first lecture, and he was working assiduously on his manuscript in his study, surrounded by the piles of reference works and photographs of flying saucers that he had prepared for slides. He was quoting liberally from several indispensable flying saucer studies, such as Kenneth Arnold's *My Sighting of Flying Saucers*, Donald Keyhoe's *Flying Saucers are Real* and William Ferguson's *A Message from Outer Space*, in an effort to make his own text as interesting as possible. Jūichirō was very tired, and his gut felt heavy.

There was a knock at the door and Iyoko came in, carrying some tea and fruit.

'Still up? It's nearly two-thirty,' said Jūichirō.

'My hands were black with mimeograph ink, and I've just washed them. I'm finished for tonight. Goodnight, then.'

For years, Iyoko had not been one to overstay her welcome in her husband's study. Jūichirō stopped what he was doing and urged her to sit.

'Stay for a while. I was just about to take a break.'

When they were alone, there was always a rather prim atmosphere of camaraderie between them, of the kind found among liberal married couples during the 1920s. Maybe because Iyoko never spent much time in the study, she tended to be most fascinated by her husband in this environment.

An electric brazier, her husband dressed in a woollen cardigan and some corduroy slacks, the tiger-shaped paperweight on the table carved from jade, a pen tray holding a line of anxiously sharpened pencils. The scene offered no hint of the greasy carnal smell that most women Iyoko's age might pick up from their husbands.

'I suppose the kids are in bed.'

'Ages ago.'

In this house, there was always something else going on underneath such domestic exchanges. Iyoko buried her mouth in the sleeve of her jacket as she whispered:

'Actually, when Akiko was out, I read all her letters from that Kanazawa boy. They're full of passion, but there's something strangely cold about them. He doesn't exactly spell it out, but I'm telling you, they saw flying saucers together in Kanazawa.'

Iyoko, noticing how deeply her words had cut Jūichirō, stopped talking. Her husband's cool, pale cheeks flushed, and quickly paled again.

'Don't be stupid . . . They can't have . . .'

He felt that his daughter had committed a terrifying act of profound betrayal. If the two had really witnessed flying saucers *together*, this was evidence indeed that the boy from Kanazawa must be from Venus. And if it was true that only extraterrestrials from the same planet were able to see flying saucers together, then his daughter was the only member of the family who was now certain of her origins. It also meant that the relative order of the planets in their family, and the harmony that pertained from that order, had broken down. In the process of ascertaining her Venusian origins, Akiko had actually committed an irredeemable *human* error. At the risk of sounding like sour grapes, the flying saucers' no-show that dawn before the entire family on top of Mt Rakan meant that the family still lacked real evidence to bind them together. However, Jūichirō actually revelled in the realization that it was now his almost super-human fate to maintain family cohesion through nothing more than mutual trust. But now Akiko had gone and intentionally reduced everything to the almost carnal level of evidence that humans pre-ferred. What is more, she had kept it from her parents out of some kind of guilt.

Strangely, Jūichirō's elevated mind was driven by indignation and agitation in a way that differed little from the lamentations of any ordinary father with a belief in his daughter's purity who now real-izes she had acted shoddily behind his back.

'Don't beat yourself up over this.' His wife was desperate to throw in some comforting words of reason. 'From the moment I realized the children were from different planets, I resigned myself to the fact that something like this would happen at some point. Kazuo is moving away from us, and Akiko is just finding her way. But all planets follow their own orbits. Even if they appear to mean-der around a bit, in the end they simply move according to fixed planetary motions. Come to think of it, I offered up my own belly to produce two extraterrestrial babies. If I'd been so inclined, I could have given birth to humans. But I just couldn't. And that's because I loved you.

'But right at this moment, I do wish I'd given birth to at least one human. It's not that I'm inordinately fond of them, but I'm certainly not adverse to the natural world on this planet. Especially in springtime, when the fields gradually turn green, when pure melting snow overflows into the Naguri River, when Mt Rakan fills with nightingale song and the soil of the vegetable plots turns glossy and black. Sure, I raised children from Venus and Mercury, but I still like to think this is a blessed land. Am I wrong to think like this?'

'Can you peel me some fruit?' said her husband, without replying directly.

The knife in Iyoko's hand glinted under the lamplight as she peeled a large crisp apple, its delicate glossy skin blurring from red into yellow, and paling further into white. Its firm exposed flesh exuded a scent laced with sweet anxiety. Jūichirō was aware that a similar, dangerous charm clung to his own efforts to save the world.

5

It was the afternoon of Saturday, the tenth of March. Masumi Haguro was waiting for two acquaintances on top of Mt Dainenji, located in the south-west part of Sendai City. They were expected at the rose garden here on the mountain peak at three o'clock.

Haguro was an assistant professor at the local university, lecturing in legal history. Though forty-five years old, he had not yet made the grade to full professorship. He was physically weak, with a pale complexion, wore perfectly round spectacles and retained a thick head of hair. There was nothing about him that others found particularly endearing. And he was certainly no favourite among his students.

Impatient for the two to arrive, he left a trail of scuff marks on the sandy earth path as he ambled around the deserted rose garden. It was a clear, sunny afternoon, and snow-capped Mt Izumigatake glittered splendidly on the northern horizon.

They had just finished early spring pruning in the garden. Haguro much preferred this flowerless season to the rose garden in full bloom. There was a reason for this. Around this time the previous year, from this very spot, flying saucers had appeared beyond Mt Izumigatake's snowy ridges.

It was his belief that humans were ugly, and the reason why flowers never bloomed out of the frontal lobes of humans was because they never got pruned. They ought to have their fingers and toes smashed when very young. His students at university were so unattractive and dimwitted . . .

Tired of waiting, Haguro squatted in front of a rose bush that bore the label 'Aztec'. Sand grated on the pock-marked soles of his shoes. He could feel his tightly fastened belt scrunching everything upwards. His sickly internal organs, the glasses case tucked inside his jacket, his thin wallet, his fountain pen that had just run out of ink. And then, just as a rising tide heightens the stink of rubbish in a river, he was assailed by the powerful stench of his own disagreeable human life.

Although the pruned stems were robustly green, they crouched in eccentric shapes, overgrown with thorns that resembled white-scaled insects. Strangely, a few small branches had escaped being cut back. Someone had neglected to remove the previous year's blossoms from their tips. The roses had coagulated into a brownish-purple, like dried blood.

These roses from the year before were small and round, like shrivelled testicles. They dangled from branch tips, swaying delicately in the breeze, and some of their desiccated petals had become crumbly like ash, yet still retaining the zigzag edge of the petals.

Haguro reached out and cupped the petals in his hand. With barely any pressure from his fingers, the flowers disintegrated, leaving his fingertips smeared with tiny fragments.

Live roses sentenced to be burned at the stake, yet keeping their shape even after they have turned into ash. The beautiful double form of evil. Haguro firmly believed that every form in this world was a fabrication. Even destruction had its form, yet that form was a delusion.

Would he actually need to use force in order to wipe out humanity? Maybe the human world would collapse like the roses crushed a moment before by his fingers with just a gentle touch. No, probably the world was already extinct, and only its shell remained. Whenever such abhorrent thoughts took root in Haguro's mind, he was quick to repulse them. They distracted from his *mission*.

'Hey, Professor, sorry to keep you waiting,' Sone called out from the arch that marked the entrance to the rose garden. Haguro was always put off by Sone's overbearing voice, so he ignored him. The burly Kurita followed Sone silently up the small path.

Sone owned the barber shop in front of the university North

Gate that Haguro frequented. He was a chubby man with plump healthy fingers, and he had a collection of commemorative poems written by celebrities on display in his shop. He had an undying love for gossip about others, and he even knew all the dirt about up-and-coming television actors. His enthusiasm was rooted, in a word, in envy for everything that passed between one person and another. For some reason, Haguro alone escaped Sone's envy.

Kurita lived in Sanbyakunin-machi, close to Hoshunin Temple, and he worked at S Bank. He had graduated from university, where Haguro had taught him, only the year before. They got to know each other outside of the classroom because they frequented the same barbers'.

'It's all coming back. Same place, same season, same cast of people as last year. The only difference is we won't be composing haiku poems this time.' Sone put on his usual airs as he spoke.

In early spring the previous year, a famous haiku poet from Tokyo had been invited to speak at the university. After his talk, on the way back to his hotel he decided on a whim to drop into Sone's place. Both Kurita, who was getting ready for his graduation ceremony, and Haguro were there to get haircuts. Sone abandoned his work and asked the poet to inscribe a commemorative poem, at which point all three locals launched into a shallow discussion of haiku. The poet, knowing exactly how to worm his way into people's affections, expressed an interest in accompanying his new-found friends, unversed in the haiku world, to some local sightseeing spot in order to find poetic inspiration. All three recommended Mt Dainenji over the vulgar Sendai Castle. The poet enthusiastically suggested meeting there at two in the afternoon the following day. He would instruct them in ways of marking a visit to a famous place with a poem, and give some advice on poetry composition. Sone was so excited he even began working on the menu for lunch.

The following day at two o'clock on top of Mt Dainenji, the assistant professor, the barber and the student ended up being stood up by the haiku poet.

They waited for ages, but still he did not come. The three finished off the assorted titbits that the barber had prepared, but they were not in the mood for drinking. The assistant professor's pride had been injured. Finally, when it was clear that the poet was not coming, Haguro abruptly rose to his feet and walked into the deserted rose garden, followed at a tardy pace by the other two.

That day the previous year, too, distant snow-covered Mt Izumigatake had been visible from the rose garden, cutting sharply into the clear sky. The three stood completely still, gazing at the faraway mountain. Haguro, decimated by the disrespectful poet who had failed to show up. Sone, with feelings of pure hatred towards the poet. The clumsy Kurita just standing there, vacant.

But all three, in their hearts, felt entangled in a haiku. Trapped in the tiny, mundane cage of an inconsequential poem. Malice. Like a small, meaningless, whimsical verse that the haiku poet had left behind in the bright sunlight of early spring. It hung around their noses, like a swarm of tiny black flying insects. An ingeniously crafted malice, like a gift of dainty cakes presented to them on a lacquer tray.

Just then, the barber uttered a shriek:

'Flying saucer! . . . Flying saucer! . . . How does this sound?

> Flying saucer:
> Scraps of snow over
> Mt Izumigatake.'

'What are you going on about?' There was a note of irritation in Haguro's voice.

Without awaiting a reply, both Haguro and Kurita caught sight of what had appeared spontaneously and unannounced in Sone's field of vision, and which had led to his run-of-the-mill poetic inspiration. It was so obviously there that no one could doubt its existence.

To the right of Mt Izumigatake's snowy, glittering summit floated a strange, round, silver object. They could tell at a glance that it was stationary, which gave some credence to Sone's claim in his crude haiku that scraps of snow had gone flying through the blue sky, where they remained suspended. But closer inspection revealed that the silver disc was spinning rapidly on the spot.

'What is it?'

Haguro pressed the middle of his glasses back firmly over the bridge of his nose.

This was not the end of the bizarre incident. A similar-looking flying saucer appeared to the left of the mountain. This one was spinning around in the sky like a whirligig. The mechanical structure of both vessels appeared in such detail that Haguro wondered if his visual perspective was playing tricks on him. The flying saucers seemed to be hovering directly in front of Mt Izumigatake.

But that proved not to be so. When the vessel on the right side suddenly tilted, its edge pointing towards them to create a slightly bulging, oscillating line (like a round, cute open eye that suddenly closed, leaving the lasting impression of an eyelash), the vessel to the left suddenly disappeared behind the mountain, followed by its companion.

They did not have long to wait before the two craft, now a beautiful apricot colour, reappeared from behind the mountain peak. The flying saucers ascended rapidly at an angle right before them, and disappeared at terrifying speed into the clouds gathered around the mountain top.

From that moment, the world was a different place for all three of them.

'There was nowhere else we could possibly meet,' said Haguro, finally rising to his feet but with his eyes still fixed on Izumigatake's glittering snow. 'We could have just met up in a coffee shop in town for a chat, but I thought it was vital for us to come back here to the rose garden and reconfirm our commitment in front of the distant snowy mountain. It looks like that "Universal Friendship Association" is even reaching out with a lecture tour. Not only that. Did you know that wherever they go they are sold out, and they have built themselves a formidable reputation in Tokyo? I took that Jūichirō Ōsugi to be a dumb-assed halfwit, but there seems more to him than that.'

'Oh, you mean the "World Peace Lectures"? All they ever do is drone on about saving the Earth and humanity,' said Kurita, without giving it much thought.

'He's such a jerk. I wonder if he's becoming a celebrity?' asked Sone. From the tone of his voice, he was clearly dying to receive a commemorative poem from Ōsugi.

'It is not a matter of whether he has become a celebrity, or not. All I know is that he has got some secret up his sleeve. If humans are attracted to that secret and seriously begin to wish for peace, then we are in trouble. He may not have much power right now, but he is still in our way. Very soon, we will have to eradicate the obstacle. It is in the best interest of humans to let them destroy themselves quickly, happily, comfortably and in such a brief moment of time that they won't even notice it. As I've said before.'

Haguro had considered his words carefully to make them easily comprehensible.

The three gazed instinctively towards Mt Izumigatake. There was no sign that flying saucers would be making an appearance that day, but vivid images of what they saw the year before came flooding back, along with the lively, evil emotions that had accompanied them.

When they spotted the flying saucers, all three recalled being definitely overcome by nostalgic thoughts of home. They all savoured a sense of camaraderie between people who shared the same, albeit unidentified, native place. But how was it that all three immediately felt like accomplices bound together emotionally through a malicious pleasure that lurked equally in each of their minds?

Haguro found himself at a rare, perfect moment, when he could effortlessly gain control over the minds of others and impose his will on them. All he had to do was to come up with a single, wild idea. It was unlikely that he had long harboured a desire to hold sway over an uncouth barber and a nondescript student, but he found himself in a situation where these two were the only ones standing before him. What other choice did he have?

The sighting of flying saucers was such an out-of-world experience that it could only be ascribed to the awakening of some former memory. By its very nature, the experience left no sensual residue. It was transformed immediately into pure memory, and then locked away somewhere deep. Therefore, it was only natural that the three should have considered the flying saucers that had appeared before them as the reflection of a distant memory from the other side of space-time. Moreover, it was also natural that the vision triggered a state of mind in which, at terrifying speed, their shared experience led to a desire to seek out those common memories that each harboured within himself. These memories were dark, gloomy phantoms, specific to each individual personality, and hidden until then from the view of others. Almost simultaneously, they discovered both within themselves and within each other the extent to which they had hated humans throughout their lives. It was an ecstatic discovery.

Now was the moment for Haguro to come up with a concept that would illuminate their common past like an instantaneous bolt of lightning and terrify them to the core of their being. A concept that would touch everything with the same purple tinge expressed in a flash of light.

He gazed at Izumigatake, etched into the horizon beyond the valleys, the woods and forests, the neighbourhoods and the suburbs. It wore a crown of glittering snow and spread out deeply in all directions with heavy, luxuriant mountain folds that opened into wings, like a huge white swan resting with its beak nuzzled in its feathers.

White swan. The shape of pure, sparkling evil. An assortment of memories and visions clashed in the assistant professor's mind. White pages from a notepad fluttering in on the breeze through the classroom window. The name of a star that had stayed in his ear like an eerie refrain since middle-school days. A multitude of thoughts came and went until he finally hit upon the words:

'Don't you see? We come from an unknown planet somewhere in the binary star system 61 Cygni, in the constellation Cygnus. The flying saucers just now prove it. Like it or not, we never were human beings.'

The idea immediately lodged itself firmly in the heads of the other two. Haguro had expressed himself in a dispassionate, professorial tone, but the words betrayed his delight in his own discovery, which flooded his companions like light. 'Oh, I get it.' With that, all questions melted away. All the reasons why they loathed humans had been resolved.

'I see, so we came to this Earth . . . But for what purpose?' asked Kurita. Haguro's reply was crystal clear:

'To exterminate humanity.'

Soon after those events the year before, something happened that strengthened their conviction. Two days later, the haiku poet, who had left Sendai and was on his way home to Tokyo, had a stroke on the train and dropped dead.

To celebrate this first victory, the three had met up in a coffee shop in the Higashi Ichiban-cho district. The assistant professor of legal history was a great fan of making up regulations, so he established some rather finicky internal rules as a way to take his revenge on the campus politics that had excluded him. One rule was that group members should split the bill. The three raised their coffees, paid for separately, in a toast.

'Well, that's one of them out of the way,' said the barber, licking his lips.

'Just one person is nothing to celebrate. That's only one out of three billion, and the world population is increasing by more than thirty-five million every year.'

'No, I was talking about our immediate enemy.'

'Speak for yourself, Sone. The whole of mankind needs to be destroyed. We should feel something close to what humans would call "humanism".'

'But, Professor. It's just one person we're having a toast about today, isn't it?'

'You've got me there.' The three laughed merrily.

It was only in hindsight that things had become clear, but there was some sort of bond between the three of them – so different in character, occupation and age – from the moment they set eyes on each other. They had various things in common. For example, none of them was much of a looker, they were all driven by constant hatred towards people, and they had equally harboured a long-standing vague hostility towards the whole of mankind.

Yukio Mishima

Kurita scrutinized the dating couples dotted around the shop. 'I can't tell you how happy I'd be to take aim at the whole lot of these dummies and shoot them dead.'

'That particular method simply proves there are remnants of humanity left in you. Of course, it is only natural we should feel pangs of nostalgia for the human carcasses we have been carrying around for so many years. But, rather than waste time over it, our task is to employ a *universal method*. Small events like Auschwitz or the hydrogen bomb, or bigger ones like shifts in the Earth's crust that will lead to earthquakes and floods.'

'I wonder if there were extraterrestrials among the top echelons of the Nazis?'

'It would seem so. But they failed to model their methods on *nature*, so they sometimes got carried away by human savagery. Their hatred was a dead-end because they were consumed by the infantile notion of "ethnic groups". But for you two to become intoxicated with genocidal fantasies is plain selfishness. Notions like that are just diversions from the workaday world for us, like a game of golf. The path of our illustrious training is to temper personal malice, and to rise to the level of hatred towards all humanity. In order to accomplish that, I would like to propose an idea. We could make it a habit to meet up in this noisy place at least once a week, and meditate on the crowd around us in utter silence for about thirty minutes. What do you think? How about starting right now?'

The three had window seats on the first floor, so they enjoyed a clear view of the bustling night-time crowd below. At the end of the northern end of the street was a sudden wall of darkness, but out of the gloom arose the municipal office clock tower, where the orange neon hands of its clock face appeared to be wobbling. One of those fierce night winds of early spring must have whipped up outside. The colours of the fluorescent lighting in the shops of Higashi Ichiban-cho were still too cold for the season, while big, bright bookshops faced each other across the street, their contents on display like the insides of a refrigerator.

With their empty coffee cups set before them, the three fixed their gazes on the places most conducive to meditation, and lapsed into silence.

For some time, Haguro had been aware of the drooping leaves of a potted gum plant brushing his hair inside the heated shop. The unpleasant, seductive feel of earthly plants on the skin . . . His imagination turned to the slaughter of intellectuals.

The entire world's intellectual elite – its scholars, eggheads, religious figures, artists – gathered in a single room and stripped naked, then jammed into a high-walled enclosure and starved to death. That lot would never attain a heroic death. Starvation was the best thing for them. Stuck in their studies all their lives, the ugliest forms of human flesh revealed in their nakedness. How Haguro would delight in pressing his ear to that huge enclosure wall day after day. The occasional piercing cry. The long silence that follows. As the hours and days pass, can you hear the sound of their science and religion and philosophy and aesthetics – all those things supposed to be a crystallization of the human spirit – crumbling in the face of starvation? Is that the echo of human culture, like a desiccated sandcastle, collapsing? The beautiful custom of feasting on humanity begins to flutter its wings . . . Piercing shrieks, long silences . . . The ultimate god of human culture, the final god, the god who devours human flesh, stands upright, attired in robes of gold brocade. Those who have survived so far listen to the proclamation of their god. *It is historically inevitable that the ideals of human culture all end in cannibalism.* This is the last poem that those remaining will hear. A dark, resplendent, beautiful wind blows. Perhaps salvation lies in the wind, thrumming like a *koto*, or in the predilection for human flesh. Above them, their final glimpse of the blue sky. The most perfect sunset glow in all their days. Lyrical clouds reflected on their polished thigh bones. Practical reason spilling out like teeth . . . He puts his ear to the wall and waits. Finally, a full day of utter silence. This is how humanity – the most freakish and ugly of species – is wiped out!

Sone's eyes were darting restlessly from place to place. Ever since he became aware he was from outer space his previous feelings of envy and jealousy had been replaced by the attitude of an impeccably fair public prosecutor. He was in the habit of nodding to himself and making harrumphing noises through his lips, a tendency that only intensified as he meditated.

'Hmm. Famous people, people with money, young, good-looking men who can pull girls. Hmm. They all have to be destroyed.'

All barbers on Earth should be mobilized and assigned the task of executioner. Every barber's chair in the world should be put in a line, and the famous and the rich and the good-looking men made to sit down in turn. With white capes over their bodies, and steamed towels applied to their faces. And then, one by one, their windpipes carefully slit with a razor. Barbers are very proud of their sterilized blades, and even in this situation they are not likely to neglect disinfection. Hundreds of thousands of red-white-and-blue striped barber poles rotating cheerfully, side by side, embodying what they originally stood for. The red of blood, the pure white of a sterilized towel, the blue complexion of the corpse . . . As far as the eye can see, a gorgeous row of nicely polished barber chairs . . . And when all the executions have been carried out, all those barbers in the world, Sone's business competitors, will be led to a huge public bath in thanks for their hard work. And once they've enjoyed a good soak in the tub, they will be suffocated with a sudden blast of steam.

Kurita's eyes were fixed on the backside of a young woman sitting on a chair across the room, eating a large cake. Her rear was covered in a tight, pale-green striped skirt, and it bulged in a way that seemed to invest her with really sinister designs.

Every woman sticks out some part of her body in order to ensnare others. This is what leads to the shackles of the human world. All he had to do was to cut those shackles. By sterilizing all women on Earth. No real hurry. Mankind will go extinct within a hundred years. For sure . . .

A clear vision of humanity, stripped of its reproductive cycle, rose up in Kurita's eyes. Illusions about the future, second chances and rebirth all completely smashed. Humans realizing that all they can depend on is the one-time nature of their existence, like a work of art. That moment when people dispense with their yearning and craving, and move towards their beautiful finale. In other words, they come to endure existence far better than they do now.

'Right, time's up. Why don't we tell each other what we've been meditating on?' said Haguro.

They all had great fun talking things over.

'Let us work on enhancing our feelings of hatred.' The assistant professor adopted the tone of mentor. 'The main thing is, we need to practise time and time again until our hatred is indistinguishable from our love of humanity. Ultimately, we are aiming for the euthanizing of all mankind. It is because of our kind-heartedness that we can no longer bear to watch people suffer.'

Sone interjected hesitantly. 'I wonder if you could possibly make one small exception?'

'Exception?'

'It's just about my immediate family. As you are aware, my wife and kids are human, unlike me. But I wonder if you could turn a blind eye at the moment when all humanity is destroyed? I'd like to take them with me to Cygnus when everything goes pear-shaped on Earth.'

'That should be fine.' Haguro's response was immediate. 'Just make sure you don't change your mind before the final day of destruction.'

'Oh, thank you so much.' The barber was beside himself with gratitude.

It was now a year after those events, and at today's get-together, which Haguro later dubbed the 'Rose Garden Meeting', the group discussed various ways to terminate the activities of the extraterrestrial family in Hannō. After that, they went back into town and went Dutch on dinner. Haguro had some entrance examination papers to finish marking, so he returned rather early to his home in the area around Sendai Castle where the American troops had been based. Crossing Ōhashi Bridge over the upper reaches of the Hirose River, home was on the right-hand side of the broad, paved road that led up to the castle. After the army withdrew, the collection of plain, Western-style dwellings had been reassigned as housing for public servants such as judges, public prosecutors and university professors.

The homes were either symmetrically built semi-detached bungalows, or two-storey tenement blocks divided into four. They were set among lawns, flower beds and American-style laundry-drying spaces, but the land had been rolled flat and was charmless, lacking any view. In the summer, however, children just needed to cross the bridge over the river in order to reach the new municipal swimming pool in Nishi Park.

Haguro lived in one of the tenements where, being single, he employed an old housemaid. He had turned his ten-mat upstairs room into a study, while the four-and-a-half-mat room served as his bedroom. The maid had a six-mat-room downstairs. No matter how late he returned home, his neatly attired maid would always be there to greet him when he rang the doorbell. Haguro offered a few words of appreciation, and shut himself away upstairs.

Once alone, he looked keenly into the wall mirror. The face of a scrawny, forty-five-year-old intellectual. It never changed, no matter what angle he looked from. He breathed onto the mirror. The fog erased his face. At the same time, faint traces of the halitosis he had been unable to shake off for decades stung his nostrils. He was rather attached to his own bad breath by now. The nauseating smell was totally unconnected to any vital life force, and might be more closely described as the rotten stench of academia.

Unlike other single people his age, Haguro did not keep a dog, or cat or small bird. He was his own unkempt dog, his own cunning cat. His life consisted simply of keeping himself entertained, and taking care that he had enough food to eat . . .

From the semi-detached bungalow opposite, which was occupied by an engineering professor and his family, came the sound of the daughter doing her regular evening piano practice. Haguro pushed the curtain aside a little and peeped at the bright light shining from the house. It spilled onto the parched lawn as the piano notes, which seemed to have been designed especially to convey utter simplicity, artlessly scattered happiness all around.

'That's humans for you, spattering their grubby happiness all around. What a pain! Like a car on a rainy day drenching the clothes of an innocent passer-by.'

But Haguro believed that humans were locked in eternal suffering, so he did not hold too much ill will against what happiness they had.

There were many possible thrillingly childish pleasures, but only one thing occupied his mind. And it was something he mulled over every night.

'Who would ever guess that I'm an extraterrestrial, of all things! Would anyone at university possibly suspect that I'm not human!'

He sat down in the old easy chair in a corner of his study with some nail clippers in his hands, and started to cut and file his nails carefully, as if he were a gigolo. He would often waste time in such trivial sensual activities before getting down to work. He was determined never to forget the physical aspect of being human.

His nails cut easily, like paper, but they tended to break under the file. Haguro paid increasingly careful attention to his pale fingertips as he lost himself in memories of the time when he was still human. His loveless adolescence. His loveless childhood. No matter how far he thought back, there was no love to remember.

He glanced over to the exam scripts piled up on the table. He had not even read them yet, but he was already bored. All those scripts squeezed out from the worthless, unoriginal minds of a new generation of 'youth'. The greasy, finger-stained papers were always poorly written and riddled with the pretensions and lack of self-awareness of the young.

Haguro himself had examined common rights with the intention of doing a doctorate at some point. His bookshelves were full of old documents. Though he had been studying for twenty years, he was yet to produce a book. He had, however, written a couple of papers for a quarterly journal called *Legal History Essays* . . . He should have just stuck with Japanese issues, but he developed an interest in comparative jurisprudence, and once he engaged with the ideas of Josef Kohler he was lost. Starting from a study of 'commonality', through which popular common law was most abundantly preserved in

Japan, he buried himself in the dark recesses of ancient folklore related to common law in each country. At university, he gave a perfunctory introductory lecture on legal history every year, while the wheels of his own research got stuck in the mud, leaving him unable to advance or retreat.

He had been a pale child, full of himself and argumentative. At school, his nickname was Brussel Sprout. His mother once dreamed that countless stars sprang from his head. He stubbornly believed he was incompetent, but everyone regarded him as a malicious genius. In his mind he would soar, as he gazed at the night sky, fantasizing about the day he would change into a star. Every star struck him as a frozen, sparkling brain. The insides of his *geta* sandals were painted silver. There was no significance in this, but his mother took it as an unlucky omen. They lived in an old, dark, multi-roomed house in the Kita-Rokubancho district. His cousins considered him a useless relative. When they came to play, they would tie him to the phoenix tree in the back garden. They would spit in his face, laughing with delight and dance rings around him. His mother was dead now . . .

Haguro once again pushed the curtain aside a little and peered out. The light from the professor's house was already extinguished and the piano sound was no more. Frail moonlight fell onto the parched lawn.

He finally turned to his desk, but he did not reach for the exam scripts. Instead, he reread the express mail which had arrived that morning. It was a private message from a member of the Universal Friendship Association. This young and enthusiastic member always filled him in with the latest information, having no idea that Haguro and his two companions had joined the association merely to spy on them. The association bulletin was published irregularly, so private mail was a way for news to reach them about a month earlier.

Dear Professor,

I am writing to you, so far away, to keep you as up to date as possible about the splendid developments of our association here in Tokyo.

The lectures of our chairman, Jūichirō Ōsugi, have been a resounding success. When I went to hear him, I was deeply impressed. His message appears to have been picked up by several magazines, and it would be fair to say that it has advanced our association towards a new stage of development.

An outline of the chairman's talks will eventually appear in the bulletin, but he spoke eloquently about peace for mankind and the salvation of the world on the verge of destruction. His tone was dispassionate even as he depicted with breathtaking force the catastrophe that humanity would encounter in the event of World War Three. As he expounded upon the supreme bliss when mankind establishes true peace and becomes one with cosmic harmony, his pale features flushed, and his audience was caught in a reverie as if that supreme bliss had already materialized before them.

Our leader is peerless in his ability to demonstrate conclusively that 'flying saucers' are emissaries of peace, friends who have come to warn us. The first thing we must do is learn to be brave, and discover a peace within ourselves that does not cower before mankind, the world and the Universe. The fearful and suspicious heart that trembles before the Universe, before the world and before humanity is the source of all wars.

The slides of flying saucers that Chairman Ōsugi showed were all taken from highly credible photographs. The photographs authorized by the Brazilian Navy Ministry were exceptional. The images of pure, white flying saucers hovering above the azure South Atlantic next to a cliff in some South American location elevated our hearts away from everyday matters and the world's conflicts to the distant heavens . . .

'The idiot doesn't know what's going to hit him!' Haguro spat out the words in contempt.

The next day was a Sunday, and Kurita remained cooped up all day at home, lost in melancholic thoughts. It all began two years previously when Fumiko Takarabe was killed. Whenever he got into this state, others family members could only watch over him anxiously from a distance. It was early spring, a particularly tough season of the year. Fumiko's death had taken place exactly this time two years earlier.

Fumiko Takarabe was a beautiful twenty-eight-year-old divorcee, who had returned to her family home in Gojūnin-machi, close to Kurita's place. She was living with her elderly mother, and she earned a livelihood teaching doll-making. Kurita could recite from memory the exact words inscribed on the plate next to the sliding door of their modest gate:

TAKARABE DOLL SCHOOL
PURE JAPANESE DOLLS HANDICRAFT LESSONS
YOU CAN DO IT
CLASSES: TUESDAYS, THURSDAYS AND SATURDAYS, UNTIL 4 P.M.

Fumiko was such a renowned beauty in the neighbourhood that even some men expressed an interest in taking up doll-making, but Fumiko only accepted female students. Nevertheless, she had a reputation for being a loose woman. It was true that she had several male friends, but whether it really went any further, or whether jealous people were just spreading rumours about her, was not clear.

Kurita flipped through his diary from the year before last.

For the second Sunday of March, today's date, there was an entry describing the time when Fumiko asked him to go with her to buy a flowerpot.

Fumiko was waiting at ten in the morning at the bus stop in the triangular park in front of Hoshunin Temple. What possessed Fumiko always to choose the most conspicuous places to meet her man? She was comfortably draped in a black velvet coat that set off the collar of her white kimono, with its navy-blue-and-olive chintz pattern. Her small, pale face, almost entirely taken up by large, almond-shaped eyes as she looked around restlessly under a dusty evergreen plane tree, emerged vividly from the lines of his old diary.

Kurita closed his eyes, unable to contain his shame. The moment they met, the talk had turned to children. Whenever she dragged along this lumbering, ugly university student, Fumiko would end up going on about how she wanted to see the child she had left with her estranged husband. And when the two were alone together and Kurita made a move, Fumiko always said the same thing:

'I have a child, so it's not going to work. That's why it's so hard-going for me and for the kid. There's no way I can stop seeing the child. Actually, I shouldn't have had a child, but I did.'

Fumiko would always voice this mood of rejection in a dull, sing-song tone.

And then Kurita discovered that he was not human. Which meant that the melancholy he was experiencing even now was a hangover from the past. He was an extraterrestrial indulging himself by playing the role of a suffering human. Two years earlier, however, he definitely had been human.

And yet, he constantly dreamed of finding himself in a position that would afford him a bird's-eye view of human suffering. It was a double structure that he fantasized about. Evil glittered nobly in the heavens like the sun, while another version of himself, smeared in filth, was tucked away in a human body. At some point, his murderous impulse would purify the stench that clung to his body. But what a distance there was between the negativity of his own mind and the actual desire to kill!

No matter how negative his thoughts, they never bore fruit. Only slaughter would produce a result.

The two entered the gate of the nursery garden, along with the rest of the Sunday crowd, on the other side of the railway bridge, diagonally opposite Hoshunin. Its original name was the Date Clan Nursery Garden. It had been established by Kunimune Date in 1900 in order to improve and advance agricultural produce in the Tōhoku region around Sendai. Later, it came into the possession of Sendai City, which turned it into a teaching farm for the local agricultural industry. Most people would visit during this season in search of a bargain. Potted flowers, grown in the greenhouses, were sold at cost price.

The garden stretched all along the railway embankment to the point where the track sloped down to ground level. Dotted with dreary orchards, lifeless vegetable plots and little patches of parched lawn, it bore the brunt of a cold early spring wind blowing in from the plains. Kurita suggested that they take a walk before buying some flowers. He could not think of anything else to suggest.

She kept up her usual conversation about the child. Her estranged husband gave the child a good telling-off whenever it mentioned its mother's name. The child tended to call the television, 'tevelision'. It was convinced its mother had turned into a terrifying monster.

Fumiko constantly ignored Kurita. She did it by never for a moment forgetting to press her own concerns right into his face. It was freezing on the walk, and Kurita regretted not having worn an overcoat over his student uniform. Bracing himself against the cold, only the opportunity to walk alongside Fumiko steeled Kurita against one unbearably frozen second to the next.

It was not raining, but the wide sky was full of clouds. The Chinese palm trees in the little park were wrapped in woven straw matting, and ripples flitted across the tiny round pond in the park's centre like goosebumps over skin. Fruit trees, yet to bud, crouched above furrows of dry earth. The pair were walking directly into the powerful wind as it rolled in from the plains. They eventually reached the embankment planted with a row of cherry trees and a wooden bridge that crossed the river. Bamboo grasses rustling on the riverbank were reflected on the greenish-brown river surface.

Fumiko came to a halt on the bridge. And then, curling her lips, she addressed Kurita with no particular intent other than to impose her will upon him:

'I've had enough of walking.'

Kurita had a clear recollection of Fumiko's face at that time, chilled in the cold. The pale sun filtering through the clouds had cast a faint shadow of her hair, fraying in the wind, across her forehead. Her eyes had become a little bloodshot in the teeth of the wind, and the corners of her eyes were smeared with tears. At the moment she was murdered, she must have looked up at her killer with the same look.

The words that came out of Kurita's mouth at that time were, as ever, weak and ingratiating.

'OK. Let's go back, then. To the greenhouse.'

He really despised Fumiko at that moment, but it was not he who murdered her. The vexations of human life were engraved on his forehead like a gaudy coat of arms. If he had already ceased being human back then, he would have viewed things from the perspective of the icy clouds, far above the withered cherry branches on the river embankment. In that scenario, Fumiko's refusal to walk any further written on her face would have looked very cute, as if it belonged to a starving doe. And he could have played the role of hunter, shooting an arrow into her breast without the slightest hesitation.

The greenhouse was located close to the nursery garden gate, where crowds of people came and went, each holding their favourite potted flowers in their arms.

FLOWERPOT PRICES: CYCLAMENS (150 YEN), TULIPS (120 YEN), HYACINTHS (100 YEN), CROCUSES (60 YEN), SWEET PEAS (150 YEN), BEGONIAS (80 YEN), PRIMULAS (100 YEN). PLEASE SELECT A POT AND PAY AT OFFICE.

Shrinking pansies were in bloom around this poster erected in the sunny lane outside the entrance. Compared to the path they had just walked, even in the amount of sunshine it received this spot felt richer.

The greenhouse was flooded with steam, and it was mercifully warm inside. Fumiko was making her selection of flowers. A bee rested its wings on a purple hyacinth. In contrast to the desolate outdoors, it was a riot of colour inside the greenhouse. Snapdragons, yellow-and-red Venus flytraps, blue watering cans, scarlet tulips just come into flower.

Fumiko finally held high a pot of cyclamens with their crimson velvet petals and strongly gradated leaves.

'I'll have this one! I've decided!'

That was the moment she selected flowers that would match the colour of her own blood, a perfect bedside companion for her death. Kurita watched Fumiko utter a cry of delight as she raised the 150-yen pot in her hands. The quagmire of love in human life, the struggle to make a living, coquettish purity and brutish maternal love. All these experiences came together in that instant when she lifted a cheap pot of cyclamens to the heavens. It served as a full-throated defence of herself and as a beautiful crystallization of everything phoney in the world. How much more appropriate it would have been if those flowers had been artificial!

'I hate this woman. I really hate her. How happy I'd be to return to the past and make her barren. If the child she left with her estranged husband were a fiction, if everything she told me were a lie, then her rejection of me would be an act of utter purity. If I knew that all the human shackles Fumiko used to protect her body with were built on lies, I could kill her without any qualms. But Fumiko has a human scent about her that makes me hold back.'

Such were Kurita's thoughts. Fumiko's spiteful cry of delight. The exaggerated way she pressed her cheek against the flowers. He was offended by the small-minded way she adhered to these acts of human life. The vivid earth-red of the unglazed flowerpot rang out its clear song of life like a polished brass trumpet, and he was tossed aside as if he did not exist. Fumiko's small, almost expressionless face said only one thing:

'I'm alive. What do you think you're up to? You ugly, oafish student. I can't see you ever grabbing yourself a woman and getting her pregnant.'

Three days later, Fumiko was murdered at home. Splashes of blood were found all over the small neck and limbs of the doll she had been working on. A few drops even reached the petals and leaves of the cyclamen pot placed in the decorative alcove. Her mother fainted at the sight, and died almost immediately. The culprit was caught straight away. He was a road labourer, without any regular employment. The newspaper headline spoke of a crime of passion.

After it happened, Kurita had a nervous breakdown that persisted for ages. Physically, he gradually improved, and about one year after the incident he, along with Haguro and the barber, saw flying saucers in the rose garden on the mountain top.

★

Sone was in the habit of going for a walk and a packed lunch with his children on a Sunday. They had already visited most of the places that interested them, so now they tended to hang around the university campus a lot, only a stone's throw from where they lived. One advantage was that there was nothing to spend money on around there.

The family consisted of two boys, in Years One and Three of elementary school, and a girl in Year Five. Plus Sone and Hideko, his petite, modest wife. Their elder daughter was in the second year of middle school. This was how the barber's family lined up on their day of rest as they brazened their way through the north gate of the highest institute of learning and walked along the broad path dotted with old pine trees. They used to have lunch on a bench in the sports ground which gave them a view of students playing baseball.

The eldest daughter was very self-conscious about these walks, and she hated being made to carry unwieldy baggage. She would bring up the rear, grudgingly, at some distance behind. Even when they began eating, she never dug in with her chopsticks, instead remaining glued to the magazines she had brought along. These publications were invariably large, richly coloured entertainment magazines, and she would slowly turn each page very deliberately.

Sone sat down next to her and, even though he knew she would disapprove, put his arms round her from behind to rest his chin on her shoulder. He pored over each page, all the time making a chewing sound in her ear.

Garish colour photographs. Young people dressed in loud shirts, dancing and prancing about, embracing each other under artificial cherry trees, doing the twist. The boys' hair exemplified 'the most vulgar and subversive style' that Sone's boss had warned him against when he was an apprentice. 'These guys spend shedloads of dough. They've been spoilt rotten by society, they eat whatever they fancy and wear what they like. They have fun all night, drive around in sports cars above their means, and know as many girls as there are stars in the sky. And they're just eighteen years old!'

The daughter's dreamy gaze and the father's look of righteous indignation focused, in parallel, on the faces of the pop stars, dressed in their red-and-yellow shirts. Sone knew all their names by heart:

Henry Niimura, Jō Asano, Dicky Yamada, Susumu Tori. A bunch of impertinent youngsters with weird names. The fact that Sone remembered what they were called made them more famous than they actually were. They cast a gaudy light over Sone's glittering dream world.

He should just line up the whole lot of them in his barber's chair and slit their windpipes. Their racket would disappear from the face of the Earth, and silence would hold sway as if the planet were dead. In other words, elegance would reign supreme. That would be the moment when the Earth might turn into a *beautiful star*, and people might revert to 'the refined, moderate hairstyle of a typical gentle-man' that followed established hairdressing aesthetics.

'That Henry Niimura started off at the Tokyo Home for Juvenile Delinquents in Nerima. He was an inveterate petty thief.' Sone pointed to the photograph of the wan youth that his daughter was eyeing with conspicuous enthusiasm. The youth's smiling white teeth resembled a plaster of Paris tooth mould.

'Liar! I just don't believe you!' she said, brushing aside her father with her shoulder.

'It's true, you know. It's spelt out in black and white in the weekly magazines that adults read. Everything they write in those maga-zines is true. Hmm. After he left the home, a fifty-year-old woman took him under her wing, and he gets by as her toyboy . . .'

'Hey!' His wife interrupted him with a plaintive cry. 'What are you doing, talking to children about things like that?'

Sone turned around and looked intently at his small wife. Just then, Sone felt as if his plump body had abruptly floated up into the sky. There he was, clothed in the comfy silky clouds of early spring, looking down at his own family. This family was the only one worth saving among all humanity.

Hideko had been pretty when she was young, notwithstanding her pug nose, but she was already forty and her constant doleful frowning had destroyed her looks. Hideko loved her husband with all her heart. There was something about her love for him that resembled the unadulterated affection a child might have for old bent nails and receipts stored in a little box.

Hideko seemed conscious that her husband harboured an exceptional degree of jealousy and hatred, and she was aware that his affections were focused on anyone but her. But, like every banal housewife who tolerates the husband's harmless pastimes, like cultivating bonsai or a mania for baseball, she bore no grudge. Hideko always seemed too busy for Sone to have the opportunity to speak to her. She had mountains of housework to do, and in the barber's shop her job was to toss well-wrung hot towels towards Sone and his apprentice when they were at work.

On top of that, all the children wore sweaters hand-knitted by Hideko in red, yellow and other primary colours. Piles of snot and homework to deal with . . .

'At least I put food on the table for them.' Sone, the extraterrestrial, felt pleased with himself. 'So, it's my responsibility to save them by taking them with me when mankind is on the verge of being wiped out.'

Viewed from on high, the family looked rather like small scraps of multicoloured yarn. The world still had no idea how important they were. There was nothing at all 'famous' about them.

The two youngest said they had had enough. They were bored by the students playing a half-hearted game of baseball in front of them. And they immediately ran off towards the semi-circular terrace of the central auditorium.

This auditorium was an old European-style building, with Spanish wings spreading out to the left and right. Slate roof tiles combined into precisely overlapping blue scales, and a complex, beautiful wooden façade rose above the terrace. Where the north transept of the building cast its shadow, slushy remnants of melting snow gleamed.

It looked like the two boys had suddenly stumbled, but in fact they were squabbling over some pine branches that had fallen onto the path. They started a sword fight with their improvised weapons on the terrace bathed in the pale light.

Sone was completely absorbed in the scene. On just such a lovely Sunday as this, the rich, the famous, movie actors and pop stars will all be obliterated in an instant. Members of happy, lovable, smug petit-bourgeois families – the whole lot – will be struck by malicious rays of light unleashed onto the world. Every one of them, without exception, will fall in agony like skittles.

The children were fighting with 'swords' that were nothing more than misshapen, brittle old branches. But their child's minds had invested them with the illusion of the real thing. The branches that they brandished above their small heads had turned into towering blades, catching the reflection of the gloomy early spring sky. Silver blades soaring into the heavens.

'Anything can become a lethal weapon!' thought Sone, in a fit of dizzying joy. He was a barber, and fully aware of the thinness of the human skin.

When they thought about it, the three had achieved precisely nothing during the past year. At the time of the Berlin Crisis, they were all thrilled in the knowledge that the world was about to meet its end, to such an extent that Sone made his doubtful wife cook some celebratory red-bean rice and send it to the Haguro household. But the crisis was over before they knew it. The constellation Cygnus, which had sat proudly at its zenith from summer to autumn, retreated to the edges of the northern horizon at the same time that the world crisis was resolved. The same thing happened to their own 61 Cygni and its invisible planet.

One evening the previous summer, the three had climbed Sendai Castle and with some difficulty managed to make out their native star in the neighbourhood of the Milky Way. Haguro pointed it out to the other two using a telescope he had borrowed from the university.

Though an unremarkable sixth-magnitude star, it stands out as the first star whose distance from Earth was successfully measured, by the German astronomer Friedrich Bessel in 1838. The distance, of eleven light-years, makes it the fourth closest of the stars visible to the naked eye. Haguro explained to them that 61 Cygni was a binary star, and he had no doubt that an invisible planet was in orbit around one of those stars. The planet that all three of them came from. It was not until 1942 that the existence of astronomical objects equivalent to planets outside the solar system could be proven.

Identifying the star through the telescope lens drove all three of them crazy. They felt suddenly divorced from their everyday forms, as if they were transformed into complex monsters with eight stomachs and five pairs of lungs. All their internal gears felt out of joint, all harmony was lost, a mechanical rumbling arose in their digestive tracts, everything grew distant from them, and they seemed to have been thrown into the cold void of space. They instinctively reached out to each other, but their hands on that midsummer night were as cold as ice.

It was then that Haguro had said: 'War will begin very soon.'

But on this day, six months later, Haguro was obliged to repeat the same words, laced with disappointment.

'War will begin very soon. Whatever happens, it is inevitable.'

One evening, a few days after the Rose Garden meeting, the three met up in a beer hall in Higashi Ichiban-cho and hit upon the idea of going shopping for some bargains at the nearby Fujisaki department store. They had reached a childish decision after several rounds of beer, and they hurried excitedly to put their new plan into practice.

Haguro had suggested that they each think of an implement to buy that could destroy the world, on a budget of less than one hundred yen.

They were not fans of department stores. They all hated the idea of consumption, they had an aversion to the coquetry of all material things, and they had no time for the promise of eternal human life proffered through such physical objects. Whenever a rice bowl at home was broken and needed to be replaced, cheap bowls in the same style were always on display at the tableware counter, thus preserving the veneer of eternal life. If a broom became frayed, a replacement awaited. Such objects signified utter contempt for everything that Haguro and his companions stood for.

Haguro went first. He visited the kitchenware counter to buy a small screwdriver for ninety yen.

'Damn it!' exclaimed Sone, holding his hand to his forehead. He had intended to go for the same thing.

Next, Kurita went to the pharmacy counter and asked for some sulphuric acid. Such an eccentric request made Assistant Professor Haguro uneasy, and he slipped away behind the backs of his companions to the cosmetics counter, where he closely examined the expressed milk bottles that women used. When the lady assistant asked Kurita the reason for the acid, he brazened it out, saying it was for industrial purposes. He purchased a 500-gram bottle for eighty yen. Sidling up to Haguro, who had fled the scene, Kurita put his mouth to his ear and said, 'I'm going to fling this lot in the world's face.'

Now it was Sone's turn. He took the other two on a tour of the counters, racking his brains before buying some nutcrackers for exactly one hundred yen.

After the thrill of their shopping spree, they left the department store with happy looks on their faces. The passers-by under the street lighting suddenly appeared more ephemeral, like shadows on a revolving magic lantern.

'These poor suckers won't be around for much longer.' The drink had lubricated Kurita's tongue. 'I'd like to see the expression on their faces when they wise up. Eh, Professor?'

'That'll knock them for six.' Sone spoke up in place of Haguro, who just frowned. He had a suitable cliché on hand for any cataclysm. 'Knock 'em for six, poor devils.'

The office girl carrying a handbag with the fashionable phrase NO PARKING written in large print. A spruce, young salaryman self-consciously sporting his spring coat. Students dressed in unfamiliar suits. Children being dragged along by their mothers. All of them steadfastly marked by the shadow of death. Everyone looked as if they had unwittingly joined a death cult, and now strutted around with a badge, displaying a brilliant star of destruction, pinned to their breasts.

'Let's take a taxi. It's on me. How about going to Sendai Castle? We've actually gone and bought these things, so why not try them out?' said young Kurita, emboldened. Never ones for putting a damper on things, his two older companions exchanged silent glances and acquiesced.

'Sendai Castle! Sendai Castle! Take us to the rundown castle!' exclaimed Kurita, his large frame rolling in the small taxi. The driver was used to this kind of drunken whimsy. He careered up the sharp pitch-black slope overgrown with tall spear-shaped cedars, flinging pebbles against the tree roots and scattering wild headlamp beams between the trees and into the night sky.

Sone held the department-store item, still in its wrapping paper, firmly in his sweaty hands. Quite a while had passed since he made his purchase, but he remained intoxicated by his own ingenuity.

'That's a pretty smart idea, to use nutcrackers to crush the Earth. That makes me the winner. No one else could have come up with that on the spot.'

Nevertheless, he was beginning to sober up, and as they passed below the starry sky and the lower beam of the huge, looming Torii Gate at the Gokoku Shrine war memorial came into view, his body tensed with the kind of invigorating vanity experienced by one about to participate in some major cosmic enterprise.

The nights were still a bit chilly, and the castle's inner bailey was deserted. The doors of the tea shop were closed, and noticeboards dotted along the public path that alluded to the Great Hall remains and the Noh stage were clearly silhouetted in the dark. The top of the majestic Shochu Tower, showing off the castle to its advantage, caught the rays of the sinking crescent moon. The gigantic copper eagle atop the tower spread its wings, bearing a malign dignity that spoke of night.

The three sat in a row on the viewing platform with their backs to the hackneyed, rotund, hoary statue of the castle founder, Masamune Date, and listened as the night wind passed through the conifers. Sendai at night was laid out fully below them. The Hirose River meandered darkly in front of the town, and neon signs flickered restlessly among the countless lights in the down-town buildings that spread beyond the station between Hirose and Aoba avenues. The Pacific horizon, due east of the city, was blotted out by nebulous lights that bled into the mist.

Now completely sober, the three gazed absent-mindedly at the town in which they had grown up. A putrid accumulation of bygone days and conventions. Its sparkling blanket of lights resembled luminescent fungi spurting across the body of a gigantic fish. Here, writ large, was the human world they had formerly inhabited. The sooty lights around the tower of the red-tiled courthouse near the Hyojo-gawara Bridge. Lights dotted among the dark cluster of buildings at T University. Parallel lines of fluorescent lights in the Higashi Ichiban-cho district. A mass of neon spinning into every corner of the sky above . . . The more abundant the light, the lonelier it all became. The occasional hoarse hoot of a car horn. Everything else fell securely into the normal pattern of dark night. Above them, in the eastern part of the starry night, thinly veiled in cloud, spread the calm outlines of Virgo and the Herdsman.

'War will begin very soon.' Haguro's gripe never changed. 'Not one of those troublesome lights will remain. And when that happens, all the stars in the sky will fall in relief upon the Earth.'

Haguro's loneliness was rooted in every one of those human lights before them. He somehow had an innate belief in human suffering, but now that he had been expelled from that particular human world, now that the location of suffering was becoming clearer to him by the day, now that he was no longer human, he found himself living cheek by jowl with suffering. His condition would need to be remedied sooner or later, and that was exactly what was going to happen. In other words, human beings and their world were going to perish. In that way, his compassionate heart would find salvation!

'We can expect a sudden outbreak of war any moment now. With one push of the remote-control button, anti-ballistic missiles, Nike-Zeus as well as solid-fuel ICBMs, and Minuteman missiles will blast off at 23,000 kilometres per hour. Not a single person will have time to escape . . . There will be no time to suffer. They have suffered too much already, so that is a good thing.'

Haguro appeared to be speaking to himself.

'So, what can we do to make it happen as soon as possible?' There was still something of the student in the way Kurita spoke.

'The general conclusion I have reached is that we ought to oppose the peace movement. After all, look at the way they do things, with their endless demos and signatures, and their dependence on numbers and groups. We are hardly going to incorporate people like that into a *war movement*. Because the coming nuclear war will arise not from mutual hatred between groups, but from a completely unconnected individual whim, from some confusion or "unfortunate" coincidence.

'Do you see what I am saying? The age of the masses is over. Contemporary history is all ostensibly about standardization. But its most terrifying secret is actually the fact that the age of the masses is no more.

'It is not our way to make appeals to the masses, or to depend on them, but rather to meditate on ways to shake the very core of human evil and allow humankind to destroy itself. Evil has become a solitary poem, and poetry a solitary evil. This is the real state of affairs in the present age. Everyone assumed that war would begin once massification and standardization had reached their climax, but this is an age when war will arise from the small poem of a single individual.

'All you need is a poem, like a fleck of pollen, to steal into the hearts of the whole lot of them one day – the world's leading politicians, the commandants of ICBM bases, the non-commissioned officers whose job it is to press the button – and make them sneeze. That is how war begins.

'So, how can our meditations find a way into their hearts without relying on the strength of the masses? That is the question. The only possible method is to cut off the present avenues of communication, which human logic makes almost impossible to achieve anyway, and find our own way to communicate. But we should never forget that we come from outer space. In addition to communication through education, which takes time, and through radio, television and printed matter, which take space, we possess a fourth-dimensional communication route. As we continuously refine our meditative practice, you can be sure that its power will engender within the hearts of the mediocre non-commissioned officers, the button pressers, some sort of vacant cavity in the rough mesh of human reasoning.

'Let me give an example. What we felt when we saw the flying saucers, when we sighted our native star, and our consequent sense of isolation from all earthly objects, would be mistakenly described by earthlings as poetry. In the heart of a non-commissioned officer, such feelings would immediately turn into the fluttering of a white sheet hanging up to dry, or a primrose in flower. That is what they understand by poetry. But, despite any sentimental appearance, at that moment he would actually be experiencing the sensation of his own physical body being cut off from everything around and projected into outer space. The sheet and the primrose merely hint at the urgent necessity within him to return to the world of things. In a panic, he simply jumps at the most immediate "thing" to hand. And, you see, the thing closest to hand is the button. Do you understand me now, Kurita? What I call human evil is simple. It is merely the human "relationship with things".'

Upon hearing these words, Kurita recalled in his heart the pot of cyclamens in the nursery garden. Sone, meanwhile, looked totally bored as he stifled a yawn. He removed the department-store wrapping paper, allowing the nutcrackers in his hand to catch the light as he looked around. He then picked up a table tennis ball he had spotted under a light on the ground. A child must have hit it there during the daytime, and forgot to retrieve it.

'Look. This is the Earth. Here.'

Haguro and Kurita were still deep in their thoughts and hardly took in what Sone was shouting about, but they were suddenly brought back by the sound of the celluloid ball being crushed.

'Smashed. The Earth is smashed. I'm so happy. There's nothing left of the Earth for you two to destroy.'

Sone laughed to himself and appeared to give a little dance.

This encouraged Kurita to approach the railings of the viewing platform. He poured the contents of his bottle of sulphuric acid over the tree branches, their buds still closed, as well as the bamboo grass undergrowth.

'That's messed up the face of their precious *beautiful star*! Isn't that right, Professor? Now the Earth can never show its face in public again.'

Sone and Kurita broke into meaningless laughter, as if their drunkenness had returned to life, and they danced about arm in arm, causing their shadows to stretch and contract across the ground.

Haguro took the screwdriver from his inside pocket, turning his back on his boisterous companions, and leant against the railings from which Kurita had just rained down acid.

He pointed the tip of the screwdriver towards the distant view of the glittering city streets. With one turn, a cog in the mechanism of human society comes loose. A few more turns, and the cog falls out and rolls onto the Earth. The neon tower of the Denryoku Building flickers erratic speckles of blue and white. Its windows throw out a hard, expressionless glint . . . One cog falls. Followed by the falling of another cog, until the whole mechanism ultimately collapses and dies. A vein stood out on his pale forehead, and there was a slight pain in his nostrils. His palms were damp with cold sweat, fish-like. Everyone knew him as an incompetent man, but no one was yet conscious of the dark power coiled up inside him.

6

It was a clear, chilly day in the middle of March when Akiko was taken by her mother to the new hospital in the Shiba district of Tokyo. They had to wait for ages. This would not have happened in Hannō. But her mother was nervous about attending a local hospital.

Akiko looked around at the faces of the other patients, all of them female. The modern, windowless waiting room bathed in fluorescent lighting felt like the bottom of the sea.

All these women, dressed in their finest, awaiting their turn to be called. Human females showing flashes of guilty, yet cunning, delight and pride. There they sat with heads lowered, cherishing their human shame and guilt, in a way that suggested excessive familiarity with their warm inner parts. Any bond of female solidarity seemed to have been totally discarded.

Akiko was disappointed that even her mother appeared despondent, in fear of what others might think. A woman from Jupiter could not be outdone by a human woman when it came to banal, animal instincts.

Akiko's chest alone swelled under her springtime suit as she glared down upon these women who had sunk even lower than humans. These women who had come to hospital sporting their wedding rings in search of remission of their sins. Tawdry gold on their ring fingers catching the light. What could Akiko offer up for the remission of her own sins? Of course, nothing could compare with that silver artificial lotus blossom. It all began with that flower . . .

*

One morning, after Father's extensive lecture tour had come to an end and they were all at home relaxing, Mother approached Akiko as she sat before her triple mirror. Spotting a silver artificial flower in a bud vase in front of the mirrors, Iyoko frowned.

'What are you doing with that? That flower is for funerals.'

Akiko did not respond. The silver of the lotus blossom gleamed in the morning light. Tough, resilient petals displayed an arrogant extravagance greater than any found in a real plant, and serried images of the lotus stretched from the depths of one well-polished mirror into another. Akiko never forgot to spray it every morning with a perfumed mist. Man-made flowers, too, it seemed, were liable to wilt unless they were watered.

Akiko said nothing because she was feeling uneasy. Takemiya had always responded to her letters immediately, but her two latest had gone unanswered. Consequently, Akiko had lost weight, and when that rough young fellow accustomed to carrying coffins on his sturdy shoulders unexpectedly presented her with a flower she had fretted that it might be some kind of message. Perhaps Takemiya had gone to gaze upon the world of the dead, mistaking it for Venus, and was now unable to make his way home.

'It's got nothing to do with funerals. It just happens to be an unworldly flower.' Akiko's response was rather high-handed. 'When I picked it up, it reminded me of the flowers on Venus. I realized that this single artificial bloom from Earth was modelled on Venusian flowers. You see, Mum, all flowers have a metallic hue on Venus. They reflect silver under moonlight, and gold in the sunshine. When the wind passes through flowers in the fields there, they all tinkle against each other with the sound of little bells.'

'You look terrible,' said Mother, staring into the mirror.

'That's because Dad's lecture tour wore me out.'

'You really worked hard on it. Its success is partly thanks to you.'

Takemiya's admonition was the only thing that had kept Akiko working in support of her father's tour, but all the efforts she poured into it, and its successful outcome, helped prevent Jūichirō from broaching the subject of Takemiya. Her mother had not taken the problem very seriously from the start.

'But you really are looking under the weather,' repeated her mother. With that, Akiko covered her mouth in confusion, got up and left.

Iyoko was unsure what she had said to so upset her daughter, but the vivid image of her daughter's fingers covering her face really concerned her. She stood up and went after her.

'What is it? Akiko! What is it? What's wrong?'

Akiko came back, and mother and daughter sat face to face, speaking in low voices. Iyoko had always given her children a thorough grilling about even their slightest physical ailments since they were tiny, and neither Kazuo nor Akiko had ever been able to keep anything from her.

'I'm no longer a child.'

Her mother employed some straightforward logic.

'If we were all fellow humans from the same family, that would be fine. But ever since I found out we all come from separate planets, it's been my responsibility to gather as much knowledge as I possibly can about the different physical characteristics of people from Venus, Mercury and Mars.'

In the end, Akiko was subjected to a vigorous interrogation until she was made to confess that she had seen none of the usual signs since the previous December. The fact is, she had never been particularly susceptible to the influence of the moon shining down on them every night. Her periods had always been irregular, and ever since she discovered her Venusian origins, she took pride in the way that distant Venus exerted its constant influence by warping the moon's strength so as to cause irregularities. The ocean tides susceptible to the moon obviously had some modest effect on Akiko's body, by disturbing her periods without revealing the actual source of control. But when Akiko saw the pale glow of daytime earthshine reflected on the unlit part of a crescent moon, she felt it likely that her own influence and control were exerting themselves upon the moon.

Since her encounter with Takemiya in December, Akiko had managed to escape the moon's shackles, that monthly bond that no human woman could avoid. The bloody chains that tied women to such a beautiful, yet vulgar, celestial orb had been broken by the distant, lofty power of Venus, and Akiko was now in thrall to purely Venusian principles. In January, and again in February, there was no sign that the moon was reasserting its power. It was almost too natural to be believed, but Akiko was not particularly surprised.

The defiling blood ties of the moon would never threaten Akiko again! Venusian purity had finally destroyed the humiliating reality of the wicked, shining heavenly body that tended to govern the ebb and flow of menstrual blood in the bodies of women on Earth. The moist, monthly blood-red culvert in the gloomy recesses of Akiko's body, endlessly responding to the winks and nods of the moon, had closed . . . Compared to the pleasure and relief, what did a little discomfort and nausea amount to? Just some light harassment from an abandoned moon.

Mother pursued her interrogation with dispassion.

'December? . . . So, that's after you got back from Kanazawa? Meaning that, in Kanazawa . . . I'm not angry. Just tell me. I'm sure you're holding something back. In Kanazawa . . .'

At first, Akiko could not fathom what her mother was getting at, and merely looked blankly into her eyes. Iyoko's words tumbled out like moths fluttering madly around the heart of the matter, circling a fire. When Akiko saw the nature of that fire, she was beside herself with anger.

'Mum, what on Earth are you trying to say? Please, don't allow your thoughts to sink so low. We didn't hold hands, let alone kiss.'

That evening, Mother teamed up with Father to prevail upon Akiko with a range of blandishments. Akiko endured her mother's ridiculous endeavours with a cold smile. For the first time, she was encountering the frighteningly crude way in which people from Mars and Jupiter thought. In the end, she gave in. And the following morning, she accompanied her mother to this hospital.

'I'm different from everyone else.' With this thought, Akiko gazed around brazenly at the other patients. On the other hand, the ordeal and baseless humiliation she was about to experience sent a shudder through her. There was not a single pure woman in this waiting room apart from Akiko. Why could she not be saved from her predicament right now by an act of grace from Venus? Akiko prayed for it with all her heart. Perhaps one of the doctors might be Venusian. His pale, radiant face would appear at the door and, after surveying the waiting room with frighteningly clear eyes, he would cast a smile in the direction of Akiko alone, and exclaim:

'Miss. There's no reason for you to be here. You should go home right now. I can tell at a glance. I swear to God that you are pure.'

At that point, the doctor's glowing face would turn into Takemi-ya's beautiful countenance, the gloomy hospital walls would become transparent, the defiled women would tremble before this miracle and prostrate themselves, while the silver medical instruments and the white gauze would go scattering all at once into the cold starry sky.

'Miss Ōsugi,' the nurse called out from the reception desk, her white hat pointing towards Akiko. Iyoko gave her daughter's back a gentle squeeze. Akiko stood up with a look of cool contempt in her eyes.

The young doctor avoided looking Akiko directly in the face as he spoke to her. It was a simple interview, with the mother supplying any answers that Akiko failed to provide.

'This way, please.' The nurse led Akiko to an area surrounded by curtains. As she got herself ready, the doctor kept his eyes averted. Akiko was made to sit on an oddly shaped internal examination table. An electric heater sent a hint of warmth across the area around her waist. Once both of Akiko's legs were fitted into the stirrups, which had sprung into position, the nurse artlessly drew a grey curtain in front of Akiko's chest. The voice of the doctor was immediately audible on the other side of the curtain, along with what sounded like a washing of hands.

Akiko closed her eyes and contemplated the pure twinkling of stars that she often sighted from the train window on the Seibu Line on the way to school. Forced to adopt the guise of a persecuted wild beast, Akiko had attained the highest form of spirituality. In the inexorable shame that humans felt towards the physical body there lurked something that enraptured Akiko. Akiko's flesh had endured so much humiliation that it was unclear whether it was hers any more. But the indignity of human flesh to which she was now being so casually subjected allowed her to attain a sense of affront towards the whole of mankind. She had, in other words, become divorced from her own body.

Akiko eventually lowered her eyes and stared at the whispered intimacies of the fine lace of her blouse, fluttering across her chest. No earthly handicraft presented a more beautiful and delicate deception. She allowed her fingers to toy with it gently. Both her breasts were firm, like small animals forced into a corner.

The doctor stuck his foot under the examination table to push the pedal. The table gradually changed angle until, had it been night-time, starlight would have flooded directly into Akiko's exposed body. 'Calm down. Keep calm,' said the doctor. He pushed something right inside her with a dark, heavy force. What had made that metallic popping sound just before? Maybe it was one of the oddly shaped silver instruments on the medical trolley that she had noticed earlier? The flying saucers had been made of pointed metal. And they had forced their way through the murky, dense, soup-like atmosphere that encircled the Earth. How fierce their lights had been. The doctor had his light turned towards her. The bottom of the curtain in front of her appeared to be on fire. All of humanity, fled in confusion. Akiko's body, transformed into a silver lotus blossom.

The examination was over. When Akiko tidied herself up and emerged, the doctor was just finishing her clinical chart at his desk. She took a peep as she passed by. There were some abbreviations – P., M.m., Ut., g., c., Add., Er., L.F., Sek. – next to which he had filled in some numbers and German words in sloppy handwriting with a flourish of black ink. The doctor was just stamping the word *unmarried*. Akiko also saw him stamp another word in vermilion. *Pregnant*.

Her mother rose from the chair with a shudder, and sat down again.

'She's pregnant. It's four months, so there's no mistake.'

'Oh, my word!'

In contrast to her mother, Akiko remained self-possessed. The doctor seemed to recoil from the unsettling assuredness that shone in Akiko's eyes. It was unusual for a patient stamped as *unmarried* to display such serene pleasure when informed she was pregnant. For the doctor, the man whom he fancied he saw behind Akiko's shining eyes took the form of a monster.

When they walked out from the hospital into the bright sunshine, Iyoko was a little unsteady on her feet, so Akiko supported her. The sight of a smile crossing Akiko's face brought a heated response from Iyoko.

'What are you playing at, smiling at a time like this? You're giving me the creeps! I implore you. Never frighten me like that again.'

Mother and child settled into an old, dreary tea room nearby and ordered something cold to drink. Iyoko chewed on the straw in her mouth as she gulped down the garish bright red soda water they brought her.

'Where to begin . . . ?' Iyoko spoke loudly, thankful for the noisy television. 'For starters, you're not surprised at all?'

'I wouldn't have been surprised if I'd known.'

'If you'd known?' Iyoko was dumbfounded. She did not understand what her daughter was suggesting. 'What do you mean by that?'

The same smile that had disturbed her mother a moment before reappeared on Akiko's lips.

'Until just now when I got examined, it felt intolerable. But when the doctor confirmed the situation very clearly, I understood for the first time. I'm relieved now. I feel like I've woken up. Now I see what it was all about.'

'I don't understand. Spell it out.'

'That was the moment I clearly understood I'm pure.'

'Pure?' yelled Iyoko, unable to contain herself.

Akiko's lips now assumed the most natural of beautiful, deeply etched smiles. It reached beyond her face, spreading all around in ceaseless, quiet ripples, while the usual heavy gloom of her lustrous hair suddenly became a forest enveloped in a mist of smiles.

'Mum, I don't know why you're so surprised. It's an immaculate conception.'

'Don't be so stupid.'

'Remember what you once said? *We are not humans*, we must never forget that. *Not for a moment.* An immaculate conception. I didn't mention it to the doctor because trying to explain would have been pointless.'

'But you're . . .'

'Mum, you're not qualified to talk about it. I'm the only one who's experienced it. Now I finally know how Venusians produce offspring.'

The two sank into a long silence. Their ears filled with the sound of people singing on television. They gazed through the dirty window at the street outside where numerous cars jostled impatiently to be first off the mark, as if they were at each other's throats.

It was a pain-filled, bitter moment in which a miracle was gradually revealing itself, like letters written in invisible ink emerging from an everyday, dusty picture.

After much thought, the mother turned to her saintly daughter, and timidly broached the one question that remained:

'I won't trouble you with any more questions, but at least make one thing clear. You and that young man saw flying saucers in Uchinada, didn't you?'

'How do you know that?'

Akiko had never said anything about it until then, so how could her mother possibly know?

However, Iyoko deflected her daughter's question by immediately turning the tables.

'People from Jupiter understand that sort of thing.'

'But how . . .'

'Listen, that's not what we're talking about. I'm not interested in whether it was two of you who saw it, or three. The exact details of what you witnessed don't concern me. I just want to know what it felt like when the flying saucers appeared.'

'It was marvellous. I'd never experienced anything that made my heart tremble like that before. Three appeared before us out of black clouds over the Japan Sea.'

At this point, Akiko dried up. What more could she add?

It had only lasted four or five seconds. The vessels had been cruising above the sea when they came to an abrupt stop in the air, looking like three alluring pupils embedded in the blackness. A moment later, they all began to shudder and, right in front of them, their fuselages turned an incandescent apricot colour. They suddenly soared skywards at terrifying speed, perpendicular to the surface of the sea, and disappeared from view.

What did Akiko feel at that moment?

She was conscious of having experienced some kind of ecstasy. But upon deeper reflection, her memories had become entangled in something else, just as a grassy trail gradually narrows until it gets lost in the undergrowth.

It was only natural that flying saucers should have appeared at the most intense instant of lofty spiritual connection and cosmic solidarity. They simply had to appear then. Failure to turn up would have resulted in the instantaneous disintegration of the world.

Perhaps Akiko's heart was filled with an expectation beyond the capacity of the human heart when she saw the flying saucers. She was privy to something outside the range of human vision. For that reason, even if an earthling had been by their side in the sand dunes, they would not necessarily have been visible to the human eye. Be that as it may, what was not in doubt was the fact that the flying saucers had appeared before the young couple.

How on Earth could Akiko describe the supreme bliss and the clanging of her heart at that moment? That heart of hers followed in the wake of the flying saucers, cutting through the low-lying clouds over the northern lands, ascending through the surging cirrus formations and the pearly glow of the stratospheric clouds, and even beyond the upper atmosphere, where noctilucent clouds drifted, ascending perhaps as far as the fluttering crimson aurora's embrace. Her body remained on Earth. *For quite a while . . .* How could Akiko possibly know what happened to her earthly body during that time? A human witness might have been able to comment on the physical actions performed while the spirit was absent. But no one was about.

Akiko's essential nature had taken flight with Takemiya during that time. Her spirit became utterly content, like a piece of music. Purity in its highest form interwoven with ripples of carnal desire. At her very core, Akiko had been enveloped in dazzling, pleasurable, amorphous splendour. The two held hands as they flew on to beauty's further shore.

But what exactly was the nature of that pleasure? What generated the ambiguous rapture that seemed to transform body into cloud? Her memories appeared with great clarity, yet dimmed when she probed them further.

. . . Akiko lowered her head and flatly rejected self-analysis, that vulgar human practice tantamount to checking the contents of one's own purse. She reassured herself that there was nothing else she needed to get off her chest in front of her mother.

'That's all,' she continued. 'We didn't hold hands and we didn't kiss. What do you think, then? Is there some rule that says you at least have to kiss to make it an immaculate conception?'

Her mother grew even more restless. Like most inhabitants of Jupiter, she recognized the baleful influence of humans when it came to all transcendental speculation. Words like soul and spirit stank of humanity, as surely as a dog smelt of dog. The meaning of those words reeked of the straw in which humans slept.

'I perfectly understand. What you say is true. But in the human world, when the secret gets out it will be a big deal. Our quiet home in Hannō will be surrounded by TV cameras and radio tape recorders and weekly magazine reporters, and you'll end up a laughing stock in the human world.'

'I just won't tell anyone.'

'It's our secret. But the best thing is to get rid of the secret. You know, even the fourth month isn't too late.'

The expression on Iyoko's face as she spoke revealed the ruthlessness of a housewife who was happiest when rinsing her chopping board under the tap. Akiko cut her off with a callow look in her eyes.

'I can't do that.'

'Just think about it, Akiko. When you begin to show, you won't be able to go to school any more. And our little local neighbourhood will be out of bounds. The humans around here will look at you with contempt. Do you think someone as proud as you will be able to display your unsightly body to others, and subject yourself day and night to these foolish earthlings and their scornful laughter?'

Akiko turned her head away in silence. In her heart, she was contemplating the humiliating vision set out by her mother.

Akiko already had a fancy silver hairpin stuck in her hair, decorated with lotus blossoms and bearing the name *immaculate conception*. Perhaps her fate had been decided from the moment she descended from Venus. That she should walk every avenue of the human world with this glittering pin in her hair. From her very first step until the world's ending.

Akiko's tummy would begin to stick out. A tummy that would provide both unassailable proof of her own purity, and the most egregious evidence of lost purity as far as humans were concerned. On this planet, the peerless poetry of Venus would turn into an obscene spectacle. They would parade her with her bloated stomach, swaying like a beautiful festival float. And her colourful, much-derided sacred ornaments would tinkle as she walked . . . This was, after all, Earth . . . Akiko looked around. She had never experienced such a sensation before. She felt like she was in the middle of some hideous nightmare.

'I can't believe this place. Earth!'

Even inside the tea room, Earth was baring its dreadful, grubby fangs. The world had previously been filled with harmony and peace and a sense of unity. The image of supreme bliss had descended upon the Ōsugi household following the appearance of flying saucers. But that was all gone now. Dusty seats, garish crimson ice left at the bottom of the glass, lurid peremptory numerals on the calendar, brutish ears on the faces of movie actors plastered higgledy-piggledy onto the wall, fly eggs from the previous year still glued here and there to the ceiling, the insipid, insane drone of the TV screen . . . Akiko watched uneasily as her mother made a show of drawing her spring gloves, made from black lace, through her hands before putting them on, as if enacting some kind of curse.

'Right, let's go home. Your father's waiting for a report,' said

Iyoko, encouragingly. Akiko replied with not the slightest sign of apprehension.

'Never speak to me again like you did just then. I'm prepared now for any eventuality.'

Akiko had a mission. To walk the route of her own sacredness to the very end, no matter how precipitous or scorched that route might prove.

'It's because she's beautiful. It's her beauty that got her pregnant,' muttered Jūichirō again and again, pale with anger. It was an anger that overflowed with absolute paternal love. An anger that displayed ill will towards neither his daughter nor her young man.

But Jūichirō was opposed to Akiko's uterus being scraped out with a curette, and he worried about entrusting her to a procedure that had even one chance in a million of going wrong. Moreover, he believed that, for extraterrestrials and humans alike, it was not right to extract their generative buds. Personally, he was fully prepared to stand defiant in the face of criticism and ridicule from the human world, but it was solely murky intrigue centred around his tender young daughter's beauty that had landed her in such a predicament. Akiko had lost sight of peace for mankind. Seduced by a beauty that belied the world, she had sown the seeds of her own tragic fate. Those flying saucers that had appeared in Uchinada surely represented the shoddiest form of beauty.

The successful lecture tour had led to an increase in the Universal Friendship Association membership, more work at the association office, and many more visitors all needing attention. And now, this matter with Akiko was weighing very heavily on Jūichirō's mind. Meanwhile, Kazuo was returning late every night, and the assistance that their father hoped for from his children during the spring holiday had failed to materialize.

On top of that, spring arrived laden with lethal fallout. Radioactive material, the product of frequent nuclear tests, had danced up into the stratosphere where strontium 90 and caesium 137, both with long half-lives, floated undissolved until, in time, the material settled back onto Earth in the form of dust. When spring reached the northern hemisphere, leading to an abrupt temperature rise in the atmosphere, the fallout, which had been suspended in the stratosphere, leaked through gaps in the tropopause around the mid-latitudes, and ceaselessly scattered its flowers into the troposphere. In this way, spring saw a doubling of radioactive fall-out, and scholars gave it a name. *Spring maximum*. It appeared that the Soviet nuclear tests during the previous autumn had led to an unprecedented level of material raining down.

Jūichirō was left speechless in the face of humankind's slow-motion suicide.

Death now enveloped earthlings in the form of beautiful clouds. The high crimson and violet banks glowing in the evening sky were all toxic. An incessant seepage of invisible death. This springtime poison, scattered throughout the highest reaches of the sky, was falling to Earth, passing through vegetables and milk, and finally lodging itself deep within human bones. Tiny flecks of death on a tireless journey, weaving their way through the structures of radiant flora and fauna in the fields of the Earth, in search of some dark abode. Death's eventual resting place within human bones spoke loud and clear of an unperishable core within the body of living people. Bones generally go unnoticed until death, but now they were singing out even in life, like trumpets. Death blossomed from the beautiful vegetable fields bathed in sunlight, from pastures hemmed in by streams and green woods, from landscapes overflowing with flowers and honeybees. Picnickers felt the bones in their bodies resonate with a death intimately woven into nature. In humans, only their bones are imperishable. Deadly fallout may destroy the flesh, but the beautifully desiccated, modest structure of bones will never be lost. A gentle duet was striking up between fall-out and bones in their victory over nature . . . There was the song now. For Jūichirō, it was a deafening roar. Humans, on the other hand, could hear nothing.

An insurrection against nature had already broken out within the human body. The people who stoked that insurrection were, it goes without saying, the inventors of the hydrogen bomb. Have you never noticed the adorably coquettish nature of your bones as they usher in the radioactive material? America, too, had failed to learn its lesson and was about to restart nuclear testing. The conditions Jūichirō most feared had come to pass. Bones form an alliance. They predict that the day to escape the fleshy bonds is near at hand. They scramble to provide a lodging for their microscopic liberators. They take every opportunity to exchange meaningful looks and engage in flattery. They dream of the day when they can stretch out lazily, unclothed, under the starry sky, beside the flowers and the woods, drenched in dew.

Not surprisingly, flying saucers were now ubiquitous and humans were waking up to their existence. Jūichirō's desk was piled high with letters attesting to flying-saucer sightings. As far as he was concerned, however, he had not managed to spot another since that one time.

Letters were filled with serious eyewitness accounts coming in from all parts of the country. At just gone seven in the evening, two middle-school students from the village of Ogawa in Sakawa-cho, Takaoka District, Kōchi Prefecture, reported having seen an elliptical object, enveloped in a thin membrane, fly through the southern sky at incredible speed from east to west, and disappear into the mountains. Someone claimed to have sighted an orange-coloured luminous body around nine at night in Yatanomachi, Komatsu, Ishikawa Prefecture, emitting what looked like various shades of light and dark, and floating due west through the air at an elevation of 30 degrees. Another reported a Saturn-shaped flying saucer that suddenly rose up in front of a car as it was driving along the Kawagoe Highway. And there was a report from Bihoro-cho, Abashiri District, Hokkaido, that a huge soybean-shaped object had hung, glittering, in the western sky around five in the evening.

The integrity of these people was not to be doubted, and they were clearly passionate about peace. The Friendship Association joined hands in a huge circle and prayed to save mankind from the fate of extinction. But at the same time, they were trying to bring about harmony and unity on Earth at a stroke.

One day, two members of the Anti-Nuclear Testing Council came to visit Jūichirō in Hannō to say they had heard good things about his lecture tour, and they would love him to join their group. They were both rather well-known scholars, and quite shrewd. They surreptitiously flattered him, using very rational language.

Jūichirō had previously read their articles in general magazines, where they would offer their considered opinions on the popular arts and working-class ideas and beliefs. They were so keen to bring everything strange and popular in the world into their own camp, it was almost vulgar. During their visit to Jūichirō's house, they really made a show of treating him as a fellow intellectual.

Jūichirō could not bear this kind of elaborate charade, so characteristic of humans. He talked exclusively about flying saucers, and was surprised that the scholars appeared to take him seriously. Eventually, firmly convinced that the present company could be trusted, he casually alluded to the secret he had kept hidden from even the most intimate members of the Friendship Association.

'It appears that you're speaking to me as a human being. I'm sure you can keep a secret, so let me be frank. The fact is, I'm not human.'

'Really? So, what are you?' One of the visitors thrust forward his slightly stubbly chin and asked in a serious tone.

'Well, actually . . .' Jūichirō looked around and lowered his voice. 'Actually, I'm . . . Martian, and I came from Mars to save the people of Earth.'

The two scholars exchanged glances. They were probably thinking that such a claim went a little too far beyond the limit of the popular arts that they loved. They made some vague comments and prepared to take their leave.

Jūichirō pushed his case further.

'I guess, from a human perspective, it makes sense not to allow people like me into your fold.'

'Human perspective?' said one of the scholars, wide-eyed behind his thick spectacles. 'That sort of thing doesn't help in our struggle against nuclear testing. We're not so easily taken in.'

As Jūichirō politely led these earthlings to the door, he was pleased to see how instantly they had been rattled by the expression 'human perspective'.

★

One day, very unusually, Jūichirō departed on a trip without announcing where he was going. He looked worried. Iyoko knew, but she did not let on to the children.

The head of the family was on his way to Kanazawa.

As he sat in the train, his mind repeatedly returned to his daughter's beautiful looks. It made his chest tighten.

Jūichirō was determined to endure any embarrassment if it could save his child from misfortune. If he was ordered to prostrate himself before that little brat from Venus, so be it . . .

He had an incredibly strong sense of duty to save mankind, yet he lacked any concrete plan. So how was it, when it came to saving his sole daughter from Venus, that he was able to come up with immediate emergency measures and get down to business? It would be a human error to ascribe that resourcefulness to paternal love, and a denial of normal logic to identify Akiko's beauty as the reason. Perhaps it was simply easier to save one person rather than three billion. Or possibly, living this life on Earth incognito was a fundamental affront to himself, and he was doing his level best to compensate by acting 'like a normal person'?

As the *White Swan* approached Naoetsu around one in the afternoon, Mt Myokosan came into view through the carriage window on the left. He observed the sharp, silvery mountain ridges thrusting impatiently into the lightly clouded sky. Country-style grey wooden public halls. Grassy fields on the cusp of turning green. Rows of poplars, skinny and stunted, yet to bud . . . The sky embracing this desolate landscape presented a vision of Akiko's face. In low spirits, her clear gaze had turned inwards, eyes plunging straight downwards like a dark lead weight. Her hair, the bridge of her nose, her cheerless, taut lips. Her features, superimposed upon the pale colours of the spring sky, like a religious icon adorned with a single phrase. *Immaculate conception*. The words laid an invisible crown on her troubled brow, studded her forehead with invisible gems, dangled unseen pendants from her earlobes . . . Just at that moment, a patch of faint blue in a tiny clearing in the sky seemed to bleed into Akiko's cheeks and eyes, leaving only the faintest impression of her profile on the surrounding clouds.

As he gazed out over Toyama Bay, it started to rain. From there, the train turned west towards Takaoka, crossed the base of the Noto Peninsula, and passed north-east of the Kahokugata Lagoon before arriving in Kanazawa.

Jūichirō spent a restless night at an inexpensive hotel in front of the station. Given the nature of his business, he felt uncomfortable with the thought that he might seem threatening if he paid the young man a visit at night-time.

When he pulled back the faded floral hotel curtains the next morning, it was still raining. In silence, he carefully opened his pocket umbrella and ventured into the drizzly streets.

He had brought along the address that Iyoko had made a secret note of after going through the bundle of Takemiya's letters to Akiko. They were all signed the same way:

TAKEMIYA KAORU
36-1, NIBANCHO, NAGAMACHI, KANAZAWA

At his hotel they told him it was a residential area full of old houses, the remnants of samurai mansions. In one letter, Takemiya spoke disparagingly about his family, stuck in their ways. His parents, his siblings, his uncle and aunt, all of them mere humans.

On the Korinbō-bound tram, Jūichirō went over the plan of action he had rehearsed several times in his head since the previous night. If his parents answered the door, he could hardly cut straight to the chase. First, he would need to convince them that he was completely versed in the commonsense ways of the human world. That he was a likeable, trustworthy man of property. He could broach the matter of marriage later.

He had lost his appetite since the night before, as if some rusty iron sheet was stretched around his stomach. His rain-sodden body felt heavy. His malaise did not presage a happy outcome during the course of the day.

The equinox had just passed, and spring in the northern provinces, when the plum, peach and cherry trees all blossomed at once, had yet to arrive. There were remnants of snow on the north side of town. Jūichirō got off the tram, opened up a city map under the eaves of a nearby shop and searched for his destination. He got lost and made a long detour before he arrived at what looked like the right area.

A willow tree, just beginning to bud, stood next to a stone bridge alongside a stone and mud wall that followed a stream. He was struck by the freshness of the waving green waterweeds in the stream.

Crossing the bridge, he entered a winding path. The houses were all old and looked like they had history, with bamboo poles placed across their mud walls, on top of which straw matting was heaped to protect them from the snow. The matting was still there, despite the arrival of spring. He could see apple trees on the other side of the walls. Rain had brought a glint to the glazed-lacquer roof tiles of the houses. Inside each gate was a small front garden where trees stood silently, supporting snowy skeletons. There was one gate to a small tenement block. It had lattice windows, but it was dark inside and seemed deserted.

At each gate, Jūichirō lowered his umbrella to check the name and number on the nameplate, but Takemiya's name was not to be found. He paced up and down the path, stopping several times in front of the same gates. Wondering if he might be in the wrong place, he walked over to the adjacent area to make a careful check of the houses there. On the way, he met hardly anyone in the road. Only once did he hear the faltering, rusty sound of a bicycle bell pass by.

Jūichirō was exhausted by his walk and close to collapse. He decided to return to the area he had gone to first. Finally, he noticed a place with a nameplate he had missed the first time. It was a cheap hotel completely out of keeping with the area. A lamp displaying the name, Meiji Hotel, was hanging from a breeze-block wall at the gate. There were pines and palm trees in the dreary front garden used for cars to turn around, as well as a sign advertising a billiard hall that blocked out all the windows on the first floor of the crude two-storey wood-and-mortar structure.

A small nameplate with the name 'Takemiya' in faded black ink, was nailed onto the bamboo fence next to a side door. Jūichirō immediately opened it and went in. The gravel path led to the hotel kitchen area.

Jūichirō called out. Three or four grubby ramen bowls were hanging up at the dark counter. Rainwater had soaked halfway into the entranceway, reaching as far as some carelessly discarded *geta* sandals.

'Mr Takemiya! Mr Takemiya!'

A diminutive man emerged from the back, dressed in a grey jumper.

'Can I help?'

'My name is Ōsugi. I wonder if Kaoru Takemiya is at home?'

'Kaoru? He's no longer here.'

Jūichirō sat down at the counter, shattered. Sensing that this might take some time, the little man sat on a little yellow vinyl chair. He was around fifty, with thin hair coiled on top of his head and a small, mousey, innocuous face.

'I'm sure this is the place the letters came from.'

'He left just over a month ago.'

'But Takemiya is on the nameplate.'

'Oh, that. That's my name.'

'You're a relative?'

'No, sir, I'm completely unrelated. Although this place is called a hotel, it also serves as apartments. Kaoru stayed for about a year. He was a ladies' man, and quite vain with it. He asked to use my name so that he could have letters delivered here. Any letters addressed to "Takemiya, c/o Meiji Hotel" would only ever be for him. His name was Kaoru Kawaguchi, but even that may have been made up. He sent letters to all sorts of places under the false name, and goodness knows how many girls he hoodwinked. I didn't see any harm in it, so I let him use my surname for free . . . I don't know what kind of business he was in, but he read all sorts of books, and sometimes he practised Noh chanting. Writing letters seems to have been his pastime. At any rate, there was a lot of coming and going of girls. Ah, one of his fellow Noh students, a woman who runs the Senkaku Inn, helped him out in various ways. Why don't you go and ask there? He might have shacked up with her over there . . . After all, his rent for this place was six months overdue, and she paid it off for him last year . . . Not that he left for that reason. He just packed up and went. I haven't heard a word from him since. I guess he's the type who keeps very much to himself.'

Jūichirō made his way to the Senkaku Inn, the same place where Akiko had stayed previously. When he announced himself as Ōsugi from Hannō, he was given an unexpectedly warm reception. The maid brought him a selection of food and drinks to the tea-ceremony-style room overlooking the river. But there was no sign of the landlady.

Midday chimes from a loudspeaker echoed through the streets. Jūichirō showed not the slightest inclination to pick up his chopsticks and tuck into the titbits on his tray. The river view was misted in rain, and the room was filled with the scent of strong incense. At last, he felt able to sit up straight.

He was kept waiting for thirty minutes before the landlady turned up. She was plump, with a touch of grey in her hair, and she wore a gaudy, finely patterned purple kimono. She greeted him politely at the door, ordered the maid to withdraw and proffered a sake bottle with her own hands.

'Come, Father, how about a cup of sake? You are so kind to come all the way to see us. We were fortunate enough to have your daughter stay in this very room.'

It felt odd to be addressed as 'Father'. In order to pour, she kept her left arm tucked in her sleeve while her fully exposed right arm gave off an unusually dull, white, fleshy glow in the gloomy room.

The landlady would not let Jūichirō get a word in. He had barely put his lips to his cup before she slid back on the tatami mat and gave a deep bow of greeting, planting both hands on the ground. As she raised her face, it was already soaked in tears. She said:

'There's something I need to say. I fully appreciate your feelings but, I beg you, please take pity and return Takemiya to me. No questions asked. That is my only desire.'

★

It took some effort for Jūichirō to convince the landlady that he, too, was looking for the young man. Without touching on his daughter's pregnancy, he described in detail how he had ended up here.

Changing tack, the landlady suddenly adopted a coarse tone as she related at great length and without any sign of self-recrimination how she had worked hand in glove with Takemiya in his first meeting with Akiko. She had first met him the year before last during a recital of the Noh drama *Himuro*. She was enchanted at the time by the figure he cut in his white kimono, splashed with indigo patterns, and his formal skirt. They went out together for less than two years. Sometimes she had to put up with his infidelities, or make excuses about his being the son of a good family whenever she found herself face to face with one of his other lovers. His chanting was so good that he ended up making a stage debut in *Dōjōji*.

The landlady was unable to shed any light on where Takemiya had disappeared to. But she did offer some food for thought. It seems that he had been seeing a cabaret girl behind her back. The girl was from the Sanbanchō area of the old Itsusaka red-light district. She was not familiar with the name of the girl or the establishment where she worked, but someone did once spot Takemiya rubbing shoulders with a girl who fitted the description one early afternoon among the hills of the Itsusaka area.

Thinking all along that Takemiya had run off to Akiko's place, the landlady never pursued the matter.

Jūichirō was almost faint with fatigue, so he asked for a mattress to be laid out in order to take a nap. He slept only lightly, but whenever he tried to awaken, his body refused to move, as if he were encased in clay. When he did occasionally open his eyes, he caught sight of an *ikebana* arrangement, mostly involving rape flower buds, in a small black vase by his bedside. But whether this was reality or an illusion, he was unsure.

When people take a nap straight after such a shock, they sometimes have surprisingly happy dreams. Jūichirō's dream lacked a definite narrative, went through richly coloured changes and was dotted with moments of euphoria, as if he had abandoned himself to a speeding sleigh.

When he arose to take a bath just after three-thirty, a cloudless blue sky was visible through the bathroom window. He made a quick departure, map in hand.

The Itsusaka red-light district had many houses built in the Kyoto style. Even a casual visitor like Jūichirō could immediately distinguish the pleasure quarters, along the upper reaches of the narrow stream, from the old-fashioned, more transactional red-light quarter downstream. Small greengrocers and fishmongers stood between the two areas and, at this time of day, those were the only shops, with their fresh produce on display, that showed any activity. There were additional shops specializing in stationery and cheap sweets, as well as a lending library. Two or three children were engrossed in a game of kicking stones around in the middle of a sunny backstreet. As they played, their kneecaps, scarred with all sorts of little wounds, caught the sun and shone the colour of ginger.

The old red-light quarter was being refurbished with new bars, cabarets and inns. But the half-completed repairs to the original tiled entranceways, with their apologies for door curtains hanging outside, gave the whole area an even more dodgy feel. Jūichirō stole glances at the cabarets with their American-style names, and at the bars with their cabaret-like pretensions, but all their front doors were closed and there was no one about. Some faded artificial cherry blossoms, still dripping raindrops, and a rain-stained nude on a signboard advertising the 'Cherry Blossom Festival' gleamed in the setting sun that emerged after the rain.

A woman, her hair bundled high and sporting a man's nylon jumper, appeared out of nowhere and looked back at Jūichirō, eyeing him suspiciously. She was probably returning from her bath. The clatter of retreating *geta* grew so faint that every step sounded grainy.

Jūichirō walked aimlessly. He felt that the least he could do right now was to keep walking until he collapsed in exhaustion.

It eventually dawned on him that he had no idea what Kaoru Takemiya, or rather, Kawaguchi, looked like, let alone his girlfriend. Even if he struck lucky and bumped into them in the street, would he actually be able to tell? But weariness clouded his judgement, and he was fully confident he would be able to recognize Takemiya from a hundred paces if the boy really was from outer space. Assuming, of course, that he really did come from there.

The pleasure quarters further upstream had preserved their olden days charm, with rows of red-ochre-painted lattice windows and the area in front of the entranceways thoroughly swept. The sun was low, and evening sunshine pressed in from an angle.

After trudging up and down the hills, he finally reached the top of one hill close to a street where the trams ran, and an unexpected view opened up to the west. He saw a scattering of houses that turned into fields and, way beyond that, the sun on the point of dipping below the horizon. The rumbling of the trams blurred in his mind into the sound of the setting sun.

Just as the sun completely disappeared from view, he observed a single white dot shining among the banked clouds in the sky, like the scale of a little fish between the waves as it caught the light. It was Venus, the morning star. During this transitional season, it appeared in the evening time. Its angle of elongation from the sun appeared to be no more than 10 degrees.

The chances of finding Takemiya were zero. As her father, what could he tell Akiko? 'Turns out he was from Venus. He's left you behind and returned home.' Should he say that? 'Turns out he was human. He deceived you and now he's vanished into thin air.' That might be better. The evidence pointed both ways. Jūichirō did not believe that Takemiya was Venusian, but a human father would go out of his way to repress that truth and lie to his daughter in order to preserve her dreams. The latter, blunt response seemed more appropriate for a family of extraterrestrials.

If he were an earthling, he would have made it look as if Takemiya was a Venusian without any hesitation. But even from the perspective of an extraterrestrial, Jūichirō could appreciate that Akiko, an extraterrestrial herself, had committed the mistake of harbouring fantasies about an earthling, and one way for her to atone would be to remain ignorant of her own groundless illusion. Fundamentally, Akiko had gone astray by defiling beauty with a false reality.

'I'll make that girl pay,' thought the tender-hearted Martian.

After returning to Hannō, the exhausted father knew what his line was going to be:

'Turns out he was from Venus. He's left you behind and returned home.'

His circuitous sympathy was in no way a compromise with the human understanding of reality.

7

'Give the young ones a dream.' So went Katsumi Kuroki's slogan.

Its appeal to many young people was premised on the vagueness of its actual meaning and the fact that present-day youngsters had lost their dreams. But Kazuo saw things differently. The only thing that satisfied him was a *sense of reality*. Namely, the reality that he hailed from Mercury. The reality that Earth was a delightful planet, that its nature was beautiful, its women graceful, and in so many other ways worthy of preservation . . . For him, what other reality was there?

Since he held this sense of reality so close to his heart, he impressed others as a young man filled with bright hopes. He felt confident that, compared to other youths of the day with their nervous disorders, he came across as likeable, with a lot of promise.

'I get the feeling you're the only one with a strong vision about the future of Japan and mankind. I'm not just saying that. It's the impression I get from you.' Kuroki's comments were actually way off the mark, but Kazuo liked the sound of them. If things carried on like this, earthlings would unknowingly vote for an extraterrestrial at some point, and fall under extraterrestrial control. What greater state of bliss could there possibly be?

Whenever there was any incident in the world, Kuroki would send off what they call a 'full and frank' letter to high-up American officials. He would eventually receive back a two- or three-line note from some administrative assistant, which he would then print up with relish in a pamphlet. Kazuo found Kuroki's naivety rather hard to take but, on the whole, he liked him.

The various ways in which Kuroki won popularity among

earthlings, especially among the Japanese, provided Kazuo with an unparalleled opportunity to learn. Within a very short time, Kazuo even came to pity his father's poor understanding of human psychology.

Jūichirō's lecture tour had gone very well, but it owed its success to 'sick' people. In that sense, it resembled the pathetic success of artists.

When the end-of-term exams finished at the beginning of March, Kazuo handed over all his duties for their father's tour to his sister. He had heard that a politician should be visited in the morning, so he called on Kuroki's house in the Setagaya district at eight-thirty, clutching the business card he had accepted previously. He was surprised how small the place was, enclosed by a sooty hedge and filled to overflowing with visitors. Kuroki needed to attend a parliamentary committee meeting from ten that morning, but before that he was receiving callers in no particular order.

Kazuo announced the purpose of his visit to the student who greeted him at the door, but of course Kuroki could not remember someone he had only asked to drop by in passing. Kazuo found this hint of insincerity rather refreshing and appealing.

Kazuo filled the student in with details about his activities at university lectures. This first visit to Kuroki's front door taught him how necessary it was to advertise oneself cheerfully and without a scintilla of shame.

He could hear the student convey the message on the other side of the sliding-screen wall. And then, Kuroki's sharp voice cut right through the visitors' commotion.

'Oh, that student! That guy has promise. Show him straight in.'

Kazuo had made a point of coming in school uniform, and his gold-buttoned chest filled out as he went through the ordeal of being introduced to the group at large.

'This is Kazuo Ōsugi.' Kuroki spoke loudly, his eyes skimming Kazuo's card. 'During a talk at A University, he very skilfully tackled a commotion by some left-wing students. He won me over. He's a fine young man.'

Even so, Kuroki spoke not another word to Kazuo.

Kuroki was wearing a youthful black sweater, which showed off his faultless athletic physique. His head was small for a Japanese, and his thin, sharp face responded with quick wit to his visitors whenever the need arose. But hardly anyone spoke to Kuroki. Most just remained silent, as if they were soaking up the pleasure of sharing the same space. Four or five young women were numbered among them.

Kazuo noticed that visitors spoke to Kuroki in ways that would baffle an outsider. It was only afterwards that he gradually came to understand.

'Sir, I wonder when you'll sort that matter out?' What the director, from a company which sponsored Kuroki, actually meant was: 'Sir, can you please grant that machinery import licence as soon as possible? We're stuck because the Ministry of Trade and Industry is moving at a snail's pace.' When an official from Kuroki's electoral district in Miyagi Prefecture said, 'Sir, please pull out all the stops. We're worried about this year's rainy season', his real meaning was, 'Sir, get the flood defence works for the R River finished as soon as possible.'

There was a single political journalist among all the visitors. The direct tone he used when speaking to Kuroki, as if they were friends, identified not only himself but also the newspaper he represented as rather 'cool'. He did address a few words to Kazuo too, using marvellously vulgar language.

For little less than an hour, Kazuo sat all alone. Eventually a car turned up, and it was time for Kuroki to take his leave. Only the journalist, who seemed to have the right to tag along, got ready to follow after Kuroki and his secretary.

Kuroki changed into a well-tailored grey suit and appeared at the entranceway. He walked up to Kazuo, who was standing in his school uniform, jostling with all the others in the narrow space to see him off. The politician turned to him and smiled.

It was a particularly sweet smile that passed across his angular face. Kazuo could completely understand how he would appeal to a television audience. He even felt his own body melting. Kuroki gave him a generous tap on the shoulder.

'Sorry I was so busy this morning. I meet with a group of students at my Toranomon office at four o'clock every Friday afternoon, so come along to the next one if you're interested. I make time to chat for an hour to the young ones there. I love those Friday get-togethers.'

. . . Kazuo took up his offer and went to the meeting, and this time Kuroki gave a one-hour non-stop monologue. But Kazuo, sat with arms wrapped around his knees in the cramped office, listened spellbound to what he had to say.

Kuroki embarked upon an eloquent discussion about civilization. He started from Indian Ocean civilization (as he described it), then moved on to Mediterranean civilization, to Atlantic Ocean civilization (the shift of European civilization to the Americas) and finally he came to the age of Pacific Ocean civilization during the last few decades. He spread out an impressive sketch map with Japan at its centre, and explained how the Japanese military clique's wartime cry to 'unify the eight corners of the world' had trivialized his own prediction regarding the history of civilization. It was inevitable that a world federation would be established at some point, but the principles of this foundation would not be based on the kind of dead-end misguided equality espoused by the United Nations. Instead, they would need to rest on the prophetic insights of the tide of civilizational history in which the individual nation of Japan and the world at large embraced each other to forge a multidimensional collective (!). World peace floated, like a bubble in a spirit level, at the very core of consciousness about the present-day crisis, at the very heart of a Japan that seemed adrift on the raging waves of world politics in a way that truly reflected the spirit of a new world community.

He saw young people as the embodiment of fresh aspiration among the Japanese people. While he tied his hopes to the future, the present corrupt crop of politicians was deplorable. He reproached the Ikeda cabinet for its attitude of sitting on the fence, and he denounced its economic and diplomatic policies. He also drew from Switzerland's example to advocate the establishment of a national defence army, and he lamented the left-wing anti-patriotism into which post-war new education had sunk. A lack of patriotism in its true sense meant a failure to recognize the spirit of the age, what the Germans call *Weltgeist*, and he had set himself against the nationalistic façade of the left and degenerate cosmopolitanism alike.

Kuroki's youthful physique and tone of voice endowed his rough-and-ready opinions with a bright, healthy, energetic glamour. During that hour, the students sitting silently in a row were totally recharged, and even Kazuo could appreciate the surge of ideas that flushed all of their cheeks.

Kazuo received another special favour. Though a newcomer, he was assigned the task of acting as guide for a group of peers from Kuroki's electoral district who would be visiting Tokyo the next day.

And then again, the following week, when Kuroki's formal secretary went down with a bad cold, Kazuo was asked to step in and take one of Kuroki's prominent supporters, an assembly member from Miyagi Prefecture, on a tour of the parliament. Afterwards, Kuroki made a point of informing Kazuo that the assembly member had spoken well of him, describing him as 'an energetic young man with lots of promise'.

Kazuo barely had time to return home to Hannō any longer. On a rare occasion when he did make an appearance, the house was noisy with strange visitors, his pale-looking sister had confined herself to her room and his mother finally had a quiet word with him to announce that Akiko was pregnant. He simply saw this as the sort of dark affliction that affected a typical family.

One day, Kuroki showed Kazuo a delightful way to use money as a way of clearly demonstrating a reputation for integrity.

'Go and see the Senior Managing Director of Oshima Shoji, and bring back 300,000 yen. I've called him about it, so all you have to do is go and get the cash.'

With these instructions, Kazuo visited the company in Ōtemachi, where he showed Kuroki's business card and met the director. He was ready with the cash, but conscientiously counted it again and put it in an envelope before handing it to Kazuo. This was the first time Kazuo had personally received what are known as political funds.

When Kazuo returned to Kuroki's office, one of his protégés, a parliamentary member in financial straits, was waiting. Kuroki took the envelope and handed it straight to the man in front of Kazuo. Kazuo had never before seen someone accept money by holding it reverently over his head.

'Poor guy. He didn't have enough money to pay for his wife's hospital expenses,' Kuroki informed Kazuo once the man had left. For Kuroki, the sense of reverence he saw in the young man's eyes at that moment was surely a source of nothing less than pure, unadulterated joy. Kazuo could not help but look up at Kuroki with eyes innocently ablaze, and view himself in the role of a maiden.

'I get the feeling you're the only one with a strong vision about the future of Japan and mankind. I'm not just saying that. It's the impression I get from you.' That was the moment these words passed Kuroki's lips.

One evening, Kazuo accompanied a party of guests from the electoral district on a night bus tour, and then took them to see a performance of *The Mikado*. Kuroki had grown bored with a reception he was attending in Akasaka, so he decided on a whim to drop by and say hello. He ended up accompanying them all the way to a show performed by traditional courtesans at the Matsubara Geisha House in the Yoshiwara district, which thrilled the guests. Kuroki was heading home, so he gave Kazuo a lift once the guests had been escorted back to their inn. The night was late, and Kuroki continuously hummed some ditty.

Just as they were approaching the politician's house in Setagaya, Kuroki felt a desperate urge to relieve himself so he had the car stop next to a large, unlit garden shop. He took a long pee against a thicket of miniature cypresses.

Kazuo was waiting in the car. It was a magnificent starry night. There were lots of shrubs among the trees in the shop front, and a cliff could be seen on the far side of the large plot of land, beyond which spread the limitless sky.

The sound of Kuroki passing water against the soft spring earth went on for ages. The budding branches of the man-made forest intertwined under the starlight, and the fir buds looked as if they were coated in white ash. One corner of the shop was reserved entirely for a collection of camellias, whose scarlet blooms had blackened in the night like dry blood. The withered branches of a few lofty elms soared above the evergreens and spread delicately into the starry night.

From their position, the sky stretched beyond the woods in a southward direction. The Milky Way was flowing low to the east while, right ahead, the constellation Hydra, the Water Snake, rolled on and on. The quadrangle of four stars in the constellation Corvus, a familiar feature in the springtime southern sky, twinkled distinctly just a whisker above the shrubbery. Almost perpendicular above them, Leo was retiring eastwards as it gazed upon the Earth below, its brightest star Regulus displaying its brilliant pupil.

Kazuo was so absorbed in this magnificent view that he failed to notice how Kuroki had not yet returned to the car despite having finished his business. It was highly unusual for Kuroki to turn his back on an audience, even of one, and remain silent and lost in thought like this for so long. Or perhaps Kazuo was simply unaware that Kuroki was in the habit of facing the star-filled night and reworking it into his own unique cosmology.

'Ah, sorry to keep you.' Kuroki sprang like a phantom back into the car. For a moment, the swiftness of his shadowy movement struck Kazuo as odd. Kuroki's face was obscured in the darkness and the glint in his eyes was indistinct. Just then, Kazuo wondered if he might also be from outer space.

When they had settled in the car and set off, Kazuo nonchalantly asked:

'Do you like the stars?'

'Stars? You mean, stars? Sure, I do,' Kuroki responded assertively.

When Kuroki suddenly set off for the Tantan Academy in Miyagi Prefecture, Kazuo was upset not to have been asked along. His unhappiness was compounded when he read in the newspapers that the purpose of his trip was to prepare for the forthcoming House of Councillors elections on the first of July. But Kuroki's close associates opined that the purpose of the trip was to expand the academy. Kazuo was afraid he might have been cold-shouldered because he had guessed Kuroko's secret recently when he was looking up into the starry night.

The Tantan Academy was a bastion of anti-Japanese Teachers Union education, run by Kuroki and renowned even among people in Tokyo. It was located in the village of Nanakita-mura, which was tucked away in the mountains of Miyagi, and an ideal spot for study, hard work and physical education. It had more than 700 students, some of whom were young fans of Kuroki from Tokyo. Kazuo had hinted to Kuroki how desperate he was to visit, but he had been excluded.

Instead, with the spring holiday over, Kazuo found himself as a university student who was also in receipt of a monthly salary. Before he knew it, he had become a junior employee of Oshima Shoji, which paid him in his capacity as Kuroki's private secretary. He put the first salary he had ever received in his wallet. The cherry blossoms were about to peak, so he went to view them at the university. A female fellow student called out to him, but he pretended not to notice. He was enthusiastic about the new world of politics, and no longer felt as captivated by girls as he did before.

The commute to Hannō was inconvenient, so Kazuo had been staying in some lodgings for students who helped Kuroki. But once he received a salary, he moved into a private boarding house he found in the same Setagaya district. It was only a four- or five-minute walk to Kuroki's house from there.

After Kuroki returned to Tokyo, everything went on as before. With his boarding house so close, Kazuo was even entrusted with doing the private shopping for the ever busy Mrs Kuroki.

One time, Mrs Kuroki pointed to an article and photograph in a magazine describing his father's lecture series.

'I understand this is your father.'

Kazuo blushed.

'Who told you that?'

'My husband. Oh . . .' She seemed bemused, and went on. 'Didn't he say anything to you?'

The fact that Kuroki knew about it but had said nothing hurt

Kazuo. Was Kuroki contemptuous of him? Did he pity him? Or was there another reason?

'Act like you're an ordinary guy. Ordinary, no matter how distasteful you may find it. People superior to others have a duty to act like that. And it's the only way to protect yourself.'

This was the wise counsel his father had previously given his son, but now he was posing as a martyr and had become a laughing stock to the world. Of course, Jūichirō had never disclosed his extraterrestrial origins to anyone, but the mere mention of 'flying saucers' was enough to make people have their suspicions.

He may be my father, but I'm a grown-up now and he has no right to make his son blush in public, thought Kazuo, consumed with anger. The way he and his father did things was now miles apart. Just being a father did not give him the authority to obstruct his son's actions.

The utter bliss when setting eyes on a flying saucer. The instantaneous healing of a fractured world. The clear and unadulterated sense of harmony and unity . . . Such feelings were certainly hard to maintain in everyday life, but once savoured, it became hard to shake free of the conviction about how the world ought to be. The whole Ōsugi family were of the same mind. This striving towards blissful harmony was an endless search for the origin, a tracing back to the very source of things. Their dreams would be realized if this bliss, like dew covering an orchard of a summer's morning, existed not only at that instant when flying saucers appeared, but for ever, so that the pleasure of the origin of things could be experienced on a daily basis.

Of course, Kazuo wished for the same. But his way was to remain as discreet as he could about himself, to throw himself into what humans call 'reality', and to purify that reality through practical control. In short, he was interested in 'politics'.

Once Kazuo had seized power, he would promulgate the Universal Constitution that had been brewing for so long in his heart. In order to maintain permanent peace on Earth, the Constitution would probably need to institute a ruthless international police organization with almost unlimited real powers.

Kazuo was riddled with shame, even viewing his pathetic sister's pregnancy as punishment for their father's naive view of human life. He hated his father on his sister's behalf in this matter too.

Ever since his mother had told him about the pregnancy, he found himself unable to look his sister squarely in the face. The happy sibling fights of yesteryear would never return, and Kazuo even began to wonder how to address her.

All the misfortune began from their father's lofty idealism, his prominent nose, his professorial spectacles. It arose from the sad shadow of his intellectual aloofness that mesmerized the people around him. Even when he advocated peace on Earth in ecstatic tones, how effective was the lonely pallor of his complexion in bringing a smile to his audience? Incidentally, the very intellectual loneliness that Jūichirō claimed to repudiate was actually something he had picked up from humans on Earth.

Kuroki said nothing upon his return to Tokyo, but a weekly magazine immediately raised the issue of the Tantan Academy. It was only after reading it that Kazuo became aware of why Kuroki had made his trip. The article was interspersed with a few photographs.

Trouble at Tantan Academy
Academy Head Kuroki Deals with 'Rights of Common' Problem

Benefiting from an increase in student numbers and unexpected largesse from the financial world, at the beginning of this year Kuroki set about expanding the Tantan Academy in Nanakita-mura. The school building needed to be extended, and fields at the back have been cleared to increase the school grounds by almost an acre.

It is public land owned by Miyagi Prefecture. Kuroki had already submitted a purchase request, and the prefectural assembly was fully intending to approve it, but some concerned locals have formed a movement to appeal for affirmation of 'rights of common' relating to the land.

Rights of common go back to the old Tokugawa Period when villagers cut the landowner's grass and chopped down trees from his forests and fields in place of paying annual tribute. The practice of communal earnings turned into real rights. This happened because Meiji Period legislative policy treated officials as more important than the people, and therefore did not consider the formal granting of such rights to the people as amounting to anything of practical significance. But after the war, from 1957, when the Japan Self-Defence Force was hoping to use the East Fuji Manoeuvre Area, things became heated. In line with the mood of the times, rights of common came to be viewed as a traditional form of democratic rights.

Kuroki was in a fix, but fortunately he knew of an assistant professor at Sendai University, Masumi Haguro, who specializes in rights of common. Kuroki went to Sendai and visited the professor straightaway to obtain his opinion. Haguro carried out an immediate land survey and checked the archives. Since he happened to be familiar with the same area from his own studies, he managed to obtain proof that overruled the villagers' claim. The indignant locals are seeking compromise and it looks as if they will come to an out-of-court settlement. A delighted Kuroki has returned to Tokyo. While taking leave at the station, Kuroki shook hands vigorously with Haguro and promised to meet again. They looked as if they had already known each other for years.

Reading this article, Kazuo felt intuitively that there was something a bit fishy about it.

He had an inkling that clever manipulation was at play in order to make this small incident and the resultant friendship seem natural. Possibly Kazuo was overthinking it, and it was all just a coincidence. But even if it were, Kazuo remembered well something his father had previously discussed at length: 'We just have to remain on constant watch about what's happening around us, and take note whenever any apparently trivial coincidence arises. My prediction is that cryptic signs of small, insignificant coincidences will become increasingly common on Earth from now on.'

There was no clear link between Kazuo's intuition and Kuroki's strange attitude when he gazed up at the stars before his trip to the Tantan Academy. But Kazuo could never shake off the impression he had been left with that evening. He tried to brush the idea away, but it kept coming back, and finally became deeply embedded. As a result, he now saw Kuroki in a totally different light.

When Kuroki had returned to the car after looking at the heavens, he had carried himself in a way that did not give the impression of someone simply running over the ground back to the car. Instead, he seemed like a creature that had swooped down upon this little patch of ground in the night, folded up its wings and rushed to the car as if it were perfectly natural.

'This evening, Professor Haguro and two of his friends are coming to Tokyo from Sendai. They are staying at the Ōgiya Ryokan, so I'd like you to go and meet them at the station, and take them to the inn. You'll also need to be their guide for tomorrow's matinee in the Kabukiza Theatre. I'll be entertaining them in Akasaka after the performance. I'm very indebted to the professor for his help with the academy, so he deserves top treatment. That's why I told him to bring along as many friends as he wanted when I invited him.' With these instructions from Kuroki, Kazuo went that evening to Ueno Station to meet the guests.

When Kazuo saw the three men alight from the first-class carriage of the express train, he immediately picked out Haguro. Kazuo had been given a little flag bearing Haguro's name, and the plan was for Haguro to identify the flag and approach him. But Kazuo had already spotted him even before he was fully off the train. Sickly body, pale face, perfectly round spectacles, boorish suit and tie. The whole look gave him away as an assistant professor from a provincial university. However, Kazuo's sharp intuition homed in on something more fundamental. You know, he thought, maybe the provincial university professor look is a bit too perfect. Perhaps he's faking it. Not only as a professor, but also as a human being . . .'

His two friends were unlikely companions, one a large, ugly young man, the other, tubby, uncouth and middle-aged. They lined up together in a way that gave the impression of three exceptionally unsavoury men at a trade fair.

'I've come to meet you on Mr Kuroki's behalf. He's looking forward to tomorrow evening. Right, let me take you to your inn.'

'Young man, you must be Ōsugi.' Haguro's voice seemed to hang slightly in the air. Kazuo was surprised that Kuroki had already conveyed his name to these visitors from afar.

Kazuo took Haguro's old briefcase and walked on ahead, aware that the three were all eyeing him from behind. Their gazes seemed to cut through the station clatter and pore over every move he made.

Even in the car, Kazuo sat in the front passenger seat, and so was forced to keep his back turned to them.

'I guess the night-time cherry blossom viewing at Ikenohata is over now? What a pity. It's been five years since I was last in Tokyo,' said Haguro. Kazuo looked through the rear-view mirror at the dry cheeks of this timid, exhausted man. Neon signs were flowing past the car on both sides, and there were still quite a few people about in the Hirokōji neighbourhood.

'There are so many people in Tokyo. We'll have to sort this out,' said the chubby, middle-aged man. But he appeared to get poked with an elbow, and he fell silent. After that, the three hardly spoke a word until they reached the inn in Akefunechō, Shiba.

The next morning, Kazuo went to pick them up in plenty of time to make it to the Kabuki. Kuroki had pointed out that Danjurō XI's performance this month officially marked his succession to that prestigious stage name, and it was only because of his prominence that he managed to get his hands on some tickets.

They had third-level box seats on the west side, but they were a pretty unprepossessing group as they sat there. Even after the curtain opened on the play, *Shibaraku*, none of them showed a flicker of interest, and they were attracted as much to the audience as to the stage. Predictably, the only time they excitedly craned over the low railing of the box was to watch the new Danjurō do his renowned 'six leap' exit during the dance, 'Kanjinchō', which was performed on the stage that extended into the stalls directly in front of them. The final piece was a new work by Yukio Mishima, entitled *The Sardine Hawker and the Dragnet of Love*. When the professor opined that this kind of new work, written like a novel, was not worth watching, the other two concurred.

'Ōsugi, how about taking us for a stroll around the Ginza? I'm sure we have lots of time before meeting up with Kuroki.' After spending half a day together, Haguro's tone had turned rougher and more familiar, and he addressed Kazuo as if he were a student.

It was a clear spring afternoon, and the Ginza crowds appeared to be full of incident.

'We wouldn't be able to meditate here, would we, Professor?' said the large young man, towering above the others.

'I'm so happy to have met Kuroki. It's finally opened things up. I did hope to be able to meet someone from *the same place* at some time.' It was an oblique reply from Haguro.

'Look at that. No surprise, the roses they sell in Tokyo are all fabulous. Hmm. All those rich show-offs buying them with their quick bucks. I bet all those arty types spend their lives buried in roses.'

'You can't be so sweeping. Of course, it's different when you're in a coffin.'

Gradually, the three lost their reserve about speaking in riddles in front of Kazuo.

During the last month, Kazuo had become accustomed to dealing with visitors from the provinces, but this time he was out of his element. As they wove their way through the jostling crowds dressed in their bright spring finery, Kazuo occasionally entertained a fantasy that their small group was following a solitary path through a field in broad daylight with no one else around. At times, the street noises in his ears suddenly ceased, and he could only hear the far-off humming of countless flies.

'Shall I take you to a café with pretty girls?' said Kazuo, unable to bear it any more.

'Sounds great,' the professor agreed affectedly.

But even when an unsmiling beauty clumsily placed coffees before them in the dark booth where they were sitting, none of the three guests showed the slightest pleasure. The large young man glared at her harshly, and the chubby middle-aged man fixed his eyes on the nape of her neck, harbouring unpleasant thoughts.

As they slurped their coffee in a desultory fashion, Haguro turned a smiling face towards Kazuo.

'I barely know you, so forgive me for asking, but you're the son of Jūichirō Ōsugi, aren't you?'

Thinking he must be an acquaintance of his father from school-teaching days, Kazuo said, 'Yes I am.'

'Actually, I've been reading about your father's activities recently in magazines with real interest.'

Kazuo burst out indignantly, 'Father is Father, and I'm my own man.'

'All young people say that. That's fine. It could hardly be any other way.'

The conversation abruptly ended, and the three guests fell into a conspiratorial silence, as if they were cats training their pricked-up ears in each other's direction.

Haguro kept his eyes averted as he sprang the question: 'There's something I'd like to ask. I wonder if your father might be an extraterrestrial?'

8

Kazuo's eyes shifted anxiously as he tried to work out the true significance of Haguro's question. It sounded as if he was simply asking out of curiosity, yet he might also be posing a serious question under the cloak of nonchalance.

Be that as it may, this involved a secret relating not only to his father but also, more importantly, to the whole family. The rather gloomy, downcast atmosphere and the absence of any tone of ridicule in Haguro's words rescued Kazuo from the humiliating rage that he usually fell into. He finally recovered enough composure to reply in a matter-of-fact way:

'Well . . . It's all so stupid. But then, Dad's gone a bit nutty recently, and I have no idea what he's on about.'

His expedient response gave him some breathing space, and it was soon time to accompany the three to the restaurant in Akasaka. Normally, that was where Kazuo's duties ended. He had never attended a smart dinner party, and guests were generally sent back afterwards to their hotel by hired car.

'It's been wonderful to meet you,' he said at the entrance, turning to leave. Haguro asked him to wait for a moment. The three guests went inside, and the hostess emerged with a message from Kuroki. 'He'd like you to eat your dinner at the Edoya Restaurant close by, and wait for him there. It seems he has something planned later. When the time comes, he'll ask me to go and fetch you.'

Kazuo had no option but to dine alone in the restaurant located in the centre of the Akasaka red-light district. The restaurant would be packed with geishas late at night, but right now there were just a few discreet punters and groups of people from the local TV company, so there were lots of tables laid, with white tablecloths going spare. He ordered beef stew and *Löwenbräu* beer.

Kazuo felt a profound unease in his heart. From the moment he set eyes on Haguro at the station, his usual ineffable calm in the company of humans had deserted him. This feeling – that he alone was different, that he lacked all responsibility even as he was submitting, albeit temporarily, to the laws of the world – provided a sense of exquisite comfort, like soaking in hot water. But his calm and his comfort had immediately crumbled in the face of Haguro.

Instead, Haguro and his companions had blasted what felt like a cold and poisonous wind from far away directly into Kazuo's face. Kazuo was not exactly sure what it signified. His only certainty was that he had never experienced such a sensation from anyone else before.

It was taking ages for the hostess to come and collect him. Even after his meal, Kazuo remained with his elbows on the table, fingers kneading his oily forehead, lost in thought. Actually, Kazuo was pretty sure he had caught the whiff of a similarly foul extraterrestrial odour before. When Kuroki had stood there gazing up at the starry night, Kazuo remembered feeling as if a malicious mist were drifting down from the dazzling stars. Every star was still fixed in its usual position, but they appeared to realign themselves into an alternative, inauspicious constellation. It was only a momentary idea that passed through his mind, forgotten the next instant.

After giving it some thought, Kazuo came up with a hypothesis. The extraterrestrials temporarily resident on Earth included other species entirely different from the Ōsugi family. Members of the same species could easily identify each other, but their eyes were clouded with dark illusions, which made it impossible to distinguish other species from outer space.

If Kazuo could see them but they could not see him, he was obviously obliged to conceal his alien roots, but he also had to maintain the pretence that he had not noticed the extraterrestrial origins of Kuroki and the three from Sendai. His own self-protection depended on it.

Kazuo could not be absolutely sure about the situation, but at least his powers of discrimination were sharper than theirs, and this gave him a sense of superiority. He was, however, aware of the need to conceal the tiniest hint of one-upmanship even more than he already did in the case of humans. Maybe extraterrestrials were more driven by jealousy than earthlings.

As he pursued his study of human politics, he felt himself confronting the essential nature of a much subtler political reality. Women were an open book, but politics was opaque. There were certainly some things he could work out, but he kept those perceptions to himself. He felt sure he was being used to serve some purpose, but he had to pretend he understood what that purpose was. All he needed was a smile to conceal his own intelligence, but he had to brandish a big stick when it came to hiding his ignorance. Kazuo felt that something was coming to fruition as he waited impatiently in the restaurant. Ripening in the face of a sweet, rich, fruity lie.

I've just not noticed it until now. There's nothing human about this situation. Hard to believe, but some mysterious aliens are teaching me about the human condition. He drank the cold dregs of his second *demitasse* of coffee.

The glass entrance door opened, and the hostess came in. She bantered with a waiter she obviously knew, and approached Kazuo.

'Sorry to keep you waiting. Mr Kuroki asked you to come immediately. You poor thing, having to look after those uncouth guests.'

With that, she appeared to brush away the surrounding air with her kimono sleeve. It was a light and easy gesture that did not quite match her puffy white face and raised, arching eyebrows. On the short walk back to the restaurant, the hostess avoided cars and walked, cat-like, close to the wall. She repeatedly and needlessly warned Kazuo, who walked ahead, about the danger of cars.

Kuroki was drunk, and his exaggerated words fell clunkily onto the fresh green tatami mats with their elegant brocade borders.

'Glad you're here. New generation full of hope!' Then he turned to Haguro. 'Haguro, great young man, isn't he? Tokyo's changed too, you know. First change is, there's a whole string of lovely young people emerging. They're pure and keen, and they're not stuck up.'

'I only met him today, but I think so too. The ones I teach in Sendai are unadventurous, yet so full of themselves. It is a real pain.'

Even as Haguro echoed the compliment, he was taking a shot at his faraway students who had never rated him highly.

Their traditional tatami room was rather large, but candlelight made it as bright as day. Five geishas were in attendance, and no sooner had Kazuo sat down than one came over to pour his drink. This was his first time at a geisha party. These women were all proud of their skills, and their thickly powdered white cheeks gleamed. Every movement of their hands was like a dance, gliding and cutting cleanly through the air. This lot don't look human in the slightest. Or like humans trying to turn themselves into aliens, thought Kazuo.

'I bet this one's underage,' said the geisha at Kazuo's side. She was getting on a bit. 'I'm worried I might get into trouble with the law if I give him alcohol. Let's stick with flirting of the purest kind.'

Oblivious to the others, Kuroki started off on one of his long monologues.

'The real reason I've got you here, Kazuo, is related to a problem with your father.'

Here we go, thought Kazuo.

'Even before meeting Haguro, I'd given considerable thought to the problem, but Haguro's done some research into the matter, and we have lots of common interests. I'm afraid I still can't spell things out here as clearly as I'd like, but there are some serious political doubts concerning the world peace movement your father is involved with. You see, if your father has promoted this movement without even being an actual extraterrestrial himself, the suspicion deepens. If he really is one, then he doesn't know how seriously he's exposed himself to danger. In the former case, there's nothing to be done. If the latter is true, well, it would attract too much public attention if I were to visit your house in Hannō, but Professor Haguro has kindly agreed to help by trying to prevail on your father on my behalf. We're so worried about you and your father, in fact your whole family. And for that reason, we're hoping you'll come straight out and give us an honest account of the secret concerning your father's background.'

Kazuo maintained a stubborn silence. He was intensely conscious of standing in a rather grand place, trump card in hand, with Kuroki before him.

He felt pressurized by the visitors' hard stares, and Kuroki was pushing for an answer, but Kazuo could smell the pleading in his words and his response was muted.

'I understand perfectly what you're saying. But I feel you are appealing to my sense of pity because you assume I'm a filial son with strong feelings for my parents. But what if I'm someone without any affection for their parents? In that case, I'd have no problem if my dad found himself under the political spotlight.'

'Interesting,' Kuroki shot back. 'So, does that mean you and your father have different backgrounds, and you just don't get on together? If so, clearly, you're human and your father is . . .'

'I have nothing to say!' snapped Kazuo.

The weight of silence gripping the whole party at that moment was extraordinary. The geishas, wide-eyed and still clutching their sake bottles, seemed dumbfounded. The visitors looked determined not to miss the slightest flutter of an expression on Kazuo's face. The body of the big, ugly fellow, in particular, trembled ever so slightly.

'This secret will go for a high price!' shouted Kazuo inside his own head. He had believed the very word 'extraterrestrial' to be a source of cheap laughter in the world, but he was mistaken. On that point, it was his faint-hearted father who seemed to have got it right.

Right now, all the funniness surrounding the word 'extraterrestrial' had been brushed away, and it had taken on an extraordinarily curious high status. The word was like an invisible crown on a black-lacquered table, instantaneously restored to its former splendour. Politics, economics and academicism crowded around it. Through the conduit of Kuroki's authority, the word permeated every corner of human life, whether in the form of bread, flowers, toffees, bicycles, sewing machines, cats or cockroaches.

Here he was, a pale young man with only a mediocre intellect, locked into a powerful play of strength. What had been a bouquet of violets in a maiden's heart was transformed into a formidable weapon in the struggle for power . . . What had happened? All those wholesome ideas that humans had worked so hard on, which had been tucked away in a drawer, had suddenly turned upside down before his very eyes.

Even for an extraterrestrial like Kazuo, it was impossible to grasp how such a sudden upheaval had come about. And yet, somewhere, those countless stars were trembling . . .

Jūichirō's large, cold, elegant nose arose in his son's mind. 'Look at that stupid nose. It looks even more ridiculous now. I'm going to turn that nose of yours into a real tragedy. It's what you're looking for.' Kazuo was redirecting the loathing he had always felt for the featureless gullibility of his own face towards his father. He was going to exaggerate the seriousness of his father's secret and talk up the price as high as possible, thus betraying his father in a spectacular manner.

He presented his empty cup to the geisha. Though taken by surprise, she managed to pour his drink without spilling a drop. The pale-yellow sake reached the very brim of the cup. Kazuo gulped it down in one go, like a real human young man, and spoke passionately:

'I might be an unfilial son, but I still need Dutch courage to spill the beans on my father's big secret, and earn the contempt of society in the process. OK, Mr Kuroki, I will speak provided you agree to two conditions. First, you formally make me your private secretary with immediate effect. Second, you relinquish your constituency to me when I run for election in future. If you can deliver on those, I'll talk.'

'Hey, hey. That's a high price.' Kuroki gave a show of obstinacy. 'Fair enough, I accept what you say.'

'So, we're agreed?'

'We are, indeed. You'll be my right-hand man from tomorrow. As far as the constituency is concerned, I'll sign a contract later.'

'Right then. I won't hide it from you, my dad is an extraterrestrial. No one outside the family knows his secret. He's . . . from Mars.'

Kazuo kept his gaze fixed on Kuroki, but the unsavoury threesome exchanged glances with sighs and muted whisperings. No surprise, they seemed to say. Sensing a relaxation in the air, the gei-shas quickly set about filling cups, but to Kazuo's ear their bustling sounded hollow, like fireworks at midday. The din reverberated through wisps of yellowish smoke and penetrated his mind, where it hung reluctantly. He spoke loudly, as if he had just come to.

'Mr Kuroki, does that mean the only reason you ever took notice of me was because you were after my father from the beginning, and I'm his son?'

'Don't be a fool. It's because you're a young man with a future. I can't bear the lefties in the All-Japan Student Federation, or the right-wing youth. It's because I see in you the face of a young man who will stand up and take responsibility for Japan in the future.' Kuroki's retort was extremely earnest.

The seventeenth of April was a beautifully sunny day. In Hannō, the Ōsugi household had finished supper before dark, and both parents were sitting together with Akiko in her west-facing room upstairs. They were gazing at the late spring sunset.

Following his Kanazawa trip, Father had developed increas-ingly tender feelings towards Akiko. A life might be growing in her womb, but he felt like he was caring for someone close to death. Once Akiko had decided to give birth, she immediately wrote to school announcing her withdrawal, confined herself at home and put all her energy into administrative work for the Friendship Association. None of them ever mentioned the fact that Kazuo seldom came home any more, and they even seemed delighted to enjoy a rare moment of communion like this after their meal.

Akiko was over her morning sickness, and once she had received her father's awkward report about his visit to Kanazawa, her worries dissipated. In her father's eyes, too, Akiko's tranquil expression and gestures seemed to lend her greater sanctity as the days went by. Her beauty had been characterized by a cool, crystalline disdain, but now it was flooded with a languorous warmth, like a full-bodied lake encroaching upon the grasses at the water's edge. Every one of her gentle expressions appeared to glow with a distant, spiritual dignity incapable of inflicting harm on anyone. Akiko was laughing a lot now. But from a distance, the clear, sad tone of that laughter brought a tremble to her father's heart.

The sun was going down beyond the low-lying streets of Hannō. All three leant against the railing as they looked westward, their eyes fixed on what would be one of the last of history's countless sunsets. The sun dissolved hazily into the evening clouds, obscured by the opaque, lyrical sighs expressed by people on Earth.

Akiko was leafing absent-mindedly through the pages of a book on celestial myths and legends, which her father had recommended as part of her antenatal training. Father was scornful of human in-accuracy when it came to astronomy, but he believed that images provided by extraterrestrials in the past were the starting point for myths and legends. Akiko loved the American Indian 'Star Maiden' legend, which referred to the stars in the constellation Corona Borealis. A hunter known as Waupee, or White Hawk, saw twelve beautiful sisters descend from the sky in a large silver basket, and he fell in love with one of them. But once the girl had become his wife, she yearned for the heavenly abode from which she came and, turning into a star, she returned home.

Iyoko worried that her daughter, left in the lurch, might cradle the infant in her arms once it was born, and bury herself ever more deeply in dream. It was a human that had cheated Akiko, so she ought to pay more attention to humans. But Iyoko had been sworn to secrecy by her husband, and was therefore unable to offer advice to her daughter.

On the other hand, years of experience had stopped Iyoko fret-ting as far as her husband was concerned. Jūichirō had become very thin recently but this was not really a surprise, given the piles of work and worries that he had to deal with.

'Dad, you're really picky about your food at the moment,' said Akiko suddenly in her clear voice.

'I think I might have become tired of food on Earth.'

'Rubbish!' said Iyoko, suspecting some criticism of her cooking skills. 'Planet Earth is blessed with an abundance of good food.'

'No, ever so gradually my palate has begun to remember the

indescribably sweet foods of the stars, and that is what's making me turn against earthly food. What I'm talking about is immaculate, unmoistened food, wonderfully scented and petal-shaped. It used to fall from the sky at night and get caught among the branches of trees. The taste of a single petal would refresh my heart, and three were enough to fill me. Now, what were they made from? Martians never cooked, but they cultivated fires in their front gardens like little beds of red flowers, for the simple thrill of looking at them. The flowers were dangerous, giving you burns if you so much as touched them. Whenever that happened, we used to say you'd snagged your finger on a red thorn. But if you held out a saucer of oil, the sweet little flowers would climb up you merrily like tame sparrows perching on their master's hand. And they'd follow you wherever you went.'

The sun was already disappearing, and below them the empty streets filled with the ringing of bicycle bells, the voices of children at play despite repeated calls to come home, the tofu seller hawking his wares with the aid of a horn, the whine of an electric saw at the mill beyond the crossroads where men were working overtime, songs on the television. In the spring air, these evening sounds seemed muffled by a flannel cloth. Only the dry, white earth of the dusty road stood out.

Just then, they heard a car come to a creaking halt close to the Inari Shrine, and from their window they could make out just one corner of a black shiny car. Three men emerged and huddled together in conversation over what looked like a map. One was thin, one was short and fat, the other was exceptionally tall. Eventually the three set off in their direction, their darkened faces set against the fading light. Just one glance made Jūichirō blanch. His eyes opened wide with fear, and even his fingers resting against the window frame trembled. The strength drained from him so fully that the flesh of his slender shoulders appeared to fall away.

'Dad, what's wrong?'

'This is terrible. It's terrifying! I was afraid something like this might come our way at some point.'

★

While the three men from Sendai were left waiting in the parlour, they made critical whispered judgements.

'This feels just like the kind of parlour you would expect in the home of a provincial family of repute. Even in Sendai, you see lots of them. But only a family that is really loaded would usher you into a tatty old room like this. This sort of household keeps its riches hidden. Ever since his lecture tour, the master of the house must be making a pretty packet from donations from his fans. But I am happy he has agreed to see us. I guess the title on my name card worked,' said the eternal assistant professor.

'If we let things go on as they are, he'll end up as a celebrity. We need to cut the root while we can,' said the barber.

'Kazuo mentioned a younger sister, but I wonder what she's like. If I have my way with her and get her pregnant, I guess she'll simply kill herself. But judging from the mother's looks when she came to the front door, she's not going to be much of a looker,' added the young bank clerk, who had taken off a few days in order to tag along.

The door opened and Jūichirō appeared. His guests were taken aback by his extremely drawn, pale face. He was dressed in a reddish-black cotton silk kimono patterned with a hexagonal design. The spectacles on his prominent nose, through which he took in the faces of the three visitors, glinted faintly like pools of water on a moonlit night. He sat down in a chair and, picking up a silver container from the table, took out one cigarette for himself before passing them around.

'How can I help?' asked Jūichirō quietly.

'It is nothing special,' answered Haguro courteously. He was struck by how extremely exhausted Jūichirō looked, in fact as tired as he himself felt. It occurred to him that they were both hoping for a situation in which at least one of them could stop being so shattered. 'It is just that you have been famous for a long time, even in Sendai, and we wanted to have the opportunity to speak with you.'

Just then, there was a knock at the door and Akiko brought in some tea and cakes. All three guests were startled by the beautiful figure she cut in her black one-piece dress. She had barely left the room before Kurita spoke up.

'I guess your daughter is human. Anyone who can carry human beauty like that must be.'

'Yes. My daughter is human.' A smile crossed Jūichirō's face for the first time. He had already guessed the purpose of their visit and, relieved by their misjudgement, played his trump card effortlessly. 'In that sense, she's different from me.'

'The fact that you have come straight to the point makes it easier to speak.' The professor pursed his lips as he sipped his tea. 'After all, the reason for our visit is to put our heads together as fellow extra-terrestrials and discuss how best to deal with the humans. By the way, Mr Ōsugi, I understand you come from Mars.'

'Ah, you already know. What about yourself?'

The barber's answer slipped out by rote.

'We come from an unknown planet somewhere in the binary star system 61 Cygni, in the constellation Cygnus.'

'Ah, Cygnus is not a very auspicious place to have come from.'

'Well, from a human viewpoint, it is not altogether inauspicious.' The professor laughed darkly. 'You see, we came to bring true repose to humanity.'

'How good of you to come from so far away to help,' was Jūichirō's riposte. 'But wouldn't it be better to leave the solar system to sort itself out?'

'That would be unfortunate for humans. It is because we love mankind that we are loath to let them carry on in their reckless way. Unlike you, we do not impose impossible conditions.'

'Impossible conditions?'

'Like this "peace" thing. But I am being too blunt. How about we just take some time this evening to ponder humanity and discuss how best to sort them out? We will reach a conclusion naturally.'

'We will reach a conclusion naturally,' echoed Jūichirō weakly. In the ensuing silence, his voice travelled as far as the unusually high ceiling of the small room, while the cigarette smoke of the aliens curled gently around the milky-white electric lampshade still bearing its load of darkish insect husks from the previous summer.

'First of all, I have considered a range of things in order to reach judgement on the flaws and evil practices of humanity.' The professor's tone was modest and scholarly. 'Humans have three fateful defects, what you might call three maladies. Their anxiety – what the Germans call *Sorge* – about things, their anxiety about people and their anxiety about God. If mankind could dispense with these three concerns, they might be able to avoid destruction. But as far as I can see, these three afflictions are incurable.

'Let me say something about how these conditions arise.

'As far as their anxiety about things is concerned, from childhood humans carefully hoard things like bent nails, spare buttons and beautiful pebbles. When they start going to school, they develop an interest in pencil cases, little satchels, erasers, baseball gloves, toy laser guns and the like. After they have grown up, they are drawn to cars and clothes and foreign revolutions. Once they marry, their interest turns to pipes, lawnmowers, stationery for the desktop at the office, and especially to money, stocks and shares. What we call human life depends upon a complex accumulation of things. Just consider the mass of empty boxes and tassels that a married woman collects. And once people have had their fill of things in the form of practical objects, they start collecting works of art and antiques. Or they develop a love of nature in its various forms. For humans, even nature, with all its flora and fauna, amounts to a kind of thing.

'Now, after a human being dies, a few prized items are placed in the coffin and burned along with the corpse. Most of the things he once showed an interest in continue to exist following the person's death. And so, whether we like it or not, it can hardly be denied that those items, once cherished or utilized, continue to exist longer than the person. Of course, a lot of things get consumed from one day to the next. However, while humans certainly live in a world of perishable things, they die without witnessing the point at which most of those objects truly come to an end. To be perfectly frank, the Nazi concentration camps demonstrated that the only objective value of human beings is in the form of soap, brushes or, at best, lampshades. Not a single human being after death has ever been converted into something as useful as an electric fan.

'Do you see? I am not only describing the material properties of the Earth as a celestial body, but also the triumph of inorganic matter. People love to gather in groups, but they cannot brush aside their unconscious sense of isolation when it becomes clear that "life" is simply the exception that proves the cosmic rules. In fact, people are particularly attached to objects and inorganic matter. Gold coins and jewels represent the epitome of heartlessness in opposition to human life and vitality, yet humans devote themselves to running after those objects, attaching human colour and the stench of humanity to them. Before long, people get used to these things and even end up discovering something essentially human within the circulation and regularity of things. Whether dealing with organic matter, a living, active cat, some incident caused by a human, or even a human being, it is only through recourse to the attributes of the thing itself that peace of mind is obtained. This is because such attributes make visible the thing's perishability, and create the external appearance of a "happiness" in which human concepts of permanence and will are jumbled together.

'In this way, human anxiety about things amounts to a constant desire to evade the irreversibility of time. It could be a gentleman with his favourite umbrella that he bought thirty years earlier in London, or a woman wearing the bathing suit *du jour* from this summer. Whether thirty years or one month, they find comfort through binding themselves to the physical representation of that time.

'Fundamentally, the human attempt to control things has always ended up with the final victory of things. If that were not so, why would so many unpleasant monuments, buildings and graves, made of stone and copper and steel, have been left behind on Earth? Ultimately, humans began to examine the nature of matter, and they discovered nuclear power. The hydrogen bomb is the most paradoxical attainment of humans, and human beings are now portraying this dangerous thing as the supreme "human" illusion.

'There is no need to elaborate on how this perversion came about. The incessant human anxiety about things has led people to imitate the solid external appearance of things, even to the point of turning humans and human relationships into things, so as to preserve human happiness. To give you just one example, the most beautiful friendship these days is between a man and his dog, while human relationships have all been reduced to committees. On the other hand, the hydrogen bomb appears on stage as humanity in its final form. That is because humans of today seem to have lost their power of mimicry, and every person attuned to the present human world harbours dreams that are inevitably hopeless.

'The bomb possesses a solitary, heroic, colossal, unfathomable strength, as well as the most modern, intellectual and modest of purposes. Destruction. It lives only moment by moment, is unaffiliated with past or present and, most importantly, embodies the exquisite ephemerality of a firework. A more idealistic form of "human" fantasy would be impossible to find. Its only purpose: the destruction of mine and thine. Ah, just like a verse from a beautiful song, don't you think? *Its only purpose: the destruction of mine and thine.*

'Humans will not be able to stop themselves from kissing this image of humanity at some point. Since the result is irrevocable, they will dance in circles around it for ages. However, there will come a time, inevitably, *inevitably*, when they cannot help but kiss that "human" limb. Let me be clear. At some point, humans will inevitably have to press their lips to it. With one brush of those lips, the dainty button on the limb will send the hydrogen warhead soaring effortlessly into the dawn sky. Ah, buttons again. *He* is not only human, but a button, too. What an idealistic existence. Humans are buttons discarded from childhood that have finally discovered their value.

'But there is more. One group of sentimental humanists wants to treat the hydrogen bomb as a "thing" to the very end. Humans have muddled heads, so they do not entirely rule out the possibility that they might consider even this "final human" as a thing, if only they make the effort. After all, humans have always done it that way. But one problem is that the hydrogen bomb still remains an incomplete thing. Human beings can only guarantee their own happiness if they live surrounded by things in their completed form. On that point, no one is less willing to compromise than humanists when it comes to their beloved pipes and walking clothes with leather elbow pads. At some point, they will inevitably invest the thing-like nature of the hydrogen bomb with a sense of completion. What do I mean by completion? Simply the act of pressing the button.'

Jūichirō looked down in silence, swallowing his sense of revulsion, but the barber responded with a light clapping of his sweaty hands.

'You are so right, Professor. The reason I cherish my wife and children, and love my beautiful family, is fundamentally because I am an extraterrestrial. It would not be the same if I were human. In fact, humans consider it good practice to be cold-hearted, especially when it comes to rich and famous families, and a really proficient gigolo regards women as things. They even say women find that more attractive. That's humanity in its most depraved form. At any rate, even when flirting with a woman you should wholeheartedly esteem her position as a human being, and shower her with warm affection. Of course, I simply take care of my own wife and children, and have no time for such things.'

Haguro flatly ignored his companion's concerns. 'Secondly,' he said, 'the malady of human anxiety about people.

'It is thought to manifest itself most directly through sexual desire, but actually sexual desire is not a source of humans' anxiety. Such desire involves the act of glimpsing into the twilight world between reproduction and destruction.

'But putting that aside, the extent to which people are constantly interested in others from dawn to dusk is astonishing. Every morning, the newspapers are crammed full of human-interest stories, and on television we see one human after another. When animals do make an occasional appearance, they are ascribed human characteristics to make them palatable. And people only talk about themselves. Even if the subject is natural phenomena like earthquakes, tsunamis or cherry blossoms coming into full bloom, everything is seen in terms of its impact on people. Nothing delights people more than to talk about people dying or being killed.

'And so, the truly universal, popular issue that really excites interest is always humans. Astronomy, mathematics, physics, chemistry. These are all left to a small handful of specialists, and they never create any enthusiasm among the masses. When it comes to "political" matters that the masses get so worked up over, whatever theory or structure you clothe the politics in, it is all about people, people, people, from beginning to end.

'For example, consider one of those dinner parties where humans indulge their anxiety about people. Words fly, there is an exchange of emotion, and everyone is happy. It feels as if they have all been old friends since the beginning of time, as if everything has melted together and everything is shared. But while that is taking place, the food picked from the same dishes and the wine poured from the same bottles make their way down each person's oesophagus to the total darkness of their stomach. The function of individual consumption continues at a pace with no relation whatsoever to the oesophagi or stomachs of others. If there is a gathering of eight guests, then the solitary, dark tubes of eight wastage systems, invisible under the bright candles, run through each individual body.

'Another example. Imagine a traffic accident in which a young woman has fallen to the ground, exposing her thighs. It happens to be a rainy night, and the rain spatters onto the blood gushing from her thighs, making it seem that she is wearing vivacious red mesh tights.'

The young bank clerk excitedly cut in with a lyrical outburst. 'How right you are! Humans are nothing but fountains of blood. If they fail to produce a fountain while still alive, the problem is just that the fountain has broken down and dried up. Pigeons approach humans in search of the fountain, but they all fly away, disappointed. Even a sweet, pure-white dove loves to splash its wings in red blood!'

'And all the surrounding rubberneckers,' continued the assistant professor calmly, 'stare long and hard at the distressed human girl with a mixture of bewilderment and delight. They are all aware that her suffering is non-transmissible, that each of them shoulders the "conditions" of suffering in their individual way.

'Human anxiety about people always takes the same form. While they share the same conditions of existence, they know very well that there is no such thing as common pain, and that mankind does not possess a single stomach. You will be familiar with how quickly women forget the pain of childbirth, and yet are convinced that no one else has ever experienced such pain. Each individual believes in all sincerity that their own experience of old age, sickness and death has no connection with the rest of mankind.

'Human beings are happy to acknowledge universality and a communal spirit when it comes to political slogans, ideas and other such things of no consequence. Harmless but pointless things, like musty old architecture and works of art, are easily categorized as a cultural legacy common to all mankind. But once suffering is involved, it becomes a real problem. If a political leader's back teeth begin to ache in the midst of a great speech, and the teeth of tens of thousands in his audience begin to ache in the same way, it means trouble.

'People endlessly discuss, watch and listen to others because it is the perfect way to soothe the conditions of human existence. People tolerate the existence of heroes because they know that every hero defecates in the same manner as everyone else.

'Humans get into a frenzy searching out other humans either in order to conclude that we are all the same, or to claim that, for good or ill, we are all different. They aim to confirm either the uniformity of all conditions of existence, or the sensuous reality of each individual.

'Let us call the former A, and the latter B. Those in the A camp all evoke thoughts of a world commonwealth. Their thoughts are rooted in nothing of consequence, they abandon themselves to a facile sense of universalism, and they espouse a unity that actually precludes real sharing. "People of the world, join hands!" "Let us eradicate racial prejudice!" These delusions all come from the A camp. But no matter how many hands you shake, as long as a white man does not fear that the pain felt in a black man's stomach will be transmitted to his own, what good is the shaking of hands? There is something a bit insensitive, yet strangely over-optimistic and saccharine, in the concept of a world commonwealth. Oh, and by the way, the fundamental ideals of a world commonwealth inevitably lead to a frightening endpoint. Since these ideals are premised upon an acceptance of the universal conditions of human existence, common consciousness will gradually find itself unable to bear the isolated circumstances of pain, discomfort and empty stomachs. Impatient people will become utterly contemptuous of a world commonwealth. Growing old alone in a world commonwealth will seem unfair. Why should it be wrong to proclaim one's own old age among a bunch of vivacious youngsters? People will find it intolerable if they are for ever defined as traitors simply for having rejected the concept of sharing. Surely the point is that people in a world commonwealth are born together, get old together, perish together. If the universal conditions of existence are the sole ideal underpinning this vast state, at some point that state will have to present the evidence.

'But people will not be able to endure returning to the isolated pain of their individual, sensuous existence. After all, a world state will have been established in which, fundamentally, it is possible to close one's eyes to such things and remain in ignorance.

'And then, they come up with the largest instantaneous, simultaneous policy of total destruction in history. *This* is the single piece of evidence of human strength that the world commonwealth can provide, and the sole opportunity to fully acknowledge the universal conditions of existence. When humans liken the suffering of that woman in the traffic accident to the universal conditions of human existence within themselves, they can only vaguely identify mutual links through the power of imagination. But with the hydrogen bomb, there is no need for imaginative power. This time, isolated suffering will cease to exist anywhere.

'Once humans have discovered the bomb as a means to carry out the instantaneous, simultaneous destruction of the world commonwealth, not much time and effort will be required. Bombs merely need to be placed around strategic points on the Earth's surface. Heads of state, either solemnly or on a whim, just have to press the button. Like throwing a garland at a ship-launching ceremony, or cramming pigeons into a festive paper ball. In an instant, the pigeons soar up and catch the dawn light . . . The end.

'And then we have those in the B camp who confirm the sensuous reality of each human individual. This group is driven by nationalistic ideals centred around both national and racial identities. In other words, their ideology is driven by pain. Unlike society at large, their ideas are disturbingly unconnected to destruction, and creepily wholesome. Their ideas are based fundamentally on individual appetites for food and sexual desire, an itchy dissatisfaction and, above all, pain. "For good or ill, I alone am different." "How could you understand the pain I feel?" These are the sort of assertions they make, and actually, there is no way others can really know their pain. Their way of thinking is for ever trapped inside their own suffering, and they are even happy to spill their own blood to prove the point. They get by without any power of imagination, but they do know how to appeal to the imaginative power of others.

'Since they believe in things that are impossible to communicate, there are even times when they forget the universal conditions of existence, confuse heroes with gods, and mistakenly interpret their own scabrous itching as a miracle. By miracle, I mean an individual sensuous entity transformed into universal form. If sticking a dagger into your own skin and producing a pain that makes you jump is the biggest exception in the history of mankind, how could that be anything but a miracle?

'However, the instinct for self-preservation provides unlimited protection for these people. Such an instinct always allows humans to feel secure in the unconditional belief they have harboured since childhood. Namely, their firm belief in the miracle that, whatever happens, they alone will be saved.

'If a man were to dash around under a hail of bullets, only he would avoid injury. If a train were suddenly involved in a collision and burst into flames, he alone would escape unscathed. If a jet crashed, only he would crawl out, uninjured, from the blackened corpses that lay scattered about. This is because the sensuous reality of each individual is something irreplaceable, more precious than a jewel, unique to the world, impervious to destruction.

'Before long, for good or ill, the ideas forged in the B camp enter upon a dangerous experiment. The miracle must be substantiated. Some trivial incident leads to thoughts of major destruction, and the scale of destruction accumulates like building a snowman. Finally, it gets to the point where, even when the destruction of all mankind looms, people can envisage a scenario in which just one person, or the single race of a nation, is saved. It is impossible to conceive of a more alluring or attractive scene than that. In such a situation, the only thing to be done is to press the button. They simply *have* to press the button.

'So, you see, when it comes to human anxiety about people, whichever side you are on, ultimately your only choice is to press the button.'

Kurita, who had been grimacing for some time, cut in before Haguro could finish.

'Professor, I don't like the way you've excluded the matter of sexual desire. It's not so much the destruction of all mankind I'm interested in, but the destruction of all women. Even while women lie on their backs with their legs open, they find men utterly contemptuous, and yet men feel the urge to reproduce with them. There's obviously something ominous and dark about mankind.'

'You're talking of women, but wives and children are an exception,' the barber broke in. 'Provided human wives have splendid husbands, they never fail to show respect, although it can lead to trouble if both man and woman are human . . .'

Professor Haguro ignored this idle exchange and continued to elaborate his theory to Jūichirō, whose head was still nodding silently.

'Thirdly, the fateful malady that is human anxiety about God.

'What we call God was a really cunning invention. It came about by placing ninety per cent of knowledge attained by humans into the realm of mankind, and by entrusting the remaining ten per cent to the management of God. The point where human knowledge shifts ambiguously into a vast emptiness was placed in the manager's hands. Humans could not bear the loneliness of standing guard at the frontiers of human knowledge. And so, the mercenaries that we call God assumed the role of guards in exchange for immense reverence and monetary offerings at the altar. As the borders of human knowledge expanded, the frontier guard outposts became increasingly distant. The citizens of the capital could no longer easily see the mercenaries' faces. However, people held firmly to the old belief that the mercenaries were still there in their distant posts, keeping people safe. Humans were reminded of this every time they saw a distant rainbow at dawn. They imagined the white-bearded mercenaries blowing trumpets in their faraway barracks, their polished spear tips in rows, as they formed lines in the compound before the break of day.

'People delight in describing God as Truth and Justice. But God is not actually Truth, or Justice, or even God. God is nothing more than a manager, designed to maintain the ambiguous seam between human knowledge and nothingness, blurring the borders between reality and the unreal. The reason for this is that humans cannot bear any chasm between existence and non-existence. Because, once the concept of "the absolute" has arisen in a person's mind, the gap between the relativity of all things in the world and "the absolute" becomes insufferable. Somehow, the border guards stationed far away seem to link together the world of relativity and the absolute. And all they have for weapons and protective helmets are the hard work and financial support of humans.

'These mercenaries have been working hard for thousands of years, and humans have never lost touch with them. The philosophers of Scholasticism prattled on about the bogus, finite existence of humans, and about God alone being in possession of true existence. Fear that the mercenaries might not exist was all that was needed to generate the feeble power of their human imagination.

'But what if every mercenary disappeared? Nothingness would immediately breach the frontier and destroy the towns built by human knowledge, inundating the houses of the capital right up to their windows. When people awoke in the morning, washed their faces and opened the windows, only nothingness would be visible out there. When they scampered downstairs, they would tumble headlong into the abyss. If they lifted the lid to the pickle tub, the jet-black face of nothingness would stare right back at them. Any attempt to arrange flowers in a vase would lead to the flowers falling straight down through the bottom of the vase into nothingness.

'Everything would lead to nothingness. If you sent a telegram, it would be delivered into nothingness and never come back. Every train leaving the station at dawn would chunter off into nothingness, never to return. Human voices would be changed into eternal echoes, and every cry would be soaked up by nothingness, like blotting paper. If you opened a window and threw a body out, it would slither down into nothingness, so that murderers would never have to worry about handling corpses.

'Such were the human misgivings and the high price that the mercenaries extracted from their masters. And humans always listened with delight to the phoney reports of the border guards. The guards were just managing things, but they made false claims about bravely engaging in endless sporadic skirmishes.

'This is my rough sketch of the web of lies centred around God in human culture. Thanks to their relationship with God, humans have somehow managed to avoid directly confronting nothingness, non-existence and the absolute. And so, even now, humans are almost entirely ignorant about nothingness in its true sense. Humanism still clings to a foolish, blind belief that the totally destructive theory of nothingness did not arise from within human culture, that human knowledge is incapable of creating nothingness.

'But is that really so? When nothingness proceeds downstairs to the ground floor, it keeps on falling straight into the abyss. You try to create an arrangement of flowers in a vase, and you end up sending them flying into the chasm. In other words, the very moment you instigate a purposeful, wilful act, that act is betrayed, the purpose is exceeded, and action tumbles endlessly into meaninglessness. You dive into meaninglessness as if that was always your intention. Every small blunder is swallowed up into a giant pool of destruction. This has been happening throughout time in the human world, and it constitutes the essence of nothingness.

'It has been taking place all over the world from the beginning of the twentieth century. But human beings, ever ignorant of the true nature of nothingness, still believed they were protected by God, by those border guards. These small events, repeated here, there, and everywhere were what you might call the preliminary *esquisses* of nothingness. And scientific technology lit the fuse of ubiquitous nothingness with eerie accuracy. Now, scientific technology is not as rational as humans think. Rather, it is an opaque impulse in abstract form, the systemization of the human nightmare since the days of alchemy. When humans dream of the appearance of an unforeseen monster, scientific technology offers confirmation that humans have already anticipated that monster. And so, the day finally arrives to realize the emptiness in which humans are already steeped. Like a crazy, giant rose with deep-red petals, nothingness is cultivated by the human hand for the first time. I am talking about the hydrogen bomb.

'However, since human beings still believe that God is responsible for the management of nothingness, they feel relaxed about pressing the button. They make the sign of the cross, say their prayers, completely exculpate themselves from responsibility and press the button without hesitation.

'No matter how it plays out, or whichever of the three maladies we examine, humans are geared inevitably to press the button.'

'Oh, poor little button!' Taking advantage of a pause in the professor's flow, the barber stifled a yawn and burst into song. 'When you press the buttons on the cute girl's boobs, Two lovely mushroom clouds spring into view. Wow, buttons so fast, they're something new!'

'Uggh!' The professor reined in the barber's little intrusion and kept his eyes on Jūichirō, who seemed about to open his mouth. But Jūichirō was not quite ready to speak.

The tired parlour was hushed, as if empty of people. In fact, it contained no humans.

Evening had already fallen outside, and the light inside the room was wrought into the window glass. The shadows of the three guests remained motionless, like three large crouching birds set against the faded wallpaper.

'What you say is correct. It's sad to say, but humans act exactly as you describe.' Jūichirō's words brought an exaggerated look of surprise from Haguro.

'So, you mean, you agree with me?'

'Yes, you've put your finger on human weaknesses. But what I'd like to ask is what you intend to do about them?'

'Can't you tell? If we are of the same mind, we should do all we can to ensure they press the button. It would be pitiful to leave them in limbo.'

'Because the professor is burning with love for humankind, he wants to euthanize the whole lot as soon as possible,' Kurita chipped in from the side.

Jūichirō pondered the matter for a while, and said: 'Can't you think of some other way to help them?'

'No, I can't. Leaving them as they are only invites suffering,' asserted Professor Haguro with a truly human degree of academic coldness.

9

The three from Sendai were surprised by Jūichirō's commendably accommodating attitude, and exchanged glances with each other. This feeble man's efforts to save the world not only cast the world in a poor light, but also showed contempt for their mission.

Jūichirō looked down at the musty woven tablecloth modelled after the Star Mandala of Hōryūji Temple. All humanity seemed to have huddled together inside the circle of the mandala, trembling before Haguro's excoriating criticisms, while Jūichirō looked down, eyes brimming with sadness, at their minuscule figures.

'It's just as you say.' Jūichirō gradually recovered his regular straightforward tone of voice. 'Humans are desperate to push the button. At a press conference on the eighth of February, President Kennedy suggested they would be resuming nuclear testing. That was about two months ago. And you can be certain that British nuclear tests on Christmas Island will restart any time now. This will inevitably encourage Soviet testing, and the world may end up covered in radioactive dust. If tests do take place on Christmas Island, I'm sure to write another letter right away to Kennedy to warn him. But I can't see myself getting a reply, any more than I did from Khrushchev.'

Haguro broke in with a confident look. 'Obviously! Humans are not designed to write such a reply. If they ever tried, all the ink on Earth would freeze up.'

'You're right, you're right,' Jūichirō calmly continued. 'I am already perfectly aware of what a strange undertaking it is to try to bring peace to mankind. At least most of the world is not in a state of war at the moment, and therefore at peace. But at the same time, there is a deep yearning for peace. People pray for it. They are impatient for it. The absurdity of waiting for something that already exists suggests that the people yearning for peace are not satisfied with the version they have at the moment. They are seeking a more complete, anxiety-free form of peace. But what may really dissatisfy them is not peace as it exists at the moment, but the essential nature of peace.

'Peace, like freedom, is a fish caught from our extraterrestrial sea. The moment it is landed on the Earth, it rots. The essential characteristic of peace on Earth is the speed with which it deteriorates, and this is what they find so dissatisfying. They constantly seek either a fresh, instantaneous peace, or a metallic, imperishable peace that will go on for ever. All sluggish, in-between versions of peace stink of phoniness.

'On top of that, their animal instincts approve of forms of peace that tend to arise only after a particular event. Peace after some victory, peace after a battle, post-coital peace. These are the only forms they intuitively recognize as true peace. The peace we have now, by the way, is a precursor to the event, extremely opaque and a total sham.

'Part of humanity agitates to stop war and to maintain peace, but their concept of peace is intertwined with this very human sense of dissatisfaction and impatience. What would really satisfy these people is instantaneous peace after the event, but their desire for such peace is premised on their wish for the event to take place. By "event" here, I am referring to nuclear war.

'Mankind is still a long way off from being able to conquer time. And so, human concepts of peace and freedom link together with, but are also fettered by, the principle of time. The irreversibility of time is a fateful factor that renders human peace and freedom extremely problematic.

'Mankind would be able to attain peace and freedom immediately if the laws of time crumbled, if the post-event became the pre-event, and the instantaneous blended into eternity. In such a moment, absolute peace and freedom would appear, and their authenticity would be unquestionable.

'To savour the future in the present age. To taste the moment in eternity. These abilities are commonplace to extraterrestrials. The reason I came to Earth was to pass them on to humans so that they can use them as weapons in the attainment of peace and universal unity.

'I have sought to give humans a clear vision, from the perspective of the present moment in time, of what the Earth would look like after a nuclear war. To let them savour right now an instantaneous rapture in their hearts that would reveal the terrifying, inorganic, eternal peace in the immediate aftermath of such a war. If my aim was successful, humans would be able to savour with their own tongues the utter freshness of peace in a post-event world. In tasting it, no person on Earth would any longer feel a need to press the button. I decided to give them some delicious sake to drink that had the force of an anaesthetic. On that point, you might say I'm just a hair's breadth away from you and your ideas about euthanasia.

'My plan was to employ the human power of imagination. But what I discovered was the amazing paucity of this faculty in them. Even the steeliest man cannot bear to portray the fantasy of total ruin. That's because people on Earth have only the feeblest understanding of the word "ruin". Even when some petty civil servant absconds with a measly three million yen of public money and is thrown into prison, they call it "personal ruin".

'I've done everything I can to inspire the fantasy of destruction in humans. And yet, they lack even the tiniest fraction of my own powers of imagination. This is true even among Japanese, who experienced the tragedy of Hiroshima, so you can imagine what other countries are like.

'I tried appealing to their imagination by emphasizing fantasies of destruction and peace in equal measure until they ended up looking like mirror images of each other. I continued until people were convinced that one side was an image in the mirror, and the other was absolutely real. The flying saucers appeared in order to evoke human reasoning. In bringing humans to a sense of reason, my purpose was to get them to rationally conclude that they were simply intoxicated with the image on the other side of the mirror. And that intoxication amounted to the final denial of human reasoning: the collapse of the irreversibility of time, the collapse of their inability to see into the future. In other words, the very denial of desire as a possibility. After all, all human desire is rooted in time. It is said that pure human reasoning is equivalent to all the innate cognitive abilities that make experiences possible, and human experiences operate in accordance with the rules of desire. Namely, time.

'I tried to sketch out for humans a sense of intoxication about which they had remained unaware until now. A rapture in which the present moment blossoms, the human world instantly blazes with light, and the dew on the grass in front of them is suddenly transformed into gems.'

'So, have they managed to understand?' said the professor, with a smirk on his face.

'No, not yet.'

'So, there you have it.'

'But I still have hope.'

'Hope!?' exclaimed the professor, as if Jūichirō had suddenly taken on the face of a pig.

'Of course, humans lack the qualifications to have hope. But *we* are qualified. Because we control time, which is born out of hope.'

'We are no different from you,' Haguro interrupted impatiently. 'So how does your foresight differ from ours? You and I represent two opposing principles in the universe, both of which conquered time and escaped fear ages ago, and the single, ultimate political principle we have been left with is a simple smile. I acknowledge that there is some difference between a dark smile and a bright smile, but if our two species share the same foresight about the Earth, we have nothing to quarrel over. But Mr Ōsugi, what about the future of the Earth and mankind *that you seem so intimate with*? Please, do spell it out tonight in black and white. What do you see happening? What does the future hold for the Earth and mankind? We have nothing to hide from each other, you and I, so please speak frankly.'

Jūichirō was not forthcoming. His face stiffened, and he fixed his gaze on a spot. The only parts of his enervated body that shone with an indomitable strength were the pupils of his eyes, in which dark flames seemed to flicker. The utter tension in his body was evidently the product of his grim determination to fasten the doors of his heart and to deny access to the secrets of his own foresight. His forehead grew sweaty, his lips dried, and he seemed to be suffering from shortness of breath.

'You know. But you cannot answer. And why is that? Because you are being deceitful. Because we came to tell earthlings how things really were, whereas you came to play some sweet little trick on them. You don't feel able to tell them about *that*, do you? You want to pull the wool over their eyes and lead them, blind, in the direction you'd like them to go.'

'No, you're wrong!' cried Jūichirō, distraught. There was an unpleasant dissonance in his voice, which seemed to emerge from a dark abyss that straddled the spaces between the dazzling, diffuse nebulae. 'I do not speak of my foresight because, the very moment I utter it, it will become the fate of mankind on Earth.

'My mission is to still the hearts of impatient humans, but I don't want them to attain that stillness as if it were preordained. My way, as best I can, is to let them discover it through intoxication, through quiet, utterly desireless intoxication.

'Human politics involves forever making obscene allusions about the future, like flashing a woman's thighs. Or dangling the bait of dreams, hopes and "something better", just as you might dangle carrots in front of a horse's muzzle. Or whipping humans towards a dark future. That's what I'm trying to stop in this twilight of the present age . . . I just need to get their politics to settle into a state of intoxication for a while.'

'Huh. Human politics?' snorted Haguro, venting his frustration in the same tone he used during his many years engaged in Sendai university politics. 'It was always a mistake to let humans govern themselves. You might as well put woodlice in charge.'

'No, you're wrong. Governing people is easy. All you need is to govern the nothingness and void within them. All humans have wind-holes, orifices in their bodies that the wind passes through. If you thread the holes with string and connect the people all together, they will follow quietly in their millions.'

'Another wacky theory.'

'It's what I've learned about life on Earth. I've often seen people on a park bench or in a crowded train looking straight down, gazing into space. They look as if they're staring into the hollowness within themselves. You can see it clearly in their eyes. As if they're facing a loneliness that will never lead to any kind of unity or consolidation. What I've witnessed is an anti-political expression typical of humans, even the most stupid of them.

'Throughout history, politics has basically centred upon various ways to provide bread, but what made politicians more savvy than religious figures was their recognition that humans live by bread alone. This insight was very precious. No matter how much religious figures bleated on, humans planted themselves firmly in the camp of biology, and they devised a range of wholesome and lucid political sciences.

'Have you never considered how disappointed humans must have been when they directly confronted the simple conditions of human existence, when they became aware that all they needed to survive was bread? They must have been the first humans on Earth to contemplate suicide. Imagine a man who, after some sad incident, determines to kill himself tomorrow. Today, with some hesitation, he eats his bread. After much thought, he postpones suicide until the day after next. The next day, too, he eats bread in some trepidation. He keeps delaying things day after day, and every day he eats his bread . . . One particular day, he suddenly realizes that he can live an aimless and meaningless life on bread alone. He is alive right now, and it is all thanks to bread. There is no greater truth than that. He is seized by a terrifying despair, but his despair will never be resolved through suicide. After all, he is not in despair about being alive, which is the usual cause of suicide, but despair about life itself. Increasingly, despair is what sustains him.

'He has to make something out of this despair. He needs to replace suicide with something unique in order to take his revenge on cool-headed political knowledge. He comes up with the idea of surreptitiously creating pointless wind-holes in his body without letting on to the politicians. All sorts of meaning spill out of the holes.

Only the consumption of bread continues unabated. The eternal search for the next piece of bread, and the next, and the next. The political rulers themselves may not know it, but they are duty bound to keep the people supplied with bread in order to guarantee the meaninglessness of their existence. But the people are obliged never to let their rulers in on the secret.

'This hollowness. These wind-holes. Before you know it, they have insinuated themselves into the very genes of human nature, spreading far and wide, leading to the anti-political expression that I've seen on park benches and in busy trains.

'Rulers love structure, and they build tasteless towers in every corner of the Earth. But, having looked deeply into things, I finally came to realize that under their splendid clothes small wind-holes exist even in the bodies of these powerful people.

'It was after I made this discovery that I found it possible to contemplate peace and unity for mankind, here and now, on Earth. I'm hesitant to say it, but during my residence here as a human being, wind-holes have miraculously opened up in my body too.

'I've even come to think that these conditions, shared by all humans as they confront destruction, are a blessing bestowed by the Universe. By which, I mean that hollowness and wind-holes represent our Universe in miniature.'

'Oh, I see. You've given me some food for thought. It is nothing but the next piece of bread, the next piece of bread, the next piece of bread. So all that human politicians have to do is to conspire together and mix potassium cyanide into the next loaf.'

'No. No matter how malicious the politicians, the moment they're in a position to form a conspiracy, world peace will be established. Your scheme would simply end up being outmanoeuvred.

'When all humans fill their inner void en masse, all politics loses meaning and an anti-political union becomes possible. They will never press the button. Because pressing the button means the disintegration of their Universe, of their inner hollowness. Even people who do not fear the destruction of their own bodies cannot contemplate the destruction of the void. After all, that void is patterned on the maternal nothingness of the Universe.'

'What led you to trust so much in these wind-holes?'

'It's from my experience as a human being. At first, I thought I was the only one who possessed them, but eventually I realized that I had uncovered an unmistakable sign of the Universe's infiltration into every member of humanity. I just waited for that void to bloom, and I finally saw it happen.'

'Stupid! Right now, people on Earth are engaged in love and pro-creation. At this very moment when you discuss unity, that lot are working hard at the disintegration of the individual.'

'Women. I hate them!' exclaimed the big, ugly bank clerk, having finally found his way in. 'If women were exterminated, the extinc-tion of humanity would be just a matter of time. It wouldn't take much effort to finish off half of humankind. But how do we manage to gather all the women of the world together? Women twitter and cackle away, but they never listen to a word they're told.'

'You could put all the world's beauty salons in the southern hemi-sphere, and all barber shops in the northern hemisphere. Simple,' said the plump barber, with a wriggle of his nose.

Jūichirō continued calmly. 'It was a political swindle, that religion of humans, which linked together love and procreation. Like every other kind of political swindle, that linkage was just a simple hum-drum method of driving a flock of sheep into a pen, pressing what originally had no purpose into a consciousness of purpose. Sexual desire towards others is like fumbling around in the slippery dark. But once you let your hands grasp the candle of love, which is sup-posed to be the pinnacle of purposeful consciousness, it creates the illusion that a clear light has been thrown on the sublime object of your desire. But there is no evidence that what you see is actually what you've been grasping for until now. Maybe the candlelight has shown up something else.

'Human beings have grown accustomed to procreating under the light of this candle. We must take them from that site of loveless, spectacular procreation to a place in the dark, ancient Universe where procreation is performed.

'And the reason we need to do that is because political swindling, which has endured for so long, is a major cause of war on Earth.

While political leaders were still young men, they learned in their beds why conflating desire and the virtual image of love was a mistake. They got wind of their barren ideals from all their shenanigans under the candlelight.

'There has never been a time like now, when the leaders of two great countries are moving away from the cool calculation which used to produce sound rulers. It's almost as if they're *in love* with something. How else could they aim for all those triumphs that offer little hope of success, like the crazy competition over nuclear testing, or producing a surplus of atomic bombs? You might as well dump truckloads of banknotes into a dark, bottomless pit every day.

'Ironically, the absurdity of love arises because what you wait for never comes, and your wishes are never fulfilled. And yet, things remain beyond our grasp precisely because love is structured by the acts of waiting and wishing. Most dangerous is the fact that neither of the two great leaders has any wish for destruction. Since they're in love, something they have no desire for will inevitably emerge. And it's already begun. Their love of destruction is growing.

'And so, as I've repeatedly warned, we've reached an age in which the powers of imagination are less tainted by madness than the powers of reason. I've tried to encourage people to move towards the imagination in order to separate them a little from the madness, but it's all been in vain. "Trust in human reason," they say. "Now we have weapons of mass destruction, there will be no war." They just don't realize the madness of their trust.

'But I still have hope. Human beings may be a different kettle of fish, but I at least am qualified to hope.

'Humans are delightful creatures. A man goes next door to complain about a noisy party the night before and is about to press the bell in an angry state, when he spies a cute little snail in the thicket inside the porch following a rainfall. The discovery delights him, and he ends up returning home without lodging his complaint. These human creatures can't stop themselves from doing things like that. Or, someone takes a stroll along a path and suddenly decides to buy a pot of flowers . . .'

'Pot of flowers? Pot of flowers? I bet they're cyclamens!' shouted

Kurita as he began to rise from his chair, face pale, training his bloodshot eyes on Jūichirō.

'They don't necessarily have to be cyclamens. In any case, this person buys a pot of flowers. As he walks along, thinking about which window he'll display them in at home, he finds himself at a street corner he doesn't recognize. He drops into a corner bar, and the sake cups pile up so that in the end he forgets to take the flowers home. That's another thing they can't stop themselves from doing.

'Fickleness is a virtue that humans obtained from the heavens. Sometimes, fickleness provides a glimpse of the sweetest substance that the heavens can offer. This substance resembles one of those sighs that the well-ordered Universal Law occasionally exhales, or a profound poem. The substance is a gift bestowed upon humans by the distant Universe. To borrow the terminology of human religion, it's the only angelic quality that humans possess.

'A human holds a gun to someone's face, ready to shoot, but just as he's about to fire, something opens in his heart and he swiftly turns away. Fickleness is so strange. He finds himself below the window of his lover, whom he is looking forward to embracing that very night. But just as he is about to climb the rope ladder, an inexplicable, breezy fickleness assails his heart, and he suddenly embarks on a long journey into the desert. Many such beautiful examples of fickleness are riddles that even humans cannot work out. Perhaps these riddles can only be solved by honey bees when they confront a mass of roses. After all, fickleness is the recognition that all roses are the same, that other roses exist apart from those directly ahead of them, that the world is teeming with roses.

'It is because I trust in human reason that I still cling to hope. Because humans put their trust in these beautiful moments of fickleness. You say humans will definitely press the button. That is a possibility. But you might also catch a capricious smile on their faces just as they are about to do it. That's what it means to be human.'

'We are agreed on that point. Sometimes they press the button out of fickleness.'

'That would be madness, not fickleness.'

'OK. If, as you say, pressing the button is madness and not pressing it is an act of fickleness, that would mean it is reasonable to distinguish between madness and fickleness when you have the button in your hands, right? And yet, you claim that reason is madness. In which case, how does the reason of madness distinguish itself from fickleness when it comes to pressing the button? I would like to hear you get out of that one. You have fallen into a self-contradiction, in which you must acknowledge that any judgement about whether or not to press the button involves the operation of reason. The fact is, you have come to realize that, if pushing the button represents the reason of madness, then coming to a decision on whether to act, by pushing the button, is the operation of sober reasoning. Don't you think it funny that there are two kinds of reason?'

Jūichirō responded. 'Human reason lacks the ability to come to a decision. It's just that they are physically capable of pressing the button. They can do it with conviction and a cool head. Like idiots.

'How strange that an extraterrestrial like you, Professor, tired of seeing human suffering, still talks in terms of human logic.

'Earlier you were kind enough to explain the three defects, the three maladies found in humans. I believe it's my turn to raise the five human virtues, the five special qualities that I'm loath to see destroyed. The reality is that humans have numerous strange traits, but there are several I'd really love to keep. In my opinion, there is value in saving the whole of mankind if only to keep these traits.

'But even if mankind does perish, at least I can do the decent thing by expressing the five virtues in a few words on a tombstone. The stone would have to provide an account of all human accomplishment, in a thoroughly summarized form, but covering every conceivable aspect of human history. Here is my proposed draft:

> Here sleeps the human species.
> They ended up lying all the time,
> They offered up flowers for both good and bad fortune,
> They often kept small birds,
> They were frequently late getting to appointments
> And they often laughed.
> May they rest for ever in eternal peace.

'Translated into your language, it would go something like this:

> Here sleeps the human species, inhabitants of planet
> Earth.
> They were highly artistic,
> They represented joy and grief in equal measure,
> They revoked other forms of freedom and, by doing so,
> only just managed to recognize the relativity of their own
> freedom,
> Unable to conquer time, at least they endeavoured to
> remain disloyal to time,
> And sometimes, for a few moments, they knew how to
> exhale nothingness.
> May they rest for ever in eternal peace.

'I expect you'd think it marvellous to set up a stone for them afterwards. I, of course, would prefer to do it beforehand. After all, I lack the interest in money-making, or in fake, shiny things that motivates you visitors from Cygnus. And besides, if we did it beforehand, we'd end up with a portrait of extraterrestrials from far and wide embracing each other with open arms, don't you think?

'Humans offered up flowers for both auspicious and inauspicious events. In the extravagant waste of these fragile cut flowers, they acknowledged the momentary nature of good fortune, while at the same time earnestly hoping that misfortune, too, might be short-lived. And they looked after little birds too. It was a small vice, but their motive was so lovely and heartfelt that the vice turned into a sweet virtue. They captured the flight of the skies in a small basket. The birds, who had once roamed carefree across the glittering sky, now lay folded up in baskets as if entangled in invisible thread. Still tied to memories of flight, the birds merely shifted uncomfortably. But human beings ultimately purified the song of birds. The birds never forgot those songs, which constituted a crystallized version of stolen freedom. The songs reduced all the blue skies for which they had ever grieved into a single concept. An endless quivering of direct, naked feeling. And they made humans happy. It was a human invention to do things this way.

'A crowd waits in the rain in front of the station. A host of people waits in a dark café. A company director impatiently awaits visitors in his spacious boardroom, staring hard at his ultra-thin Audemars Piguet watch. Is there anything more human than these scenes? Humans are gifted with the most amazing privilege. The ability to keep others waiting. Keeping women on tenterhooks was a tried-and-tested method for male sovereigns to maintain power over their female romantic interests. But even so, women preserved the maturation of time within their own physical bodies. Do you follow me? The womb is an organ of time. And in their search for freedom and peace, they allied themselves with a more profitable kind of time. In their capacity both to wait upon others and to keep others waiting, women possessed flexible natural talents that could not be equalled by men. They absorbed the laws of time into their bodies, while sneering from the sidelines at men, who are so full of ambition and plans about making history.

'Humans created the arts. They have constructed numerous vain, frivolous buildings. From our extraterrestrial perspective, every serious, tragic piece of work they ever produced seems ultimately to have emerged from one principle peculiar to humans. Laughter. Laughter is at the very root of their art. Without laughter, those endless lies told by humans would have just rotted away. Artists discovered that laughter protects lies from decay.

'All those lies associated with human life – the falsehoods, the betrayals, the insincerity – must have strengthened artists in their conviction that all reality could be substituted for lies. The artists realized that those lies humans call truth rotted easily, like fish. When searching for material that would prevent such decay, they discovered that laughter acted as a kind of mortar. But, in fact, this innate human principle was something they learned from nature.

'I bet you, the first time that humans burst into laughter was when they saw the morning sun rise above a mountain ridge to create sudden shifts of colour on its lower reaches. Because there's nothing logical in the way universal nothingness delights the human eye with its fine gradations of colour. It is strange, and it is laughable. Every time nothingness revealed its clownish shapes, they laughed. They watched how the gentle breeze, racing across the plain, made the woolly coats of a flock of sheep stand up, and they laughed. Because such a trivial incident in the great ocean of nothingness is a joke. It was only when they laughed that they experienced nothingness as a kind of absence. And this so-called nothingness cured them.

'Before long, humans began to create their own reasons for laughter. But behind their laughter inevitably lurked the shadow of nothingness. Without that nothingness, the drama of human laughter remained incomplete. Inevitably, across the stage of this drama, unnamed major players passed, whose role was to be blown away with laughter.

'. . . Well, that's my bird's-eye view of human life and history. I guess I have nothing more to say. Humans paint a rather loveable picture, so wouldn't it be a source of regret to see them disappear from the Universe?'

'You haven't finished yet,' snapped the bank clerk. 'What happened to love and marriage?'

'Love and marriage are covered by the words on the tombstone. Lying, being late for appointments, offering up flowers, keeping small birds in cages for their whole lives, and finally, laughing before they die.'

'So, what about finances?'

'The fact that they are frequently late for their appointments affects all manner of things relating to profit and laws of obligations.'

The group from Sendai exchanged looks, and then fell quiet. Jūichirō drew strength from their momentary silence.

'I'm not saying you ought to respect humans, or to consider them important. The culture they have left behind is a measly, third-rate affair from the perspective of the Universe. And if the human economic distribution system is primitive, its political system ranks among the worst in the Universe. Even so, if we do these folks a favour and save them, there may come a day when they benefit the Universe.'

'You fool,' said Haguro with a curl of his lips. 'How could we fail to pluck the dangerous bud while we still have time? Humans have already flown beyond the Earth's gravitational pull. You are out of your depth here.

'In the ancient human world, a single powerful person would take upon himself a vast amount of evil, and represent that evil as both pleasure and pain. He would win the public's acclaim. Naturally, the people were given their share. At the Roman colosseum, tens of thousands partook in the pleasure of the powerful ruler by participating in unadulterated evil. The sight of gory deaths gave pleasure to some, while other people found it painful. But in either case, it liberated life from its source. But what happens now? When the atomic bomb was dropped on Hiroshima, who among humans was filled with pleasure, or pain, and found liberation? No one.

'Instead, the wretched executioners of days past now have full-time jobs in order to provide food. Executioners became pathetic married men who handed over their pain and pleasure and responsibility to powerful people. As heads of miserable households, their numbers increased hugely, and they could be found in any office. Given the mechanical industrialization of evil, this was inevitable. People became a race of white-collar workers, and the powerful hairy arms of the blacksmith were no longer needed. At the same time, mass-produced goods became simplified, effortless and functional, while the elaborate ornaments and the overbearing master craftsmen from the age of hand-made industry were now surplus to requirements. How did Auschwitz differ from a cannery or a chemical factory?

'Evil was rendered so abstract that the direct sight of blood became a rarity, and everything was wrapped in hygienic packaging. On the other hand, no one could participate fully in evil any more. This was true even of those in power. People who threw themselves into evil acts, and the guarantors of their evil, no longer existed. What I find so interesting is the fact that this sorry state of affairs differed in no way to those human wind-holes you described, the ones that hold sway over even a sovereign.

'In the colosseum, there was such a wealth of evil that you could weigh it by the fistful on scales. But now, there is not enough to go around. No longer limited to places like the colosseum, evil has spread throughout the world and quietly insinuated itself into the hearts of all. Humans now exist in a society of peaceful, homely, submissive executioners, who enjoy doing a bit of work on the house at weekends. They discuss fertilizers and lawn-mowers, and the only taboo topic of conversation is the work they get paid for.

'The pleasure and pain of evil once thrilled the human heart, but everything has been turned inwards, like smouldering embers in a banked fire. Present-day society has been reorganized into an enormously frustrating system. The single expression that epitomizes contemporary human society, more than any other time in history, is "a society that craves blood". Human society today has a thirst for blood deeper even than the time of a cruel empire like Genghis Khan's. But while people grasp for untrammelled evil, no one really gets their full share, and evil fails to provide any feeling of liberation. On a Sunday afternoon, a man takes his family to a concert in the park even as he burns with a thirst for blood.

'This is the most unnatural society in history. If only we set our minds to it, we could easily devise ways to incite people into sudden action. One way to describe human pain nowadays is as a series of senseless death pangs produced by a shallow and frighteningly universal version of evil. Not to put people out of their misery through euthanasia as soon as possible would be a dereliction of duty. It is so obvious. We have to do it!'

Jūichirō interrupted. 'Extraterrestrials are never taken in by the fallacy of human progress. And I have my own misgivings about humans who fall for it. But that delusion is not an essential characteristic of humanity. I know where the spaceship steered by humans is headed. The fact is, it seems to be thrusting forward into the dark future of the Universe, but it is also regressing headlong into the abyss of long-forgotten human memories. It represents not only the adventure of future human experiences, but also the re-emergence of those dark, unfathomable, commonly shared primordial experiences. In human consciousness, the Universe has a double structure. The place they eternally aim for, and the place to which they forever return. It's in the same way that human men are attracted to women who also represent something maternal.

'Inevitably, every human step forward is also a step backwards. Consequently, they never arrive and they never fully return. But this is *their* Universe. We don't need to fear it, or worry about how it might harm our own. That should be abundantly clear.

'My duty is to save them, and I just need to soldier on with that task, whatever happens. I offer visions full of destruction, and I've had my fill of them. I need to persuade mankind to end all nuclear testing and to abandon all nuclear weapons. To make them understand why flying saucers visit the Earth. After meeting you, I'm convinced that the ominous shadow that has been hanging over the Earth this century is in many ways due to the activities of you and your colleagues from Cygnus. I can see the malign influence of your stars in preventing the Earth from being reborn as a *beautiful star*.

'Your species has mixed with renowned politicians, philosophers and artists from the beginning of the twentieth century, assiduously preparing the ground for present-day conditions. There are many indications to back that up. I may have been a latecomer to Earth but, let me tell you, I didn't arrive too late.

'You have inveigled yourselves into what humans believe to be their honest passion. You have wormed your way into what they call righteousness on this Earth, reducing it to nothing but an empty shell. It's ringing in my ears so clearly right now. The sound of you and your friends in this world, secretly nibbling away at the wood like termites. Actually, I began to hear that noise ages ago. Stupid humans believed that their ears were playing tricks on them.'

'He's really going for us, isn't he?' The barber was scrutinizing Jūichirō's reddish-black silk kimono as it hung from his lean chest. It was an elegant item of clothing casually worn, and Sone's tone became increasingly aggressive as he attempted to estimate its cost. 'Professor Haguro, may I give this guy a piece of my mind? He calls me a termite, but what has a termite got to do with a barber who works his guts out to earn a living? Now, someone who attracts people with a dodgy oracle and wangles donations from the pockets of the poor, that's the kind I call a termite.'

The assistant professor flashed his friend a sympathetic smile before fixing his eyes on Jūichirō, who, exhausted from talking, had sat back into his chair and raised his shoulders with a sigh. Haguro took up the discussion:

'I have lost all respect for you. There is no point being polite about it. Your attempt to help humans is an act of selfishness; but just remember that humans have already fallen into our hands.

'It is precisely because we burn with love for mankind that we are thinking of kindly ways to exterminate them. But I can see right through you. You are a despicable swindler who actually looks down on humans but uses fancy words of praise. I cannot stand your stinking, human-like hypocrisy as you adopt that intellectually pained frown and prattle on about trying to save people. Not to mention your political bleating while you constantly try to work out under your breath whether something benefits you, or not. You sprinkle a dash of cosmic seasoning to the worn-out themes of "peace" and "freedom" in the human world, present them as something new and palm them off at a high price with the verbal pomposity of a high-principled quack. In short, you are employing your own, oblique way to exterminate them. It is obvious that you are a merchant who trades in "extermination", a cosmic rogue just passing through Earth to carry out a bit of business.

'What is so wonderfully ironic is that our species planned to allow humans to take pride in their realization that nuclear weapons were the ultimate goal of human knowledge. So why are you trying to stand in the way? Surely, winning humans over to that idea would be the highest form of consolation. It would demonstrate that something precious did exist in their ill-fated history and culture. You know, it might just be that human beings suddenly developed ambiguous feelings about the value of the history and culture they had created over thousands of years. And the reason they invented nuclear weapons, capable of destroying everything, was to redeem this value. If I am correct, then what right do you have to rob humans of this huge consolation?

'With your level of intelligence, the only humans you are likely to be able to win over are irrational, hysterical women. Humans have many virtues, of some of which even they remain unaware. But if you point out their virtues, they are hardly going to thank you for it. All you have to do is to praise the defects they already know about wholeheartedly. Now that is true salvation. They would be saved without the need to change themselves, and they would be more than happy to come to the point of euthanasia. All you have to do is applaud their vices, accept every one of their deplorable acts of delinquency, liberate them from all their religious commandments, and allow them to do whatever enters their heads. This will provide them with limitless freedom for a few months. And after that, believe me, they will beg for total destruction. Vice requires incomparably more creativity than virtue, so when in the middle of total freedom that creativity suddenly dries up, they will reach their own conclusion about the total destruction of the world. You can be sure of it. So, you see, our intention to destroy them and their intention to attain destruction match perfectly, like lovers in an embrace. We can finish them off, even as they remain convinced that destruction is a product of their own creativity. And in their death throes, you can be certain it will be my name that mankind calls out in a surge of gratitude. Yours will have already been forgotten. You know I am right. I will become their final, their greatest god. But I will not seek to reign eternal, like a human god. I only need a few months. There is not much point playing God if everyone else is dead.

'The freedom I deal with is very different from the deceit you peddle in. You are nothing more than a merchant of extermination. I am the unmistakable God of Extermination.'

'How ugly humans are! How ugly!' intoned the repulsive bank clerk, as if possessed. 'Why let such ugliness remain? Ugly dinosaurs and pterodactyls became extinct, yet humans still flourish, shamelessly exposing their ugliness. If only humans disappeared from the face of the earth, its surface would be entirely covered in flowers. The world transformed into a fragrant globe!'

'What did you mean by "termite"? That's so rude.' The tubby barber had been glaring at Jūichirō all along, and now he finally found an opportunity to speak. 'Your words are fundamentally rooted in prejudice against domestic happiness. That's why you come out with all that nonsense about humans having wind-holes in their bodies. I've been biting my tongue listening to you. Your definition of love and marriage – all that stuff about being late for appointments, offering up flowers, keeping small birds in cages for their whole lives, and finally, laughing before they die – it's all a lie. My wife is human, and she's never been late for an appointment. But most importantly, whatever you claim about little birds, that woman has always been more than happy to step inside her own cage. Because I'm an extraterrestrial, and I gave her a strict training. It's precisely my willingness to employ tough love that allowed me to enforce domestic happiness. And now, when the world falls apart, I'm even thinking of taking my family back to my home planet. Your family, meanwhile, is as cold as ice, like rich and famous families everywhere. All you did was to get an Earth woman pregnant and produce a really pretty daughter. And now, you really are the typical daughter and parents. Although she did look quite sexy when she brought the tea in just now.'

'What! Say that again!' Jūichirō stood up in a rage, fists clenched, but a push on the shoulders from the huge paws of the brawny bank clerk forced him back, pathetically, into his chair. The three visitors exchanged glances, and chuntered like pans gently bubbling over on a stove.

'Ha! An incompetent extraterrestrial fights for the honour of earthlings, and look at the pathetic state he ends up in!' Assistant Professor Haguro was doing his best to make a joke of it. But he never managed to raise a laugh among his students in his lectures, and this effort, too, fell on deaf ears.

'We don't have the time,' Haguro felt obliged to change the subject, 'to hang around listening to you drone on about sparing people's lives. That's just another useless argument about whether to destroy humans, or to save them.'

Jūichirō was still breathing hard, but calm had returned to his heart. 'Whatever you think, the time that flows between you and me right now is obviously "human time". Whether we're referring to destruction or salvation, the future is on the other side of an iron wall, and on this side, we have a flicker of pure, totally unadulterated time. It's a form of time easily bent in the palm of the hand, pliant, cast in whichever way the decision falls, and yet still a spontaneous time. This is the essence of human time. Human beings are created from one such moment to another, but they also exist in the form of breaking waves. Even if humans could be destroyed in the future, how can you possibly, at this very moment, destroy them right now? You might manage to destroy the bodies of all mankind on Earth, but the time of humans before their destruction would continue for ever. Even *we* have savoured that reality during our time on Earth.'

'You are shielding yourself behind humans again. Whenever things get bad, you hide behind them. That sort of shape-shifting nature is disgusting and just not on. And in any case, what about the "intoxication" you were trying to pass on to these humans? Surely that is what leads to the cessation of human time, and a denial of the present?'

'Do you really have such a poor opinion of what humans are experiencing right now? I came to Earth in order to warn humans. To advise them not to reject the present time, not to belittle their own human time, not to throw away such a precious treasure for ever, not to get caught up in the past and present, and allow themselves to be seduced by another, non-human form of time. But I also discovered within the present human time a rich and inexhaustible fountainhead. It's true that mankind has so far failed to acknowledge the intoxication that I've been trying to convey. However, I've come to see that the shoots of "intoxication" are concealed in no kind of time other than the human time of this present age.'

'You and your sad, fancy, abstract hot air. How are you any

different from those insipid intellectuals on Earth who sit ruminating in their studies, ensnared in their own vain fantasies? Some people write huge rambling papers based on spurious hypotheses, crammed with flimsy ideals and disturbing language. At some point, they come to view themselves as utterly brilliant, and fall victim to the illusion that their writings have somehow solved all the problems of the human world. They get their names onto various committees, and make their money by deceiving humans. How do you differ from them? At least there is a logic to destruction. Salvation, on the other hand, is based at best on the logic of aspiration. Even you must recognize deep down the iron rule of the human world. That aspiration is no match for reality.'

'And sanity is no match for madness, right? But I'm sure you'll agree that this very pessimism – the argument that aspiration is beaten by truth, and sanity by madness – was never born out of the logic of the Universe. It is nothing more than a simple, logical reality created by you to serve your own interests.'

Kurita glared at Jūichirō, fists at the ready, eyes brimming with irritation and fury in the face of such incurable optimism. 'Why doesn't he acknowledge the value of exterminating them? How can he suddenly pick himself up from the depths of despair, like a legless Daruma doll righting itself?' Jūichirō had abruptly roused Kurita from his tranquil, comforting thoughts of extermination and cloaked him in another fog of rage. Kurita snapped his thick fingers threateningly, and said:

'All you think about is rescuing humans without their having to change themselves. Why don't you put some effort into purifying the human scumbags? Your failure to act means that, even if, by some chance, mankind attains unity and peace, they'll probably end up back at square one.

'You're against any progressive belief in the industrialization of evil. You're against mass slaughter by nuclear weapons. So, how about taking it a step further, and insert an extra directive in your pro-gramme for peaceful unity? *Revive good, old-fashioned evil, and liberate the desire to carry out mass murder.* The desire to murder alone would purify humanity. Only blood will wash away the stench of humans.

'What about putting a halt to the mass slaughter of humans? We could dress up the rituals of death in various complex guises, by setting them one individual against another, slowly, carefully and respectfully. They would kill each other with a shudder of pleasure, even as they gazed with utter contentment at their opponent's suffering and bloodshed.'

'That's right. An antiseptic razor would be the most hygienic choice.' The barber, grateful for the earlier support, voiced his agreement. 'A razor, a flick knife. Anything will do. And all executions would be open to the public. We could revive the use of carriages or oxen to tear men apart limb from limb, that brilliant stroke of genius invented by the Chinese they call "death by a thousand cuts", burning at the stake, kicking to death and all kinds of gory punishments. Wherever you find humans, you will find murder. On the streets, in bedrooms, even in the kitchen.'

'It is going to take far too long to wait for all humans to kill each other.' The assistant professor proffered a muted rebuke. 'Although I guess those endless days of gore would amount to the "human time" that Mr Ōsugi appreciates so much.

'Also, you are too fixated on blood. The problem with spilling blood is that it refreshes human life and can produce the illusion of resurrection. The sight of blood intoxicates humans with the image of life, and they tend to believe they will gain strength by incorporating the life force of others into themselves. It would be awkward if humans rediscovered life during the days of gore you are proposing.

'What you need is a steamroller, to level everything off. A steamroller that brooks no refusal. I tend not to go for torture. The danger is that long, excruciating pain might awaken a sense of self-respect in even the lowliest human being. All we require is a single death blow that leaves no time for suffering. Pompeii on a world scale. Look, war is coming soon. For the first time, humans will face a cataclysm.'

'With humans, I want to –'

'– save them? In which case, the most you can do is to try to save this little town of Hannō. You can start by rescuing not only your half-crazed followers, but also the local policeman, the public order officer, the head of the post office and the lady who runs the general store. They all take a dim view of you, you know. You may be a well-known figure in the town right now, and there is nothing wrong with being amiable. But they are all sick to death of your snooty pretensions. That was obvious when we asked for directions. One young woman just responded with a sneer.'

'I'm not saving people to get thanked.'

'Then you are meddling unnecessarily. Don't you see? Unlike my way of thinking, yours requires the assent of the other party. Don't even think about thanks. In order to save people, people need to want to be saved. On the other hand, my approach is straightforward. I do not require assent or agreement. I am talking about destruction. Inescapable destruction. You dangle empty words like "peace", "unity" and "harmony" that simply confirm the impossibility of fleshing out your ideas. But let me tell you how things really are. To save people you first require peace, and peace requires unity. These are necessary but unattainable steps for the "assent" that remains beyond your grasp. And most people who seek salvation are mad or invalid. Decent humans do not seek salvation. They do not come together to help all mankind remain alive. Honest, healthy humans with a hearty appetite for food and sex are disinclined to lift a finger for anything close to "all mankind".'

'That has been the nature of salvation until now,' said Jūichirō. 'Religious figures on Earth have all failed to deliver salvation. But *my* form of salvation does not require anyone to harbour religious sentiments. They simply need to have the will to live. Nothing more.'

'You are obtuse, like a turtle pulling its head back into its shell. You make no attempt to see what can be seen, or hear what can be heard,' replied Haguro. 'Your way of thinking is wrong on two counts.

'Firstly, the threat of extermination is indispensable in any form of salvation, but no threat can compete with human optimism. On that point, it is all the same whether you are dealing with hell, nuclear war, the destruction of the soul or of the physical body. The truth is, until the end arrives, no one seriously believes that things will end.

'Secondly, human beings completely lack the will to live. In humans, there is an extremely tenuous connection between that lack of will and optimism. All healthy human beings live according to the same song: *Ah, I want to die. But in the end, I won't*. This is the human song of life sung everywhere all the time. By the lathe in the small workshop, in the shade of white sheets fluttering on the line, in the crowded trains as they come and go, in the backstreets dotted with puddles.

'How do you intend to save these humans? You do not have a snowball's chance in hell of grabbing hold of them on this slippery Earth with your precious fingertips.'

'I'm not criticizing the self-satisfied state of the soul,' insisted Jūichirō. 'I believe that such a state provides insight into the beauty of the human world. There is only one difference between you and me. You aim to destroy them in a flash, while they remain in a state of unconsciousness, with no forewarning, whereas I aim to save everyone without forewarning. In fact, those humans who are perfectly content to exist in an unconscious state are easy meat for you and me alike. Every time I see such a human being, I'm seized by a child-like temptation to try out my own skills on them. While they sleep, I move all their cradles in the direction of peace and unity in the hope that, when they awaken, they will turn into ideal citizens for the new kingdom.'

'Ideal citizens? They are a poisonous bunch. You know that. They try to create an inept caricature of what you call universal harmony and unity, but this caricature is actually a portrayal of human self-satisfaction. The result is that genius and heroism are both inevitably modelled on human mediocrity, and the imbecilic masses end up victorious once more. Is that the sort of thing you want? If it is, then all you need is today's world.'

'No,' Jūichirō retorted, 'there's a difference between an abstruse peace that soars to dizzying heights and a simple peace that resides in the lower valleys. My task is simply to gather together all aspects

Yukio Mishima

of the human character, from precious stones to trash, as long as they contribute to the attainment of peace.'

'So, you mean that quality does not concern you? You do not have any chosen people in mind? Oh, that is clever. You base your movement on television. You flatter the masses, and they send you money in turn. At least that sad-looking face of yours will sell well on TV.'

'And you'll get to be famous, too,' came the barber's vituperative aside. 'Despite your age, they'll ask for your signature, or to inscribe a commemorative poem, and in the brief spell before the Earth is destroyed you'll have a whale of a time. If your hair gets long, drop by at my place. I'll use my razor to give you a neat, deep-red wind-hole in the throat.'

The tubby barber then beat time with his hands and, in a high-pitched voice, put new lyrics to an old popular song:

'Ah, lovely death's-head, hey hey, lovely death's-head, It's 'cause I love you so much I call you lovely death's-head, pretty little skeleton . . . The vultures cry like a song of love, pretty little skeleton, lovely death's-head . . .'

Sone had gleaned these words from the supplement of a popular entertainment magazine entitled *Holiday Songs* that never left his daughter's side at the meal table. Haguro had commended him on his efforts earlier.

'Human beings, drop dead right now!' The bank clerk began to curse, his nostrils flaring repulsively. 'From the moment you're born, you roll around in the shit and the piss. When older you get stuck into female flesh. Your mouths are only good for slops of food and drink, for vile filthy words, for getting your tongue into private parts. When decrepit with age, you roll around again in the shit and piss. Human existence, how filthy is that! Drop dead right now! You revel in nothing but envy and slander. Every moment of your life is a lie. Come on, humans, drop dead now! You're nothing but foul bags stuffed with filthy entrails. You're beyond the pale. Come on, die! Rub yourselves out!'

'What is the Tokyo Bureau of Hygiene doing about it?' interrupted the barber, riding the same wave. 'If it's a matter of public hygiene, they could use disinfectant and garbage trucks to dump a population of 10 million into Tokyo Bay. Hmm. That would make Tokyo the most hygienic city in the world. After all, humanity is the greatest threat to hygiene. Isn't that right, Professor Haguro?'

'On numerous occasions, when human thought has come to an end,' said Haguro, adopting the solemn tone that was his wont, 'people have doggedly returned to the idea of extermination. From its very beginning, human history has been dotted with moments when people expected the end to arrive. But it never has. But this time the ending is for real. Because everything we know as human thought is dead.

'Humans have lost their ability to speak. Omens of death pervade the whole world. The garment of language has completely rotted away, leaving humans naked to confront the coldness of the Universe.

'Your feeble hands cannot warm human bodies already gone cold. Only a nuclear explosion can heat up that lot. The gods are dead. The soul is dead. All thought is dead. Only bodies remain, but even they are nothing more than skeletons wrapped in flesh. And they approach death with no obvious symptoms. Death pangs without suffering, without pain, without feeling, like the evening calm.

'In a situation like this, the end falls naturally, like the night. The coffins are ready. Of course, everyone will see the cloth draping their own coffin when their time comes.

'Only the people themselves remain unaware of the stench of corpses spreading around the world, the stench that signals death. Nuclear war is never a noisy affair. It sounds to everyone like the gentle clink of a key in the outside lock of a door that will never open again.

'A world cleared of all humans will still burn in lingering nuclear flames for some time. Throughout the world, forest fires will continue until all trees have turned to ash. During that time, when viewed from the deepest recesses of the Universe, the Earth might possibly glow even brighter than now and appear as a *beautiful star*.

'That is exactly as you wanted. Does that make you happy? The

Earth will become a small, round festival lantern burning the whole night through. The first time the Earth has ever looked so lyrical. Just as you wished, the Earth will turn into a *beautiful star*. What is there not to like?'

'What is there not to like?' echoed Kurita and Sone in unison, with their eyes on Jūichirō, who was lost in his own thoughts.

'Human beings are finished.'

'Salvation will never come.' The three landed a monotonous stream of intense, relentless curses onto Jūichirō's lowered head, one after the other, like a passing flock of shitting seabirds.

'Human fate is already in the bag. You should know that. You're just pretending not to know.'

'You dumb swindler. You're just a looter who's been waiting for his chance.'

'You're a human parasite, a disgrace to the Universe!'

'Idiot! Idiot! Idiot!'

'Peace arrived the day before yesterday. You're too late.'

'No need for a crematorium. That business is doomed. The whole world will turn into one.'

'Blow your trumpet! Soldiers of peace are following after you. Your skin will be stripped off and turned into a battle flag, while your hideously burned face shines bright . . .'

'Hurry up and beat a retreat, before you get your hands burned.'

'Long live the death of humankind!'

'Babies gone. The swings gone. Baseball fields turned into ponds, the parliament building a sandpit. Kids, you can play anywhere now that you've died!'

'The stink of corpses will totally disappear. The air will fill with refreshing radioactivity. The sky will never grow cloudy. Stars will appear in every corner of the sky. Benches will be nothing more than burnt stones. Lovers will cease to exist.'

'The fragrant honey of radioactivity!'

'It enters your marrow like a lyrical poem.'

'Long live radioactivity!'

'Come to think of it, what the Nazis did was a mere rehearsal.

Just think about it. A few decades later, and the whole Earth turns into a concentration camp. Where exactly is that freedom you were leading them towards?'

'Asshole! You Martian eunuch!'

'It's the end.'

'History, philosophy, banks, universities. All finished.'

'It'll be endless summer holidays from now on.'

'Beautiful radioactivity!'

'Long live radioactivity!'

'You and your dimwit ears, your bleary eyes, your feeble arms! A beggar in the Universe!'

'Go on, drop dead, and take the rest of the Earth with you.'

'That's all you're good for. Just go. Traitor to the Universe!'

'Let dawn arrive with the drums of destruction. Let's pack off the humans, loaded with their burdens, into the void.'

'Everything will be gone from tomorrow. The morning toothpaste, the commuter train, the telephone's ring, the off-the-peg suit, the pachinko parlour.'

'The stock exchange reduced to a handful of dust. The world as flat as a tennis court.'

'Mankind will be no more. That's for sure.'

'That's for sure. That's for sure.'

'Humans extinguished . . .'

Iyoko and Akiko were startled by the sound of the front door being thrown open and the scuffling of shoes. When they went to look, the guests had already departed. They heard a car start up in the distance and reverberate along the wide, silent Hannō street, already cloaked in night.

Mother and daughter anxiously opened the parlour door. As head of the household, Jūichirō was generally scrupulous in seeing off his guests at the main entrance.

He had collapsed to the floor. His daughter rushed forward to embrace him, but her father simply held his stomach and informed her that he was not feeling well. With the help of both wife and daughter, he got up and stretched lengthways across the couch. But he lacked the strength even to readjust the hem of his kimono. Iyoko got a good look at her husband's face under the lamplight. She was startled by how terribly haggard he had become in just a few hours.

10

Even with the aid of his family, Jūichirō was finding it very hard to stand, so he eventually agreed to attend the major hospital in Tokyo where Akiko had previously undergone an examination in the Obstetrics Department. Jūichirō's test results were yet to come back, but the doctor suspected a stomach ulcer, and ordered him to be admitted immediately.

Upon receiving the news, Kazuo came to see him, but he found it hard to look his father in the eye. He was informed that his condition had deteriorated following that evening visit from the Sendai three. Since their last meeting, his father had become shockingly haggard, and the wrist that pushed aside the blanket and reached out to him was pitifully thin. Kazuo hurried home under the pretext of a heavy workload, although in reality Kuroki had given him nothing to do recently. After leaving the hospital, he tried to kill time as best he could by watching three movies in a row, none of which interested him.

Jūichirō had a series of tests lasting several days, followed by an operation. Kazuo came to sit with his mother and sister in the waiting room, but it was all over in less than thirty minutes. His father's body was returned, still under anaesthetic, to his hospital room.

Kazuo was about to follow his father when a doctor casually stopped him and asked for a light. With lit cigarette in hand, the doctor asked: 'Are you confident you can really handle this without letting on to your mother and sister, let alone the patient?' In response to Kazuo's nod, the doctor announced that Jūichirō had stomach cancer, and it was untreatable. They had operated, but closed him back up immediately. He did not have much time left to live.

Kazuo did not fancy facing his mother and sister with the news still ringing in his ears. He decided to wait for the shock to pass by going out onto the third-floor balcony, which overlooked the early summer streets. Once alone, his tears poured freely.

He recalled how his father's nose had stuck out even more than usual from the cloth that covered his eyes when he was being wheeled out from the operating theatre. 'Look at that stupid nose. It looks even more ridiculous now. I'm going to turn that nose of yours into a real tragedy. It's what you're looking for.' That was the silent oath Kazuo had taken before Kuroki, but it was bearing fruit much quicker than anticipated. And this was not the way he wanted it. Somewhere along the line, the threads of his hopes had become frayed and entangled, leading him into an unforeseen situation. Maybe this is what humans meant by a sense of sin, he thought. This was the first time he had ever looked deeply into human emotions.

Since it was early May, *Koi-nobori* carp streamers, with their glittering decorative spinning wheels on display, fluttered in the wind in celebration of the annual Boys' Festival. Generally, this would have left Kazuo dry-eyed as he viewed the gayly billowing streamers with a cool sense of detachment, or even antagonism, towards humans. But right now, his feelings were very different. After all, Kazuo's own sadness seemed to describe circles according to the same melody that inspired the carefree red and black carp swimming in the sky. Fierce sunlight and shadow etched bold patches of light and dark into the high-rise downtown area. Everything was involved in a gentle, cyclical dance of emotion. Something went into the shade, and took the form of sadness. When it emerged into sunlight, it became a carp, fluttering its vibrant, wind-filled tail. Just thinking about it gave him better insight into the major bonds between humans and extraterrestrials.

Kazuo had every reason to feel overwhelmed by his personal emotions. There were two contradictory things going on at the same time. The death of his own father versus the simple disintegration of the transitory body of an interplanetary alien. Kazuo felt betrayed by Jūichirō as an alien, but he grieved for Jūichirō's death as his father. He could appreciate that his own incongruous tears constituted a fragmentary ruffling of the major links between the two realities. The very thought led Kazuo to weep even more as he leant against the balcony railing.

He failed to notice his sister approaching him at some point from behind. Turning around in surprise, he allowed her a clear view of his tear-stained face.

Akiko stood, apparently oblivious to her brother's grief. Her beautifully composed face had lost all traces of its recent languid warmth, and the old familiar cool disdain appeared once more etched across her almond eyes and well-formed lips.

'You're crying . . . I get it. It's cancer, isn't it?'

'No.' Kazuo's denial was so clumsy that silence would have been more effective. Aware of this, he tried to make amends.

'The doctor asked me to say nothing to Dad, obviously, but also to you and Mum. It's too late for Dad. He hasn't got long.'

'OK, I don't think we should say anything to Mum. She's sure to get upset and take it really badly.' Akiko recalled her mother's reaction in springtime in this very hospital.

'I'm so glad you understand,' said Kazuo. But a moment later it occurred to him she had not mentioned their father, and this made him a little uneasy.

'And don't tell Dad, either. It would be awful if you do. You do understand, don't you?'

Akiko said nothing.

Thinking Akiko must be choking back tears, he looked away and held his tongue for a while. But there was no sound of weeping. When he glanced her way, there was not a tear in her eye. The look on her face made Kazuo shudder. Akiko appeared to be peering into a room for signs of life from the other side of a windowpane frosted with the delicate crystals of her emotions.

'Do you remember what Mum said last November, that dawn on Mt Rakan? *We are not humans*, we must never forget that.'

'But Dad has a human body.' For the first time, Kazuo's sadness began to give way to irritation. 'Dad has a human illness. He feels human pain. So, why . . .'

Akiko's shrill voice cut him off brusquely. 'But Dad's death is not a human death. We must keep that in mind.'

It was a day when Jūichirō was enjoying a remission following the removal of his stitches. Iyoko was looking after the house in Hannō, and Akiko was sleeping at the hospital. Members of the Universal Friendship Association had offered to attend to him in place of Iyoko and Akiko, who were exhausted, but Jūichirō insisted that they refuse the offer. Even so, the members did come and help out during the daytime, taking turns to receive visitors. That afternoon, three of his old high-school classmates had come to see him: Satomi, the chief of the General Affairs Department at Tozai Denki Company; Maeda, the company director at Dainippon Rayon; and Ōtsu, the owner of the draper's shop. They were sat at his bedside, engaged in an energetic discussion about work and the state of the economy. The patient grew weary of the talking and began to nod off, but the guests showed no sign of leaving. Jūichirō awakened from his doze and sat up in a sudden paroxysm.

'You again!' he cried, staring into the void, as if something terrifying had appeared before him.

'What are you on about? "You again", indeed. That's a fine thing to say! This is our first visit. We're very busy, you know. Why would we keep coming back to visit you in a boring place like this?'

'Ōsugi, you fell sick because you're too unyielding. When you're better, we'll give you some lessons in wine and women. Hey, your wife's not here today, is she?'

Jūichirō was adrift somewhere between sleep and reality, and he had mistaken the three for the group from Sendai.

As they took their leave, they spoke into Akiko's ear with a tone of condescension:

'Young lady, we did all we could to keep things lively during this visit. Maintaining an optimistic atmosphere, as if we were still at school, is the best way to perk up the patient. It does him no good at all when visitors come and look as if they're attending a wake. Right, we'll try to come again. So, look after yourself and don't overdo it.'

Following this exchange, while Akiko accompanied them to the lift, the three repeatedly pressed her to disclose the true nature of his illness and any confidential details. Ōtsu was just getting into the lift when he suddenly looked pointedly at Akiko's tummy. Akiko could not help but catch snippets of the conversation that started up just as the doors were closing.

'It's just a matter of time now. They're hiding it, but it's cancer. Clear as day. Poor thing.'

'And did you see? Don't you think her stomach looked a bit on the large side?'

When Akiko returned to her father's room and watched him dozing, she noticed a change in his emaciated face. She wondered if it had started to fill out a little. Soon afterwards, the doctor did his round and Akiko asked about it. But his ambiguous response offered nothing positive. Akiko immediately revised her own observation. He was showing the first signs of swelling.

It was night-time. Akiko had persuaded the zealous association members to go home, leaving her alone. She sat in a chair next to the window, which she left ajar to allow in the summery night air. She could see a mass of neon below. She was particularly intrigued by the neon trademark of a soft drink, its red form swirling in a cluster of flames. Its gaudy display projected human unease into the night sky even as its nervous structure attempted to trick people by flattering their senses.

At that moment, there was a tiny movement in Akiko's tummy. Since her first experience of one the month before, she had become intimate with these sudden, unannounced micro-tremors. It felt as if the hot gloom in her belly had relaxed, and a sweet little momentary bolt of lightning was passing through. All calm again. Akiko waited. She remained totally focused, all her emotions directed towards the immense internal darkness.

She thought her father was sleeping, but he sat up.

'I'm sorry. You shouldn't be working in your condition. Make sure you don't overtire yourself. Once I recover, I'll buy you whatever you want. But I wonder when that will be. The pain after the operation seems to be improving day by day, so I guess I'll get through. I've had so much on my plate recently. Once I'm better, let's do something nice together for a change. Take a trip, or go to the theatre.'

Akiko was infuriated that he should mention getting better so many times in a few short sentences. She was troubled by her father's feeble, blind expressions of human hope. Her father's spirit had once sped around every corner of the heavens, yet here he was, unexpectedly trapped in a physical form, enclosed in a small patch of darkness no bigger than a body.

A dull pain had recently prevented her father from sleeping at night. His back and chest hurt more than the wound itself.

'I wonder if you would mind rubbing my back?' His tone was weak, almost abject. The entreaty in his voice and the words he used revealed to Akiko her father's spiritual, rather than physical, collapse.

He's become a patient just like anyone else!

Her father managed to turn in bed so that his back was facing Akiko. She drew her chair up to the bed, slipped her beautiful white hands under the blanket and reached out to his back. Those beautiful white hands, like a fine web of stars stretching into the dark void.

However, it was not cold universal space that she laid her hands on. It was a hot, enervated, smelly human back. Her hands sensed the boundary of revulsion, and she hesitated. She knew she could not reach out beyond that point. Cancer, and the sickly human spirit clinging to hope. A few walnuts, surrounded by withered leaves . . .

As she gently stroked his back, Akiko took advantage of the fact he was facing the other way to ask something she had been wanting to ask for ages, something she would never have another opportunity to ask.

'Dad, that time you came back from Kanazawa, you told me you thought Takemiya was from Venus, and he'd gone back without me.'

'I did, indeed.' Her father very slightly shifted his spine, as if he were a skinny rabbit.

'Did you mean it?'

The more serenely his daughter's hands worked smoothly over

his back, the more her fingertips overwhelmed him with a sense of how much rested on this question for Akiko, and how long her emotions had been building up. But in his present state, it just felt too much. He had been so sensitive to the structure of those emotions of other people that he loved observing from on high. But now, the emotions struck him as an exquisite, futile mechanism. He did not think before he spoke.

'Yes, of course. Your dad doesn't lie.'

'Do you really mean that?'

'Of course I do.'

Akiko's voice suddenly tensed. 'Stop being kind, Dad. I can't tell you how much I've suffered over this.

'Of course, I've tried to believe. Because if it really is true, everything becomes a dream, all irrationality is permissible, and my pregnancy is an immaculate conception. No one would be able to deny it. That's why I decided to follow the logic of my own dream and declare it to be a virgin birth. That was the only way to make a reality of the child in my belly.

'You didn't know the facts, but you understood my resolve and you were great, going all that way to Kanazawa to find the evidence. But if the reason you went there was not because we lived the same dream and we shared the same understanding of the world, but just to show me some sympathy, then I can't allow it. That would be a really frightening betrayal, far worse than telling the truth.

'I was determined to turn the child in my belly into a reality. If I had in fact experienced a romantic encounter with a fellow Venusian, then everything would be part of a dream, and the child in my belly would be made from a pure fabric spun from dreams and ideals. There really would be a child born out of absolute purity, entirely independent of its mother or father. That would be the definition of Venusian. Venusian purity would emerge from that generative act.

'But the moment I began to wonder if your words were driven by sympathy, I imagined an alternative, darker possibility. It became a source of intense pain day and night, even though I was generally good at hiding it. If it was all actually a lie, then only the lowest form of reality would remain, and my pitiful, vulgar dream would extend no further than the child in my belly. Once born, the baby would lose its reality, becoming simply the chrysalis of its mother's dream, for ever discarded and bearing the fate of an earthling. By which, I mean the fate of an illegitimate extraterrestrial child. Nothing more than a sullied dream gone bad.

'With each passing day, I weighed up the good and bad alternatives in my mind, and before long I felt the child move in my womb. When I considered that the day of the child's birth was approaching, I found it harder and harder to endure. That's why I felt the need to ask you this question, Dad, despite your illness. If it's a lie, just say so. If you do, I might be able to find another kind of strength.'

Her father was moved. Turning his body towards his daughter, he reached out and took her hand.

'Understood, Akiko. You've suffered so much. I was wrong. Please forgive me.'

'So, it was a lie. Takemiya was just an earthling, and I ended up with a defiled body.'

Her father was suffering from an ache that coursed through his back and chest. It took him a while to reply.

'Akiko, let me speak frankly. The truth is, even I am unsure whether he was real or a fraud. I went to Kanazawa. I looked all over, but I couldn't find him. That's all there is to it. That boy was certainly a liar. But I still can't make up my mind whether he was from Earth or Venus.'

'You're still trying to comfort me!' Akiko lashed out. 'I can't stand that way humans discuss things in ambiguous tones.

'The heavens have lumbered me with a double-layered lie, and I've been suffering for months trying to disentangle it all. And all you do now is act like a human father and tell me to grin and bear it because it's my fate.

'The person I loved more than anyone else shot me with an arrow of deceit. If my only father does the same, I don't know how I'm going to defend myself. You may come to the aid of Takemiya and his lies, but that does no good for my dreams. Dad, it was wrong of you to try to cover up his lies with another one, or to think of ways to pander to my dreams. You should have told only the truth. You would have given me the right to choose. To defy truth and believe my dreams, or to give up.

'Extraterrestrials are not weak creatures, so afraid to confront the face of truth that they need to cover it with a mask. And we're not like humans. Truth is the bait that allows us to dream. Isn't that so? Our dreams are actually opposed to lies, right? To live even for an instant inside a comforting lie leads to your own dreams being eaten away. The result of that is really, really terrifying. *We end up as humans.*'

'You're right. Absolutely right. Akiko. I never intended to reduce my lovely Venusian daughter to the level of a human.

'But calm down and think it through. To feel happiness in having the wool pulled over your eyes is a pitiful human peculiarity, but there's a more complex quality about the lies and truth we're now considering. For example, the reason we conceal our extraterrestrial nature from the world is because we have to keep the truth to ourselves, and show humans a deceitful mask. Our human friends are different. They tend to mask their lies with truth.

'Do you see what I'm saying, Akiko? We have nothing but truth on our side. You can think about it as much as you like, but that's the bottom line. However much of a liar Takemiya may have been, *you* became a kind of sieve in which only truth remained at the bottom, like gold dust.

'I believed in that sieve. And I presented it with rather finely worked, half-digested lies, rather than excessively coarse ones, in order for the sieve to do its work properly. Does that amount to a kind of consolation? I believed it was right to pass things on to you in the form of lies. After all, you did a great job on them. You turned them into truth.'

'I wonder. Even for an extraterrestrial, doesn't the sieve sometimes stop working?' countered Akiko, her eyes once again burning angrily in the face of her father's mild reasoning.

'No, never.'

'So, if you suddenly throw in the truth rather than lies, how does the sieve malfunction?'

'It doesn't. There might be a momentary tremble, but that's all.'

'I've been afraid of even the tiniest tremble.'

'You have, indeed.'

'OK, then. Test my sieve. Throw in some truth. Come on, Dad, be brave.'

Her father hesitated. But he was transfixed by his daughter's searing eyes, and finally spoke in sadness. 'Akiko, you lost out. The truth is, he was a human and a playboy. He took advantage of your infatuation, gave you a child and ran away.'

At these words, Jūichirō watched his daughter shut her eyes so tightly that they seemed to cave in for a moment. He feared the next instant when Akiko would open them.

But when she did, a dawn-like smile played around Akiko's mouth, and she seemed to have resolved something right at that moment.

'That felt weird. There was a slight tremble. But I'm fine now. I know it's strange, but I feel I've always known it from the very beginning. I'm sure I knew. The only role he played was to be a catalyst for me. I needed help from an earthling in order to give birth to a Venusian child on earth. He was like a mendacious breeze floating over a flower garden heavy with the sleepy drone of honey bees. I needed nothing more . . . Now, I never have to think about him again.'

'I'm relieved.'

'But it was a lot of fun. Now it's my turn to test your sieve. Are you confident yours is working well enough to chew up any lie and turn it into our truth?'

'I'm confident.'

'You really are, aren't you?'

'You bet.'

Jūichirō forgot his pain for a moment, relieved at his daughter's unexpected cheerfulness, and he felt in the mood to join in her pleasant game. Akiko's words cut through the air like the swift glint of a scalpel:

'The thing about the stomach ulcer is a lie. You have stomach cancer, and it's untreatable.'

Akiko watched a spasm of fear cross Jūichirō's face. His yellowish hue flushed red, and half-muttered words lingered in his mouth. His wide-open eyes were searching desperately for something that had suddenly been snatched away, and he looked downwards. His head sank back into the depression of his pillow, and he stopped moving.

The sight of her father in this state brought the flood of tears that had eluded Akiko until this moment. She buried her face in his pillow and exclaimed, sobbing:

'I'm sorry. I'm so sorry, Dad. I just couldn't bear you turning into a human being.'

Jūichirō made no reply. His eyes remained wide open, still housing the fear that had befallen him.

'Dad, even as you are now, do you still have the ability that no extraterrestrial can do without? To use the bait of truth, however frightening, to create dreams. Do your teeth have the strength at least to bite into the bait that has fallen so opportunely into your hands? I just don't know. Maybe I was wrong to believe in your ability and blurt out the truth.'

With that thought, Akiko was struck again by an indescribable sadness and fear.

From that time on, Jūichirō hardly spoke a word. Akiko continued to care for him, but she was overwhelmed by feelings of guilt and she lost the courage to address him, merely gazing into his face deep into the night. He would occasionally doze off, then awaken with a start, groaning, his eyes searching the dark parts of the room. When he did, Akiko repeatedly mopped his sweating brow, but he no longer complained of the pain.

Iyoko changed places with Akiko at midday the following day. Until then, Jūichirō had been happy to ignore the sign over his bed that forbade visitors, so Iyoko was surprised when he announced he was no longer willing to meet anyone. He could not bear to face any more of those empty human words of consolation.

The association helpers had been sent home, and Iyoko found herself alone with her husband in the gloomy evening twilight. The nurse brought an early supper, but Jūichirō did not even touch it.

'Try a little,' said Iyoko. 'If you don't eat properly, it'll take longer to get better.'

'Get better? Who are you trying to kid?' said the patient, a flash of derision in his dark eyes. Iyoko was clueless as to what had provoked his barbed response.

'What's wrong? Today, all of a sudden . . .'

'I found out the truth yesterday.'

'The truth?'

'Don't play dumb with me.' As a further show of consideration for Akiko, Jūichirō bent the facts slightly. 'Kazuo and Akiko were acting really strange, so I forced them to confess. I'm now perfectly aware that I have stomach cancer, and it's only a matter of time. So, there's no need to keep up this farce.'

At this moment, Jūichirō could not dismiss the thought of hanging on Iyoko's final denial. If Iyoko did deny any knowledge, of course he would criticize her for offering empty words of kindness. But if he kept going on at her, hitting her with below-the-belt questions, and she still continued to insist she knew nothing, then a sliver of hope would inevitably stir within him.

If Iyoko had known beforehand, she would probably have at least put on a show of ignorance. But this mother from Jupiter had been left completely in the dark by her children. She was hearing it for the first time from her husband's mouth.

Iyoko was blessed with the most level-headed sensitivity in the whole family, but she reeled at this direct shock, even as she unquestioningly accepted the objectivity of her husband's words. She almost collapsed in sorrow, but a peculiar vanity was also at work in her sorrow. The rest of the family had shared a secret and they had kept it from her, the mother who had been entrusted with the kitchen. It was a huge blow to her pride.

Iyoko felt that this family of extraterrestrials had conspired against her for the sake of one secret. It may have been a very human kind of secret, but they had undoubtedly clung onto it with a superhuman instinct. For a long time, Iyoko had been haunted by the fear that her exceptionally gifted husband and children secretly looked down upon her prosaic sensitivity and old-fashioned stubbornness.

Iyoko hated the thought of being ostracized, so she chose this moment to vainly reject her own poor instinct and make a desperate pretence that she was in the know.

Iyoko collapsed at the side of the bed, sobbing: 'I'm sorry . . . I knew . . . I knew . . . I just couldn't say anything.'

These words turned Jūichirō's eyes into blank, empty wells. He quietly told her that he needed no help this night so she should go home. He wanted time alone to think. Iyoko put up a strong resistance, but Jūichirō would not relent. That was his first night alone since coming into hospital.

Jūichirō became intimately aware of how terrifying it was to be alone at night in a hospital. There was the occasional groan of water flushing the toilet in the room next door. The dark, lonely evacuation of a patient. Around nine o'clock, a commotion reached him from a room a few doors down on the opposite side of the corridor. He heard a confusion of muffled sobs and the hurried patter of feet, followed by a crushing silence. He felt that death had been switched on like a lamp in that room. Switched on mechanically, like the red light on a meter.

He considered how much he had grown to love this world and its human life since first coming to live here. But such thoughts did not satisfy him. He himself had barely lived! And how he regretted that. He had left the living to the humans.

And yet, Jūichirō simply could not grasp why the deterioration of this temporary body was weighing him down with such dreadful feelings of fear and gloom. Humans were only concerned with the incomprehensibility of death, but it was their inability to understand both the fear of death and the power of death to influence things that dismayed him.

Compared to the insubstantiality of human life that had passed him by, Jūichirō was bewildered that death exerted such unreasonable force. If this weight was what human life really felt like, perhaps he was beginning to live it now for the first time.

In contrast, the image of the total destruction of mankind that once so animated his mind had abruptly lost strength, and almost disappeared. He tried many times to refocus his attention on utter destruction, but the faded concept leaked away like sand between outstretched fingers.

In its place, despite facing certain death, mankind was mustering all its grim strength to rebuke Jūichirō cruelly as he awaited his own end in his hospital room. Humans were screaming in unison, and appeared to be stumbling headlong towards fields of lascivious copulation and eternal life. What was happening? Before, it was a case of Jūichirō leaving behind mankind as they faced extinction. But now mankind was abandoning Jūichirō to his own impending doom.

Outside the window, he saw the vast illusion of humankind. Living, moving, procreating. They danced merrily towards aimless life, moving untidily forward, mingling by the roadside, standing up again with a funny shout, having a damn good laugh, or a good cry. But they never stopped moving. They sang. Their obscenities were limited only by their imaginations, and their melodies engendered life . . . Every one of their thoughts, turned into a simple, unbridled song . . . Their pupils and their lithe bodies flashing here and there in the dark. The thickets of the night resembling human hair. Was he capable of loving such things?

He recalled the various symbols that humans had thought up in their search for good fortune and eternal life. Celebratory emblems, red-and-white twisted-paper cords, cranes gliding through the sky, stooping pine trees bent out of shape by the winds at the ocean's edge, piles of seaweed washed ashore with giant turtles nestled among them . . . In these things of wonder, he fancied he saw a momentary victory over time, the eternal chains of procreation. In the distant offing, death had raised its heavy eyelids and glared his way, but he remained on this bright shore in the human realm, surrounded by celebratory objects.

How many nights had humans endured in order to gather once again on the bright shore? How often had they tried to sing the same songs? It was impossible to say. As Jūichirō gazed at the dry, wasted muscles of his hand, he dreamed of the ephemeral but glorious flesh of vibrant humanity. The tiniest scratch would cause blood to flow, yet their flesh was lustrous, like a mirror reflecting the sun. Humans were fated never to be able to step outside their own skins by even an inch. At the same time, they had turned the shell of their bodies into a fragile and unstable 'shoreline', separating the vast ocean of cosmic space from an equally vast internal continent. Strength emanated from within the body to repel the sea a tiny bit, while thin skin defended against the water's incessant encroachment. It was only natural that young glorious flesh had become a source of human pride. After all, it stood for the brightest, most splendid kind of shore, brimming with good fortune.

It was beyond his wildest expectations that humans could cast him aside and continue living, but this was unquestionably a sign that he had foiled the plot hatched by those sinister aliens from the unknown planet of 61 Cygni. Thoughts of sacrifice arose in his heart. Maybe it was the will of the Universe to save all mankind in exchange for the sacrifice of a single Martian called Jūichirō, and he had just been unaware of the plan until this moment.

The Universal Will had dispatched him here, and now he looked gingerly in the direction of that Will. A place that lay far beyond the cold, white ceiling of his small sickroom, reeking of disinfectant, towards the absolute abyss where light was dark, and dark, light.

A curtain was drawn across the entrance to his room, and through the walls he heard mutterings of patients unable to sleep. A telephone rang ominously in the distance. There was a shuffling of footsteps along the corridor, and the roar of flushing water. In this major hospital in the middle of the night, Jūichirō kept his eyes fixed on the featureless white ceiling. The white starched skirts of a night nurse brushed past baskets of wilting flowers and leaves, left by visitors, that had been put out in the corridor during the night. Every little sound the flowers made confirmed their state of languid decline.

If it was the highest Universal Will to cut through this white, insignificant ceiling and reveal the hidden significance of the plan that had brought him to Earth, he would be able to embrace his own death with confidence. After all, any necessary sacrifice of Jūichirō in order to save mankind would turn his death into something more than a simple human death. His death would carry the weight of three billion human lives. If only the Universal Will could offer some clue, he would be saved from baseless fears and anguish . . .

Despite his many attempts, his method of communicating with the Universe had failed to produce satisfactory results, so he was doubtful he would be able to get answers regarding the most profound Will of the Universe. But he only had one method, so what else could he rely on? As Jūichirō continued to stare steadily, the area around his eyes became hot and painful. His face was heavy with swelling. Pain darted around his body, sweat oozed like cold needles, and he could not stop groaning.

He saw nothing on the white ceiling, and it emitted no sound. Matter follows the material laws, and earthly time strictly adheres to the laws of time. The walls were firmly attached to the ceiling, and the newly built structure released no creak or movement, let alone dream. The ceiling was the ceiling. The cancer patient stretched out below was the cancer patient.

As Jūichirō waited, he dreamed of childhood memories, the loneliness of his youth, his joy when he first saw a flying saucer, the visit of those unsavoury aliens. He dreamed that someone had written his 'biography' in a style that reflected the simple tones of a life lived, but sprinkled with gold dust, and frilled with lilies and roses. In the midst of stupidity, defeat, agony and misery, he thought he saw something sacred. Humans were prone to all these conditions, but Jūichirō had a vague sense that, just as Akiko had insisted, it was the 'mendacious breeze' of human existence that allowed the spontaneous emergence of something sacred.

He waited. This was the time of day when the folds in the window curtains began to turn slightly transparent. There was not a sound in the hospital. It had never been so quiet since his arrival. Night was gradually retreating.

Suddenly, Jūichirō was conscious of the white ceiling gently opening up on both sides. He was partly ecstatic with joy, but he also felt he was witnessing something entirely practical and normal. He heard a voice. The voice was bright and clear, and Jūichirō was able to catch everything that was said, word for word.

★

When Kazuo took a phone call from his mother at his lodging, he assumed it was to inform him that Father was fading fast. But she merely asked him, calmly, to come to the hospital as soon as he could. It struck him as odd. Kazuo had been ready to move out of his place and return to Hannō ever since reading the previous day's morning newspaper. The banner headline announced that Katsumi Kuroki had formed a new political party. But Kazuo had been told nothing about it. And there was more. There was even an article describing how Assistant Professor Haguro had been invited to become an adviser. Kazuo had received no communication from Kuroki recently, and he was just keeping to himself in his room. He was in no mood to visit Kuroki at his home, or to go to the hospital and watch his father's face as he reached his end. And yet he was not keen on studying either. When he read the paper, he knew very well that Kuroki had discarded him.

He reached the hospital. His mother and sister were already there. Father was sat up in bed, beaming, his eyes sparkling with joy. Seeing this, Kazuo knew his father's intentions immediately. His mother and sister offered no additional explanation. They were a close interplanetary family once more.

Father issued brisk instructions. Today was Sunday, so the hospital had limited staff. They would be leaving at eleven that night, and they were holding this clandestine meeting in order to make arrangements. Kazuo was to take Mother back to Hannō to sort everything out in preparation for Father's departure, and to bring Mother back to the hospital in the Volkswagen. Akiko's role was to remain here in the room, and send away the association helpers and any unexpected visitors. Everything had to be sorted out by ten that night.

Iyoko, Kazuo and Akiko said not one word in response.

Before lights out at ten, the family were gathered around Father, checking the bags that each held in their hands. Kazuo returned to report that he had helped his mother lock up all the doors of the Hannō house. Akiko had placed a hand-knitted gown and hat, for the child she was expecting, in her small handbag, along with some personal effects. Iyoko had done well to bring all their rings set with precious stones, but for some reason she had thrown in her fixed deposit bonds and her current account bank book. She had also prepared sandwiches for the whole family, which were in her handbag, with a flask. She had remembered to bring along a torch.

Once the nurse had finished her round following lights out, the three of them dressed Father in his suit, taking care not to make any noise. He was so thin, he seemed to be wearing an oversized hired suit. The lift was available at night-time, but they would need to pass the nurses' station in order to take it. Their only choice was to go down the dark staircase at the back.

It was ten minutes past eleven. After ensuring the coast was clear, the family carefully helped Father out of the room into the corridor without incident.

It was tough going for Jūichirō to make it down the stairs from the second floor, but it would have attracted unwelcome attention if Kazuo had carried him on his back. So on the way down they supported him on both sides, letting him rest from time to time.. At several points Jūichirō's body gave way, and they had to let his dizziness and pain pass before setting off again.

The security guard at the rear entrance was only keeping an eye out for thieves, and he let the respectable-looking family go by without a second thought. Between there and the car park, Jūichirō's spirits perked up remarkably and he walked like a healthy visitor.

Kazuo was driving, with Akiko in the passenger seat. Jūichirō, barely able to sit upright in the back of the Volkswagen, was supported by his wife.

'Come on, hurry up. I told you where we're going earlier.' Relieved that they had managed to escape the hospital without mishap, Jūichirō muttered these barely audible words and closed his eyes.

The car was soon stuck in the hustle and bustle of Shibuya.

'Already late, but still so many people around.' Iyoko, who had never been out late at night, let out an innocent sigh. Supported by his wife, Jūichirō raised his head and gazed at the sea of neon that appeared like a vision in his half-closed eyes.

'You should look,' he said. 'You should all look. Our farewell to the human streets.'

'But Dad,' said Kazuo. He had already given up all hope of controlling the crowds as they pressed in around the car. 'What will become of the people left behind after we disappear?'

In the rear seat, dappled with flickering streetlights, Iyoko saw a smile cross Jūichirō's face for the first time. He spoke in a tone that was new, fearless and lacked propriety. 'Humans, they'll get by, somehow.'

Akiko was startled by the beauty of the streets beyond the windows. The thought that they were leaving these streets, that they would never see them again, made everything seem right. A picture of restless movement painted on glass, all vulgarity extinguished, the bustling night streets of early summer sparkling crystal-clear like the Buddha's Pure Land.

'Why couldn't they choose a closer place?' said Kazuo, as they sped along a dark road through Setagaya. 'It's really tough on Dad.'

'No, that's the safest close place there is. They told me they couldn't find anywhere within Tokyo that would escape people's attention. Patience, patience. Once we get there, all our suffering will end.'

There were not many cars on the suburban roads late on a Sunday night, so the drive went very smoothly. They were already in Kanagawa Prefecture once they crossed the Izumi-Tamagawa Bridge, and before long they drove over the silent Nanbu Line railway track. They turned left at the lighthouse-shaped fire station tower near Noborito Station. They were almost at Higashi-Ikuta, their destination. Turning left off the main road, they stopped in the square at the rear of the brightly lit, country-style Higashi-Ikuta Station. No one was around, but countless platform lights spilled in through their windows. Dark clumps of grass dotted the empty lot.

'Good. Stop here. Now we walk. Over that crossing there, and up the hill.'

'That's quite some walk,' said Kazuo.

'You won't know until you try.'

'Kazuo, get hold of your father. All I can do is push him from behind. Akiko, just concentrate on walking. There's no one to give you a hand. And Akiko, careful you don't fall.'

'Sure.' Akiko acquiesced meekly and emerged from the car. As the family was helping Jūichirō out, he peered closely into each of their faces in the gloom.

'And so, we have come together again as a group. We have joined forces. I've never been so happy . . . But what makes our family so special is the fact that we are about to separate just when we have bonded again so tightly. Our life together as a family has been short-lived, while we waited to return to our respective home planets. But until we accomplish that, let us aspire to attain beauty in its per-fected form, as friends and without rancour!'

Jūichirō began to walk, with his arm over his son's strong shoulder and supported by his wife. They went south, crossed the railway track and passed through some paddy fields until they reached the hill. They heard a loud gurgle of water streaming along what seemed to be a drainage gully at the base of the hill. On the other side of a small concrete bridge stood a streetlight. Even Jūichirō was able to muster the strength to walk as far as that.

But when they turned left, the path leading up the hill was over-grown with a tangle of chestnut and maple branches, enveloped in gloom. They had to depend entirely on the light from the pocket torch that Kazuo brandished.

'Yes, this is the path. Just as they told me.' Jūichirō was panting. The path was a dark grotto of young foliage, musty with the smell of heaped leaves. It was slippery, and the family watched out for each other as they made their ascent.

When they reached the top, they found themselves next to a house deep in slumber. A starry sky suddenly opened up above the swaying fields of wheat that covered the hilltop. The sky was not as clear as the one over Hannō, but Scorpio and Libra still gently beck-oned, twinkling further to the south. The whole family felt refreshed under the shower of stars. As they made their way through the fields of ripe wheat, a dog barked in a distant house, but no people were around.

'Straight south! As far as you can!' cried Jūichirō. As they advanced southwards, their path was cut off by a ridge of even higher, flat hills.

But Jūichirō's cry took the strength out of him, and he slowed down. It was not enough to hang onto Kazuo's shoulder and, every few paces, he needed to crouch down on the path, where he remained for a while, head lowered.

'Dad, not long. Keep going.'

Kazuo encouraged him, all the time walking gently forward, bearing most of his father's weight on his shoulder. Jūichirō was starting to stumble every time he stood up. The walk up the hill had taken a toll on Akiko too, and she felt a tightness in her chest. Still, she bundled all her bags into one hand and lent her shoulder to her father.

They seemed to be getting nowhere. When they entered a field lined with eggplant and cucumber seedlings, they realized there was still quite a distance to go before reaching those flat hills that had seemed so close. Iyoko kept pushing her husband from behind and stumbled in the earth countless times, but she was unmindful of her soiled kimono.

Jūichirō was barely aware of where he was walking. But his mental anguish was gone, and he heard nothing but his own panting and the racing of his pulse. All he had to do was to reach his goal. He just had to overcome those irrefutable obstructions of time and space, and get there. And throughout, he was aware of the blessing of the starry sky above. An ineffable, invigorating, disembodied blessing born from light, communication, correspondence and tranquillity. A blessing born from order and madness. Space had opened up magnanimously to convey a ceaseless liberation from the narrow, stuffy cage of physical sickness in which he had been trapped. The blessing of repudiation . . . His mind drifted between dream and reality. Even if he could not attain his goal in this human body, only ever a temporary garment, why should that stop him? The border between what was possible and what was not began spontaneously to blur.

It felt as if those iron-clad distinctions between walking and flying, between fabrication and reality, could be broken down by the simple poke of a finger.

The four finally made it to the ridge of hills. Jūichirō fell face down onto the grassy slope. With Kazuo's assistance, he managed to raise his head, now wet with night dew. He realized they had reached a large wheatfield on top of the higher hill. Further beyond was a small mound, concealed behind a tangle of woods like an island in the middle of a lake.

'They're here! Dad! They're here!' Akiko suddenly cried out.

A silver-grey flying saucer could be seen resting at a slight angle, hidden amongst the woods on the mound. The lower part of its body changed colours, as if breathing, from green to vivid apricot.